Praise for *Confessions of the Other Sister*

"Both hilarious and deeply moving, *Confessions of the Other Sister* had everything I want in a book: a fast-moving plot, some sunny armchair travel, and a ride on an emotional roller coaster. This might be Beth's best book yet!"

—Jen Lancaster

Praise for *The Cookbook Club*

"Filled with heartfelt charm and delicious cooking details. . . . A sweet tale about the true power of great friends and great food."

—*Woman's World*

"Heartwarming and fun, *The Cookbook Club* celebrates food and female friendship with a side of sweet romance that affirms the simple joy of being with people you care about. This is the book I didn't know I needed."

—Amy E. Reichert, author of *The Coincidence of Coconut Cake*

Praise for the Works of Beth Harbison

"Harbison dazzles in her latest. . . . Absolutely first-rate."

—*Publishers Weekly* (starred review)

dd Butter

D1018827

Confessions of the Other Sister

Also by Beth Harbison

Confessions of the Other Sister

A NOVEL

Beth Harbison

wm

WILLIAM MORROW

An Imprint of HarperCollinsPublishers

P.S.™ is a trademark of HarperCollins Publishers.

HarperCollins books may be purchased for educational, business, or sales promotional use. For information, please email the Special Markets Department at SPsales@harpercollins.com.

FIRST EDITION

Designed by Diahann Sturge

Library of Congress Cataloging-in-Publication Data has been applied for.

ISBN 978-0-06-295866-2

22 23 24 25 26 LSC 10 9 8 7 6 5 4 3 2 1

*To Steve Troha, my friend through the good, the bad, and the
ill-advised. Here's to you with all my love and gratitude.*

Confessions
of the
Other Sister

Prologue

Eighteen Years Ago, Halloween Night

$\mathcal{W}$hat is that costume supposed to be?" Frances Turner looked at her younger sister, Crosby, in confusion, as she had done so many times in the past. "Are you Britney Spears or something? A little cold for a belly shirt, isn't it? Mom's going to tell you to change."

"They already went to the hotel, so no, she's not. *And* I'm a ghost," Crosby said, crossing her arms in front of her bare midriff. "The ghost of me. This is—this is what I died in. Obviously." She splayed her arms, displaying naturally tight abs and a body that actually *did* resemble Britney's. So did her long blond hair, which she'd used a waving iron on.

"Good thing I didn't take that trip to Mexico like the rest of you or I wouldn't be pale enough to pull it off," she went on, reminding Frances of the guilt she'd felt when Crosby learned the theater group was going on this exotic trip and she wasn't allowed to tag along. "Looks like a win for me after all."

What she didn't know was that Frances had actually gone so far as to float the idea with the others, wanting to make her little sister happy and give her the same cool experience she was going to have, but no one wanted a fourteen-year-old freshman to come after they'd worked to earn it themselves as seniors.

"You're not in theater," Frances snapped, overly defensive from having fought this fight for so long. "You know we worked for that trip. We did car washes, bake sales"—she counted these off on her fingers—"babysitting, cutting grass, bulk recycling—"

"Calm down, you're going to expose yourself." Crosby gestured toward her chest. "What are you, the little match girl?"

Frances shifted her bustier back in place. It was too big and kept slipping down. "And you know I'm not the little match girl, I'm Éponine!"

"I don't even know what that *means*."

"From *Les Misérables!* She is the clever, beautiful, doomed girl of the streets who does *nothing* but love unconditionally and die tragically and alone with only the kiss of her pitying love!"

Crosby paused, giving Frances the fleeting hope she'd gotten through. "Well, I guess I don't need to watch it, then."

"*Watch* it? You never would have anyway, the only way to see it is as a show."

"A show? Like on TV?"

"A play."

"Okay, so a *play.*" Crosby rolled her eyes. "Forget it, then. I cannot *stand* plays. So boring."

"Great. Fantastic. I'm so glad you're here for all my friends who do shows, then."

"Stop calling them shows, oh my God."

"That's what they're called!"

"That's not what they're called! No one calls them that except you *theater* people!"

"That's what *everyone* calls them!"

"Your *everyone* is not *big* everyone—your everyone is in there." Crosby gestured to the other room.

"Well, where is your *everyone,* then?"

"Excuse me?"

"You have no friends." Frances laughed. "That's why you're always trying to glom onto mine."

"I do have friends," said Crosby, fighting back emotion.

"You do not. You are always in your room. Even your *boyfriend* isn't here."

"He's coming."

"Oh, please. Benjamin is a senior, he just thought he could get into your pants easily. Which I *hope* he didn't. He'll get bored and dump you and then where will you be? Sorry, I'm not trying to be a bitchy older sister here—"

"No, you are, you're just not trying to be *my* bitchy older sister, you're being some character right now. You're always being some character or other. The whole world is a play to you."

Frances rolled her eyes. "I am not *being*—ugh, stop, can you, why are you always interrupting me?"

"Because you *monologue*."

"I was talking for *literally two seconds*."

"You were not, we've been—look, I've almost finished my soda, and it was completely full when we started talking, or when *you* started talking."

Frances shook her head, eyes shut. "You are so *difficult*."

This sobered an already sober Crosby. She reached for the bucket on the nylon-tableclothed foldout table beside them, grabbed a Miller Lite, and cracked it. "Maybe I just need to loosen up, huh? Maybe that's what you and Benjamin both want me to do."

"Oh, good, now you're drinking," said Frances.

"*Oh, good, now you're drinking,*" imitated Crosby.

"Wow, really good. Maybe *you* should be the actress."

"Maybe I *am*!" said Crosby.

"Right. Whatever." Frances paused, regrouped, and said, "I'm just saying, please just try not to embarrass me." She glanced pointedly at the gold-and-blue can in Crosby's hand.

"Seasons of Love" started up on the stereo.

Crosby let out a genuine *ugh*.

"See, like, why do you have to always act so . . ." Frances

looked her over pointedly. "Do you think this is cool, being so *bored* by everything in front of people?"

"How could it be cool?" asked Crosby. "I don't have any friends."

Frances groaned. "You're really going to get stuck on that. Like it isn't obvious."

"I mean, yeah, since, like, I guess I didn't sign up for a club in order to find them."

"Are you talking about theater? It's a class, not a club. At least I'm a lot more social than you, always alone, in your head, reading or writing." Frances put her hands on her hips and her bustier loosened a bit, gaping a little too much.

"You better hope I don't write a book that becomes a movie someday because I will tell them *not* to put you in it."

"Ouch." Frances gathered herself, trying not to continue this argument. "Listen. Please. For once, don't embarrass me in front of my friends."

"Me? Embarrass you? That's perfect coming from the girl who looks like Marie Antoinette after being hit by a car. Sorry, *carriage*."

"It's a *Halloween party*."

There were voices then; another group of Frances's friends had arrived and were coming down the stairs to join them in the rec room. Joey, Robbie, and Lisa were the first down.

"Éponine!" Joey cried upon seeing Frances. He was dressed as a Newsie. "Perfect!"

Robbie, dressed as a mime, did a chef's kiss and a deep bow.

"Thank you," Frances said, feeling Crosby's judgment radiating from her like heat.

Lisa gave her a quick hug, then said to Crosby, "Are you Britney tonight?"

"Yeah!" She smiled.

"La Vie Bohème" came on. "Oh, I *love* this song," said Frances, turning from her sister and folding into her friends. They laughed and began to sing along.

Crosby finished the rest of her beer. It tasted like pennies in the gutter, but she was glad she'd had it.

Her friend Julie Powell sidled up next to her, wearing a cat costume that might have been sexy on someone a little more developed. "Is Fran being all Meryl Streep at you again?"

"When isn't she?" Crosby said. "I think we should invite, like, everyone. Screw it. Our parents are gone, why not? Frances doesn't think I have any friends. I do." She nodded at Julie. "We do. We do, don't we?"

Julie nodded. "Tons of friends."

"I want you to call everyone you know and say that the Turners are having a party and it's a rager. Do we know someone who can get a keg?"

"Obviously. My brother will get it if you pay."

Within a half hour, Julie had called everyone she knew and invited them. The keg was ordered. It was Yuengling. Frances knew nothing.

Frances was in the rec room dancing to a mix brought by Joey that included every belter he could burn onto one CD.

Every time Frances looked over at Crosby and Julie, who were giggling like they'd gotten one over on her, she felt seriously pissed off. Crosby was right—Frances wasn't exactly a social butterfly either.

And since the theater group kids were always rehearsing, it's not like any of them did anything but hang out together. Because when they *weren't* rehearsing, they were just watching shows, going to shows, singing in their pajamas, practicing for no reason, playing Cranium and skipping every card that wasn't green . . . it probably would have been nice to have social interaction outside of them. But she was so comfortable being understood.

She was in the middle of walking back and forth doing the "Waltz for Eva and Che" with Joey when the much bigger boom box from Crosby's room was suddenly blasting from the living room upstairs. "Swing" by Savage started ticking like a bomb with just enough preamble in the beginning that it felt like a crossover from the wholesome cast album of Frances and her friends to Crosby and . . .

Frances walked upstairs.

It was the opposite of a horror movie. Instead of descending into a dark and mysterious basement, she was ascending into an unsettlingly lit upstairs that held something she knew to fear.

Cars scattered the front yard. A keg sat in a Playskool blue tub filled with ice. There were red Solo cups. Someone was standing on the counter in his high-top Nikes—which were, as was the way, super-fresh—setting up a strobe light.

A black light went up. Big speakers went up. The place was crawling with people. It was like the hallways of school but at Frances and Crosby's home.

Frances walked through her unfamiliar house, suddenly lit blue, bright, flashing, and occupied by people who said nothing to her, and she saw nothing of her sister. At first.

Finally she found her.

She was standing there drinking from a Solo cup, looking totally at ease.

Frances's anger raged.

She went back downstairs to find her own friends looking like deer in the headlights. The musical mix had been cut off. Their party was over. The sad foldout table of snacks just seemed pathetically wholesome now.

"I didn't tell her she could do this," said Frances to her friends.

Her group told her she was right.

"I'm going to tell her," said Frances, but she didn't; instead, she crossed her arms, bit her tongue, rolled her eyes, and angrily jerked her head in the direction of the steps for about half an hour.

When the Ying Yang Twins came on, Frances announced that she was *just going to effing to do it*.

"Because she can't just get away with this," she explained.

"She can't, seriously, no way," agreed Joey and Robbie.

Frances stormed upstairs to tell off her sister. She finally found her outside on the patio. It had taken just long enough to find Crosby that Frances's ears had adjusted to the bass and the outside felt like a weird absence of sound.

Crosby stood in the yellow light near the faux-leather-covered hot tub. Ben was standing a couple feet in front of her. So he *had* shown up.

"Listen—" began Frances.

Crosby turned to her sister, who immediately understood that something was wrong. Crosby had been glaring at Benjamin. Frances had interrupted something between the two of them.

Benjamin shrugged and hung his head. Shook it. "I'm sorry. I didn't mean to hurt you. You must understand."

"Just go."

"I . . . Crosby—"

"*Go!*"

He shook his head again, said, "I'm sorry," and left.

As if synchronized, the sisters looked at each other at the same second. Frances didn't need to ask, and Crosby said, "He's leaving, it doesn't matter. He's going off to school. It's . . . whatever, yeah."

Frances thought of a hundred different answers. Thought of hugging her. Thought of leaving her alone. Thought of saying they ought to go egg his house. Thought of telling her she deserved it. Thought of saying that of course he was leaving.

Instead, she asked, "Do you want to get rid of everyone and watch *The Notebook*?"

It hadn't been easy, but within an hour, they'd gotten everyone out, decided to deal with their parents and the mess tomorrow, put the couch cushions on the living-room floor, found every blanket they could, and started watching the opening credits of *The Notebook* as the soft, sad piano score played.

Chapter One

Seven Years Later

The fire was huge. Almost terrifying, yet beautiful at the same time. It was one of the rites of fall here in the New York north. The crisp air was scented by drizzles of smoke from the burning leaves and white cedar in the bonfire. It was a heady fragrance, almost perfume to her senses, but also intoxicatingly appetizing. As she sat in the old wood chair in front of the wall of heat from the fire, she suddenly wanted a beer brat on a stick. And a marshmallow on a stick. And some graham crackers and chocolate. When was the last time she'd eaten? A couple of hours ago? She felt like she was starving. Was anyone else weird enough to get hungry from the smell of burning leaves?

She took a sip of her beer. *Maple pumpkin ale*, Billy Sharp had corrected her more than once tonight. *Not just beer.* He and his dad made it in their garage and took great pride in it. It wasn't really that good. She recognized the taste of McCormick's pumpkin pie spice and they'd put in too much of it. And there was something else, something bitter. Too much hops, maybe, though she suspected they had just used some sort of cheap flavoring. She wasn't a huge fan of IPAs. But it was beer and it was making her feel nice and light and floaty.

Across the field, she could see her sister talking to a group of people. Gesticulating broadly, obviously telling one of her stories. She looked pretty in the glow of the fire, it had to be admitted. Her long hair looked like literal gold and she'd curled it like a Victoria's Secret model's. In fact, that's what she looked like. Somehow her time at school had made her *lose* weight instead of gain it, like you'd expect. She was the perfect image of a movie star at the moment. The guys in the group looked pretty attentive. Her boyfriend wasn't among them, though. He'd be pissed when he saw. He always got jealous about stupid things like this, like he was a little kid instead of the twenty-two-year-old he was supposed to be. Eh. It was better to be alone.

Another sip and she leaned her head back and looked at the stars. There were so many, they were almost even with the deep purple sky beyond. In the distance, beyond the field party, trees lined the horizon, one long dark silhouette against the lingering glow of the moon.

She had ambitions to move far away from this small town. Other worlds beckoned. The green hills of Ireland, where a big part of their family had come from. Or maybe the Amalfi Coast, with its gem-blue water and tart limoncello and tender pastas. The South of France, with triple-crème cheese and fresh bread, and deep ruby wine to wash it all down. She smiled to herself. It all came down to food with her. Almost always.

The fire bloomed, and the tiki torches that had been set about glowed like stars themselves. Odd. But cool. She hadn't noticed that before. They were so pretty. She could just close her eyes and take a long nap in this beautiful setting. A long nap where she dreamed of fairies and unicorns and all the magic in the woods from the stories their father used to tell her sister and her at night when they went to bed.

She didn't know how long she sat there but she did know she heard "Don't get up, let me get you another one!" a few times. All at once she realized she'd had too much to drink. Way too much. She felt like she was going to get sick. She braced her hands on the armrests of the chair and tried to stand up but lost her balance and plopped back down on the wood, hard.

"Hey, you okay?"

She looked toward the voice. Oh, thank God. A familiar face. She managed a smile. "The Sharps' beer is kind of rank. And I had a ton of it. I feel a little woozy."

His face creased in concern. "Are you going to be sick?"

"I—I don't know." Her stomach swelled. "I think . . . maybe . . . so." She tried to get up again.

"Easy, easy." She felt his warm hand on her upper arm. "Just stand up. I'm here."

"I don't want to puke in front of everyone," she said, forcing a humble smile. "I'll never hear the end of it."

He chuckled softly. "Like Carl Rumbowski?"

"Exactly." She was on her feet now and walking next to him. Maybe it was the air getting clearer as they walked farther from the fire, but the nausea was ebbing. "Or that time Amanda Malone went behind the trees and peed in that clearing where everyone saw her." She felt her own face grow warm with commiseration. "So humiliating."

"We'll go in the barn," he suggested, gesturing toward what was rumored to be one of the oldest barns left standing in Tompkins County. The unpainted wood was so old, it was almost black. Normally she wouldn't go in the place for fear it would collapse on top of her but tonight she'd take the privacy at just about any cost, even if it only meant her body was hidden by wood slats.

Funny how the threat of getting sick changes all your values.

The door creaked loud when he opened it; they stepped in. It took a moment for her eyes to adjust to the light coming through the rotting slats. It was just a barn. Empty now, but not that far from inhabitable. Stall doors, open and seemingly waiting for occupants. Remnants of straw within.

He opened another door to what must have been the tack room. A single old bridle hung on the wall, the bit dull with age, next to a shredded nylon halter. There was a bag of feed on the floor, split open with corn spilling out, as if it had been dropped from some height and then just left there. She took a long, bracing breath. The room smelled like deep cold earth, leather, and a hint of molasses.

"Better?" he asked.

"Yes, actually." The world was warped, for sure, but she no longer thought she was on the verge of vomiting.

"Good." He pulled her into his arms, wrapping his warmth and strength around her.

And, damn it, it felt so good. More than that—it felt life-saving. She all but went slack and it didn't even matter; he held her up. She wanted to sleep.

Or *was* she asleep?

"You look so fucking hot tonight," he said, then kissed her, hard and wet, on the mouth.

"Don't!" She tried to draw away but was firmly in his arms. "We can't!"

"Shhh." He moved a hand up and down her back.

She relaxed against his touch. It felt good. If she could just stand here and enjoy this for a little while . . .

He kissed her again. "You don't know how long I've wanted to do that."

She floated in it for a moment, actually enjoying the security of his embrace, the smell of the smoke on his skin and hair, even the cinnamon and beer on his breath. It was almost a romantic Christmas movie.

Almost.

"No," she forced herself to say. "Really."

"You don't mean that. I can tell. You feel the same way I do. You always have."

"No. It's not okay. Don't."

"It's okay. I promise you we won't get caught. Just go with it. You know you want to." And he kissed her again.

Chapter Two

Frances

You know the party is getting stale when the topic turns to people claiming they've seen the ghost of Frank Sinatra in the bathroom.

It was impossible, of course. He's been gone, what, twenty-some years now? Thirty? I don't know. I couldn't ask him because I didn't see him, but it was the night of the Emmy Awards, at the after-party of one of TV's great divas, Jill Cameron, and the champagne was flowing. I heard at least five guests say they saw him in there, though the details varied greatly.

"I was washing my hands and when I turned off the water and looked in the mirror, he was right behind me. Right behind me, I tell you, clear as day. It was, if you'll forgive me, chilling and"—with a delighted shiver—"thrilling."

"He was sort of floating, just a faint whisper of gossamer,

but he was singing 'Strangers in the Night' right to me! I think he was flirting."

"I was takin' a whiz, so obviously I told him to leave, and the sonofabitch tried to punch me, but his fist went right through me." There's always one in the crowd, isn't there? The jerk who thought he sounded like a badass by claiming to have stood up to a ghost. "I mean it," he insisted through the laughter of the others. "I'll go back in right now, come with me!"

All of this was after my employer, Jill herself, had proclaimed that Sinatra and Ava Gardner had rented the place together when they were having a secret affair, before they were married. The story of their rental was one I had seen her devise while I was making the avocado egg rolls that afternoon.

I'm her private chef, you see.

She was watching a biography of Frank wherein a love shack was referred to, and while I admit the description—a gorgeous midcentury modern with a pool shaped like a piano—sounded like Jill's house, I knew from my own passive viewing that that house was in Palm Springs. But Jill was so excited at the idea of him having been in her house once that I didn't want to correct her.

And obviously there was no correcting people who wanted to believe they'd seen a really cool ghost.

The same documentary said he hated the song "Strangers in the Night," so the likelihood of him choosing that to serenade Missy Gaylord, known to daytime-soap fans as Phoebe Millstone, grande dame of a group of make-believe hospital staffers in upstate New York (where I happen to have grown up), with that particular number really felt unlikely. I'd come away from the documentary, and the egg rolls, with the impression that he was a man who didn't suffer fools gladly, and Missy Gaylord was most definitely a fool.

I am, somewhat embarrassingly, named after Frank Sinatra. He was Francis and I'm Frances, but it's still for him. My sister is Crosby, after Bing, which is a much cooler first name and only one of many things about her that stick in my craw.

Our contemporaries are way too young to be really familiar with either namesake, though there are always some who know them. But our parents are old-movie-and-music buffs who practically live in the past. Actually, our dad wrote the song "Happily Never After" in the early 1980s (sorry if it's stuck in your head now) and he's been living pretty well off that stupid song ever since, though he was always a bigger fan of the standards.

I'm not being disrespectful, by the way. He says it's a dippy song himself. He had a whole album and that was the only track he thought was definitely a B side, written as a pun, but it ended up being a monster hit. It was even resurrected in a cartoon feature in the early 2000s. I'm embarrassed to tell you how much he's made from it, but trust me, it would give you a new respect for one-hit wonders. I just wish, for his sake, he'd been able to follow it up with another so it didn't feel like a fluke.

My mother, Sandy Solomon, is a cookbook author, famous for her first effort, *Veg Out*, a vegetarian cookbook of reimagined comfort foods published back when a pun on vegging out was funny and not groan-worthy. She is further beloved for her ongoing series (*Veg In, Don't Be Chicken*, et cetera), which I think is now at eight books. Good recipes, by the way. I use them all the time. I can butcher an entire side of beef with quick precision, eliminating all question-able parts, and I can make an osso buco that would bring tears of joy to your eyes, but nine times out of ten, I'd rather have wild mushroom risotto or even macaroni and cheese. And yes, I use a bit of Velveeta in that. I do what works, not what's strictly "fancy."

Cooking professionally doesn't always give me a choice, however. And I love cooking, I really do, but it's not my most golden aspiration. What I want—my dream vocation—is to act. I wish it weren't. But it is.

That's why I left the East Coast and came to Los Angeles in the first place.

I started following this dream in fifth grade, dressed as a Twister game box in a (retrospectively) terrifying school play called *The Enchanted Toy Shop*. Needless to say, I dropped it for a bit in order to be a child, then, after some coercing from my eighth-grade English teacher, who thought I per-formed well in our class readings of elementary Shakespeare, I landed the lead in the terrible (but cheap, royalty-wise, so the school could afford it) *Frankenstein, Honey!* Which was a musical about the love between a monster cobbled together from clay and his female inventor (me). Again, looking back, just weird, particularly in its efforts to make the original story less gruesome. I mean . . . a clay monster? This was not the route to child-stardom.

In high school I was the only freshman and then sophomore getting leads with the upperclassmen. By graduation, theater fully defined me in reputation. There was no question when I went to college that I'd keep doing it. And I did.

In college, I was Roxie Hart in *Chicago*, A in *Three Tall Women*, Blanche in *A Streetcar Named Desire*, Martha in *Who's Afraid of Virginia Woolf?* I was in tons of embarrassing films made by film students. Everyone else—like my sister—spent their college careers playing beer pong and sneaking into bars with fake IDs. I spent Friday nights at the school's film festival or rehearsing or practicing in my dorm.

It seemed like I was off to a great start. But it turns out that no one cares what plays you did in school. You don't ride into a real audition on a list of high-school accomplishments; all you do is be very, very good. Oh, and have connections. Have multiple talents. I could sing and dance a little, well enough to get that role of Roxie, but I wasn't fit for big Broadway musicals.

So I came to Los Angeles, forgoing any potentially disappointing attempt at the lights of Broadway. I started lining up auditions. Basically, I was told that my theater roots showed. I needed to start learning to act for the camera instead of the back row.

The time between auditions got filled up quickly with restaurant jobs as I tried to make enough to pay the rent. I'd worked at a place in town as a teenager, learned I was good at cooking, fast as a line cook. Runs in the blood, I guess. I wasn't working at great places, but I was making high hourly, which meant I could depend on a steady income. Plus, I really didn't have to talk to anyone. Not like the bouncy, buzzy servers and bartenders who were also trying to "make it." I didn't have it in me to be constantly *on*.

Then I never had time to practice. I got stuck staying up late and sleeping until the beginning of my shifts. Taking doubles. I was too tired, too worn out to focus on the new challenge of acting *small*, acting with *nuance*, reeling myself in.

Suddenly I was lost. I wasn't doing theater at all, I wasn't really able to focus on learning how to change my talent, and I was just scraping by with money. My livelihood was taking over my dream career.

Still, I got a few walk-on parts, but nothing very promising. I gave Will Arnett a cup of coffee in a short-lived sitcom. I was a dead body on *NCIS*. But the forgettable roles weren't worth the time I put in going for auditions in LA; there was more money in restaurant work.

The seeming last gasp of my career came when I decided to audition for a holiday production of *Brigadoon* at a large dinner theater. I got an ensemble role. Everyone there was clearly close; it was a clique. I could even identify the *me* in the group, the shy one who quietly wanted it more than anyone. I ended up quitting. I didn't have the time to sing in the background for a musical I didn't even like.

And that was the last time for a while that I made an effort at acting. It felt hopeless. Great actors, great singers, great beauties—they're a dime a dozen in LA, and the clichés are all true: so many of them are working as servers to pay the bills. You've got to have something extra. My confidence withered to almost nothing a couple of years back.

I started working for a woman I'd met through the restaurant industry. She was opening a boutique grocery store with prepared food made daily. With her reputation, it was bound to become a quick staple. And it did. It flew to the top of lists, got great Yelp ratings. I was making great, steady money, and for the first time since moving to LA, I was doing something that mattered and I wasn't holding my breath before opening bills and e-mails from my credit card company. I wasn't drowning in late fees and overdraft fees and spending hours on the phone with customer service begging for them to be waived.

I had good hours. I had a nice boss. I worked in a pleasant environment. I was too young to compromise that hard, but . . . I needed the break. I needed to rest. I needed to breathe.

Meanwhile, through all of my lonely struggle, I was constantly at odds with my ever-happy, never-trying sister.

We had never exactly been two peas in a pod, and as we got older, it got worse. She was always off socializing, making friends, falling in love, wallowing when it didn't work out. She traveled with big groups. She drank cheap beer on small boats and champagne on big ones. And despite never once pushing herself to the limit to succeed, she was always tripping over good luck and opportunity.

She gets everything she wants, no matter what it takes. Want to try singing? How about doing a little backup on a huge Andrew Bird song because you happened to meet him around a campfire in Joshua Tree and sang a harmony on "Sister Goldenhair" that he liked? Acting? How about during one of your two nights of work at a high-end restaurant, you bring the *wrong entrée* to a big-time casting director, but you're so charming about it that he says you're perfect for a bit part in the new Judd Apatow movie. (She was a party guest in a leopard-fur coat and smeared lipstick, and the scene is often lauded as one of the funniest in the movie.)

Even the small stuff. She once got hit on by a famous, objectively hot musician (at a bar in *Florida*) and turned him down because she knew he was a player. He texted her for a month after, and there's a theory she's the inspiration behind one of his songs.

Oh, then, for whatever reason, she wanted to try her hand at being a writer because she read *Gone Girl* and thought it was "sooo good." She hit the *New York Times* bestseller list with her debut novel. It was a mystery, admittedly a damn good puzzle of a book, but it should have been—she'd been making up the story since we were kids playing Clue. Always imaginative, back then she'd come up with the idea that *everyone* had done it—*Murder on the Orient Express* but different—and even the grown-ups had told her it was clever and she should do something with it, so when she got older, she did just that. And it worked, to the tune of a number-one bestseller.

Last I heard, she was leisurely working on her second book, apparently living happily on the royalties of the first, while I'm slaving over a hot stove to make a living so I can get back to the fruitless effort of pursuing my dreams in my off-hours. Last she heard from me, I was getting a great new job that she still couldn't be impressed by because it wasn't acting.

Anyway. Enough about Crosby. (That would probably be the sad name of my sad memoir—even the title wouldn't be about me.) (I promise I see the humor in that.)

The thing is, my life is actually going pretty well. Really. It's a sweet gig cooking for Jill and mixing with the weird and diverse crowd she hangs with. A-listers, D-listers, the whole alphabet of listers. I've met people who were a big deal in this or that decade, character actors who have been in a hundred movies with tons of Somebodys. I have even met—and fed—a few Somebodys.

Plus it pays well enough to keep me in a nice place in the Miracle Mile with air-conditioning. I can afford to have good local produce in my home. I can stave off headaches with good wine. I have even started to curate a decent wardrobe with a few high-end pieces to mix in with the cheaper stuff.

And most important, most secret, I've saved a lot. I've saved enough that if I needed to, I could take a few months off. It's not so hard if you have a good salary and you're able to nibble on food at work. But while saving enough money for a rainy day seems like a good idea when you're doing it and like an achievement when you get there, you don't want to use it or you'll be right back where you started. I don't want to use up my savings and go back to zero. Yet it's hard to serve two masters—practicality and passion.

The truth is, I'm trying to get back into the acting thing. Once I was able to stop panic-working to stay alive, I found myself with time again. I started filming myself. Acting in front of the mirror, like I did in high school. I look up great auditions. I pore over the best monologues. I master them. I practice and practice. It's started to come more naturally again. I'm starting to think I could really do it again.

I haven't told anyone but Jill about that, though.

Meanwhile, I am happy, really. I go to work every day in a beautiful place with a nice boss and I'm making enough to support myself as well as put away some savings. How many people can say that?

Jill lives in a moderate-for-the-area house in old Bel Air with a pretty large property surrounding it. The house was built in the 1920s, but beyond that I've never really been able to find any specific history on it. Perhaps because even then it had been modest compared to its surroundings. It's a stone's throw from homes that once belonged to Myrna Loy, Rudolph Valentino, Lucy and Desi, and Jayne Mansfield, and it's even next door to a place where Cary Grant had lived briefly.

I love the romantic golden-era history of the place and the feel of driving into that always-sunny neighborhood. I grew up in upstate New York, so palm trees remain a novelty that I appreciate every time. Particularly the very tall, thin kind of palm with a splat of leaves on the top, giving that unmistakable Hollywood look.

They are the Harlow blondes of the tree world.

The kitchen there is also something to behold. Bright and sunny all day long, with sleek concrete countertops someone smart had talked her into when she'd replaced the old tile surface. The ceilings are so high that a searing steak never sets off the smoke detector, and each of the two counter islands is wide enough to seat twelve people comfortably. Having a workspace that makes cooking easy and having a client as appreciative as Jill makes it completely fulfilling. I think I could genuinely be happy doing this for the rest of my life. Or, if not *happy*, at least content.

Because, no.

I'm not happy.

Not really.

I still want to act. Whether it's old dreams or something in the Hollywood air itself, I don't know, but that itch isn't scratched. I'm back in the game and playing hard, getting as many auditions as I can now, basically throwing spaghetti at the wall to see if any of it will stick.

It is the most important thing to me.

* * *

"MY GOD, HOW many cases of champagne did we go through?"

It was the end of the night, and Jill had just removed her Louboutins, throwing them haphazardly into a black and red pile on the hardwood. She put her stockinged feet up on the glass coffee table.

It had been a long, glamorous night filled with laughter, and the last guest had just stumbled out to his car and driver.

"Three cases of Bollinger," I told her, knowing she measured the success of her parties by the amount of champagne consumed, "then another one of that Stardust Brut from BevMo."

"Stardust," she echoed, tipping her head back, humming some random notes, probably envisioning a romantic scene from one of the glitzy romance dramas she'd starred in in the '80s. "I only had the Bolli. Was the Stardust as good as it sounds?"

"Nope!"

She crinkled her nose and looked at me. "Do you think anyone noticed?"

"Nope."

She laughed. "I don't think so either. I'm pretty sure they drank so much good stuff early on that they couldn't taste the swill later on."

It was hard to imagine not noticing the difference between a dry, mineral-rich French champagne and the Welch's grape juice that had been pumped through a CO_2 cartridge and wrangled under a plastic cork in Trenton, New Jersey, but the fact that the entire case was gone, save for a few unfinished glasses left about, was testament that she was right.

"Do you think it went well? Do you think everyone had a good time?" Jill had another sip and swung her foot over her crossed leg. "Will they say good things about me tomorrow or are they already laughing at some gaffe I don't remember making?"

My heart went out to her. Really, it did. You wouldn't believe the skill with which I can summon the "Are they talking about *me*?" anxiety, and it was no easier for a glamorous Sorta-Somebody like Jill.

She is still thought of as a star, Jill Cameron, though she hasn't worked regularly for a while. She was a Bond girl once, and she was in a few movies that weren't exactly well received. Later she had a major role in a series of action movies based on futuristic space-opera books. It was a coup when ABC got her to play the mistress (and, eventually, wife) in a long-running prime-time soap about a rich ranching family in Texas, and that was the role most people remembered her for.

So her parties tended to have costars and guest stars from that show, and they were, by and large, the bitchiest bunch of has-beens I'd ever seen. Sure, I'd seen many of them on-screen; my mother loved watching old sitcoms with my sister and me because she thought they were more "wholesome" than the Must-See TV of our childhood. In real life, though, they were all just people. Their humanness was all too evident after they'd had a few drinks and started talking honestly about who they liked, who they didn't, and very specifically *why* in both cases.

Swill or no.

Not Jill, though. Jill was really great.

Seriously. It was funny how she always seemed to be Jill.

Here I was, the girl who couldn't even up her chances in Holly-wood by becoming a charming server, who instead cowered behind the line in the back of the house. But Jill was always on. Always Jill. Always a glamorous icon.

"I didn't see anything embarrassing." There was no point in mentioning the Fallen Grape from the Cheese Board Inci-dent; she didn't know anyone had seen and fortunately she'd just missed slamming her forehead into the counter when she wiped out. "I think everyone was more interested in try-ing to find a ghost in the house than what was going on with the living."

She laughed. "The ghost." She shook her head. "I was wrong about this house, you know. Frank was never here. I don't think anyone more interesting than . . ." She thought about it. "Than me has slept here."

She was right but there were a whole lot of people out there who would think that was very cool. Call me lame, call me pathetic, but I wanted to be someone who mattered. Not just to myself and a small tribe of loved ones. I wanted to be referred to, lied about, lusted after, and imagined. But I could never admit that to anyone. I could barely admit it to myself, it's such a childish (and psychologically transparent) aspiration.

I shrugged. "This old house has got a long history. He could have been here."

She shot me a look. "Or it could have been Don Knotts float-ing around the powder room tonight." She looked thoughtful.

"I imagine they wouldn't look that different in drifty ghost form."

"I loved Don Knotts."

"Everyone loved Don Knotts, but he was no Sinatra." She started humming "Strangers in the Night," then stopped abruptly. "It could have been my third husband. Sim."

"Sam?"

"*Sim.* Simpson Rollins. He was tall and thin, had piercing blue eyes. But is he dead?"

I watched her puzzling that out and tried to imagine what it was like to love someone enough to marry him and pledge your life to him and then, some scant years later, have to really rack your brain to recall if he was dead or alive.

"Ah, well, I don't know." She shrugged; her interest in the answer was that fleeting. "It could have been anyone. Who knows?"

"I don't think there's *any* ghost here."

"Oh, Frances. You're so practical."

"Someone has to be."

I'd been working for her for almost two years now and it had been obvious from day one that I was going to be the sensible one in our conversations. It was the role I'd played my whole life with pretty much everyone I knew. I couldn't help it. One word of caution from me, and my sister would tell me not to have a Franic attack. Her puns on my name were seemingly endless.

And the worst part was, she was right.

"I'm going to hit the road now and get some sleep because I have an audition in the morning," I told Jill. "The cleaning crew will be here at eight. Larissa will be here to let them in if you want to sleep late."

She bumped her palm against her forehead. "Oh, *that's* what I forgot to tell you! Fletcher Hall is coming for brunch tomorrow and I was hoping you'd come by. I don't know if you've heard of him, but he's a producer I really think you should meet. I think you might be able to help him with a project he's got in mind."

Fletcher Hall.

Oh, I knew exactly who he was, no introduction necessary. He was a star-maker. A major director and producer. This was like saying, *Oh, by the way, Steven Spielberg will be coming to the party. I don't know if you've heard of him but he's done a couple little films that were big hits.*

"What—" I composed myself but my heart was pounding. "What time?"

"Oh, I told everyone to be here about noon or so."

I had an audition. But that was at ten fifteen. If I hurried, I could probably *just* make it on time. It would be really close, though. Luckily, noon usually means twelve thirty with this crowd.

But what the hell. The audition was for a small, nonrecurring part on a mediocre sitcom. The kind of thing I'd take with the hopes it would get me one step closer to meeting a Fletcher Hall. This chance was way too good to pass up. "I'll be here," I told her. Then, a little awkwardly, "*Thank* you!"

"Wonderful!" She clapped her hands together. "I'll see you about nine, then, to start preparing brunch? Maybe earlier. I was thinking those little lobster Benedicts you make, they are *so* tasty."

My heart sank. I felt my face go cold. She wanted me to *work*. She wanted me to *make* the meal, not eat it. This was so disheartening. She was the one person who knew how hard I was trying to get into acting, but she didn't take it seriously. But what had I expected? She'd never invited me to a party as a guest before. We got along great, but not best-friends great; it was just a very nice working relationship.

I could cut it close with an audition and the chance to meet a big Hollywood player, but I couldn't miss an audition because I was working—that was just more of the same pattern. "Oh." I tried to find the words to back gracefully out of this despite the enthusiasm I'd just had. "I don't think—"

"Sweetie, stop, I'm *kidding!*" She waved her hand airily. "I would never let you miss an audition to work in my kitchen. Yes, see, I remember the audition. The party should go on from about noon to two and any time you can make it will be fine. Trust me, I've been where you are. The more irons you can put in the fire, the better."

Relief flooded through me, strangely chilly. "Jill—wow. Thank you. I can't tell you how much I appreciate it."

"Not at all." She shook her head and mused to herself, "And people think I can't act." She winked.

I had to laugh at that, however weakly. "You definitely fooled me."

She frowned. "Maybe a little too well. I didn't really mean to fool you. I thought surely you'd know I didn't mean it."

If I had a nickel for every time in my life something exactly like that had happened to me—the date that turned out to be for the guy's unattractive friend; the party that turned out to be a request for free babysitting—I'd be so rich I wouldn't need *any* of these jobs.

Or any of those friends, come to think of it.

"I really appreciate the opportunity to meet him," I said, hoping to gloss over what had clearly been an awkward moment. "My audition should be over well before for that." Then it occurred to me that this could be a bad omen for my job. "Who's cooking. Are . . . you?"

"Do you think I can cook well enough for guests but I hire a chef anyway?" She laughed. "No, no, no, I'm an utter *disaster* in the kitchen, as you well know. But my dear friend Mona Buhle is opening a new place and wanted to try a few dishes out on my guests. There was no saying no. You know I prefer your cooking to everyone's, but there's no way I'd spring a whole party on you with no notice."

I had to wonder if Jill had any idea how famous her friends were to the outside world. Mona Buhle owned one of the hottest restaurants in Malibu, so if she was opening a new one, it was bound to be awesome. It was cool enough as a brunch cameo, but I was genuinely excited that she had a new restaurant coming. I couldn't wait to try her dishes tomorrow. There was no way I was going to make it onto the waiting list of any of her places anytime soon.

"Lucky you," I said. Jill's head jerked in alarm and I realized it sounded like I'd said *Fuck you*. "*Very* lucky."

She smiled. "Here's wishing *you* luck with the audition tomorrow. I know you'll knock it out of the park."

I wasn't as confident. "Thank you." I gathered my things and prepared to leave. It didn't matter to me that the sitcom wasn't a huge hit or that my agent had two other clients going to the same audition; I still wanted it desperately and I'd take every single bit of luck that was wished my way.

Chapter Three

Crosby

What the hell was I going to do?

Really, *what* on earth was I going to *do*?

There I stood, in my Alo yoga pants and matching sports bra, draped in my Summersalt robe, Drunk Elephant polypeptide cream sinking into my skin—a vision of Instagram luxury and emptiness bought on credit—clutching a disconnection notice from the water company.

Listen, this was insulting for about a thousand reasons, but most of all because I knew that even in the privacy of me, myself, and I, this was a foolish, foolish moment.

In a movie, this would be my comeuppance. Maybe the star of the movie is some fresh-faced *absolute sweetheart*, and I'm the entitled bitch who got it all without deserving it— but *voilà! Poof!*

I actually don't think modern culture has ever quite de-

picted someone in this moment without the character absolutely deserving it.

I don't deserve it.

Do I?

My mother would say I don't. She would tell me the book
was good, life was pricey, and I'd just enjoyed myself a little.
But would she mean it?

My father would say I'd been true to myself and there was
no regret in that, but would *he* mean it?

Frances would tell me I should learn something from this.

She'd mean it.

But she wouldn't think I could.

When I fall into feeling conflicted about gratitude and
feeling cheated, I wallow in the fear that I'd inherited my
dad's "one-hit wonder" luck. One big burst of prosperity to
do with what you could. The difference was in our handling
of it. He'd parlayed one song into a comfortable, if not ex-
travagant, life. He had not burned through his quick fortune
with trips, clothes, expensive champagne gone in one round,
and lavish dinners at Charlie Palmer's.

To be fair, he had made more than I did, but that didn't
give me a pass on being smart with it.

I was trying. I might have been brunching and buying a lot,
but between flights to London and verticals of Opus One, I
had been trying to follow up and turn my fluke into a career.

You should see the desktop of my Mac. It would make any
sane person do a reset on the whole machine. Folder upon

folder upon folder, surrounded by scattered documents and pieces of documents that I couldn't commit to a folder. It's literally not worth it to sort through that nightmare.

Files scattered across the screen, getting smaller with every new addition. I didn't want to commit them to a documents folder I might or might not ever be able to find again, I needed them all right there where I could find them.

The background wallpaper on my computer is always mood. *This is the world in which my characters live. This is the world in which I want to live. This is the world my subconscious is going to create for me to live in as long as I keep it here where I see it daily. I am a manifester of my own destiny. I have to be; it's my only hope.*

Spotify is always humming along from some playlist I had perfectly curated before even writing the first page.

Pinterest—a shortcut for which joins the crowd on the screen—is filled with lists of atmosphere for said book.

The first book was easy. I'd been toying with the idea for years, spinning it around, tumbling it like a rock until it was shiny and smooth. It was a whodunit and what-did-they-do, and it made me into a mystery writer. Which was great until I had to write another one.

Turned out maybe I didn't have another one in me. At least, not another mystery. I had stuff to say but not stuff the world wanted to hear from me. They wanted another puzzle. And every time I thought I was beginning to have my head wrapped around one, I'd lose the thread.

And all of these change all of the time, because I consis-

tently get thirty-five pages to eighty pages in and abandon
the idea, feeling like it was embarrassingly juvenile or hope-
lessly convoluted or just plain boring. Then it becomes a file
in the myriad mistakable manuscripts on my desktop that
barely describe which concept lies within.

Book2.docx

BOOK2FINAL.docx

BOOK2.FINAL.REAL.docx

BOOK2FINALFINAL!!!OCT.docx

These increasingly hysterical document names indicate
nothing except my emptying mind, and, well, long story
short—or no story at all—I got *nothin'*.

The idea doesn't feel wispy and palpable, like some haunt-
ing melody whistled by an unseen muse; it feels like missing
car keys that I am becoming more and more desperate to
locate, and suddenly my mind is all overturned couch cushions and torn-open trash bags and I'm thinking about just
expiring in the middle of the floor.

It wouldn't be so bad if I had taken literally anyone's advice and started a savings account.

God, why did I have to be so *bad* at that stuff? A therapist
had talked to me about magical thinking once, and my takeaway was that I did a lot of that (I wasn't sure what the clini-
cal definition was). I needed money, therefore (*maneuvers to
Nordstrom.com; clicks*) it would come.

Turns out there is no magic.

I started to parse through exactly which of my credit
cards had credit left—the Amazon one? No, definitely not.

The Southwest one? No, that one was still loaded up with the expenses from Jackson Hole. Maybe the—

I was interrupted by a knock on the door. I opened it, feeling one scene away from the opening to *Schitt's Creek*.

"I'm from the water and sewer division," said the man standing on my front step. Then, when I looked blank: "I'm here to turn off the water." As if it made things clearer, he held up a large X-shaped pipe wrench.

"What is that?" I asked, distracted by the mysterious instrument.

"To shut off the valve."

I gave a small smile. "So if I can get one of those from, like, Home Depot, can I turn it back on when you're finished?"

His face went pink. "Um, I guess."

I put a hand on my hip. "How much are those things?"

The pink went scarlet. "I don't know, ma'am." He looked around, as if checking to see if he was being punk'd.

"I'm going to get one." This. This right here was the hill I'd chosen to die on. This poor sap was my opponent.

His discomfort grew. "I don't . . ."

"Why don't they just control it from some central place, like the electric company does, instead of sending you out here with a tool anyone can get? I mean, look at it." I tilted my head. "It's not even that sophisticated. It's just like an old skate key on a long tube."

"The bill," he said. "The bill needs to be paid."

I sighed. "How much is it?"

He looked at the tool again. "I really don't know."

"No, I mean the bill." I laughed, trying to set him at ease.

"Oh. That, sorry . . ."

He patted down his pockets and produced a slip of pink paper, faded from traveling around with him but legible. It was a lot. I got a stomach full of acid, the same way I used to when I was a kid and told a lie.

I hesitated. Sort of *at* the poor guy, as if a respite from the anxiety of allowing him to do his job would provide the fates enough time to manifest the miracle they hadn't yet assembled. This man did not have time to wait on my hysteria, and I had no faith that anything was forthcoming anyway. There was literally nothing that time could buy me in this situation.

"How do I pay? Do you have Square? I can just put it on my card."

I was pretty sure my Discover card still had some credit on it after I'd sent that return to Sephora.

"No, ma'am, you'll have to pay online. If I'm not mistaken, it has to be linked to a checking account. They don't take credit cards."

I felt a rumbling of fear inside. My checking account. It made me feel nauseated just to imagine looking at it. It would be lower than I thought. I knew it would. In this kind of situation, it *always* was.

I nodded and held up a finger. "Just one sec, okay? Do you want to come in? I have beer."

He shook his head and looked embarrassed again and this

time we both knew it was for me. "Uh. No, ma'am, I'm working." He held up the X-tool once more.

"Right. Just, um, go ahead, I'll be right back."

He gave a nod.

I hurried down the hall, beneath my soaring ceilings that I was paying way too much per square foot for, went into my office, and closed the door. I'd spent a fortune in time and money on that room. And it showed. It was more beautiful than any office I'd ever seen. I'd rationalized that it was the place I'd spend the most time and so it needed to have a lot of positive vibes.

I slid into the plush leather executive chair some influencer had talked me into and powered up my computer.

It was an effort, but I forced myself to open my Chase checking account. When I saw the balance it actually knocked the wind out of me.

It was *low*.

Lower than I'd let myself imagine.

In fact, the voice in my head that had comforted me had used a number *higher* than this to say, "It can't possibly be *that* low, so at least there's that."

I felt empty, punched in the gut, and I waited for tears to come. They did not, because they never did in the right moments for me. Instead, I just stood back up and recentered myself.

I flirted with the idea of not turning the water back on. I imagined some sort of camping situation, but with the consideration of just one omitted bathroom flush (I did grow up in a *yellow is mellow* household, thanks to hippie parents), I decided water would certainly have to be prioritized.

Better to let the electricity go than the water.

But I hated sleeping with the room any hotter than seventy-four . . .

I rolled my eyes at myself. Even I could see what trouble I was likely to be in if something didn't change.

I called the number on the pink slip. The whole ordeal took longer than I wanted it to, but when I returned to the front hall, I saw that the guy had not moved from his spot on the step. Almost to an unsettling point.

I gave him the confirmation number. He then gave me the *Just one sec* finger and took a phone out of his pocket. Of course, he had to call to confirm the confirmation. Not only was it certainly protocol, but I had given him absolutely no reason to trust me. Quite the opposite.

Still, I managed to feel insulted.

"All right." He put his phone back in his pocket and wiped his hands on the front of his pants. "You're good to go."

I managed to resist firing back a weird response like *I know that* and instead smiled feebly and waved goodbye.

I realized then, as he saluted me with his Home Depot wrench, that his truck might be a telltale clue to the neighbors. "Thank you!" I called too loudly. "I'll call you if I have any more problems!"

I closed the door and went back to the plush velvet jade-green Article sofa I had gotten custom-fitted with champagne-gold details.

It's probably just brass, I figured, now a cynic. *Or even painted aluminum foil*. I fingered one of them to see if they bent with a little effort, and the button came off in my hand.

God, this was a mess. Utter defeat.

Leaning back against the cushion, I touched the empty spot on my lower stomach where my cat, Figaro, should be lying. But of course, because it was the year of all things going wrong, he was dead.

He'd had kidney failure, and the vet had assured me that I was putting him out of his misery, but there was a part of me that considered the alternative timeline in which I had asked one more vet and found out that it was a total misdiagnosis, and I would have him for another decade.

Now the tears came. Heartbreak, not self-pity.

But really, it was just all of it combined.

It was the fact that there was no cat here, no sympathetic roommate who could cover the bills, no grown-up to tell me how to do it. If I called my friend Alison, she would tell me everything would be okay and then she would find an excuse to get off the phone. We didn't have the kind of friendship where we talked about real stuff.

Honestly, I didn't want to talk about this stuff with *any* of my friends. It was too humiliating. Breakups, bad haircuts, headaches, whatever—I had great friends to talk to about that stuff. But confiding in someone that I'd been such a fool with my money? I couldn't stand to confess that. Everyone always talked about how great my life was, how beautiful my home was; I couldn't admit that it was all a lie because I'd kept up the illusion well out of my budget.

Maybe I should call the psychic again, I thought. *Maybe it'll be more hopeful than last time.*

I rolled my eyes and turned onto my side. I stared at the books, never opened, that I had picked to store under glass under my coffee table. A book on seventies beauty, a biography of Audrey Hepburn, one on the style of Princess Diana, and the most recent addition, which was actually there by accident, *The Subtle Art of Not Giving a F*ck*.

Well, that pile of optimism and falsified authenticity really said it all when crowned by that heavy orange cone hat of unpleasant reality, didn't it?

I looked out the window. It was pretty out. A sunny, cool October day in New York. But it was only going to get grayer and uglier and then it was going to stay that way for longer than I could believe.

That was how it went literally every single year. Never did the nice weather show up when I expected it to.

I picked up my phone (thank God I'd paid the bill last week so it was still working for now) and leafed through Instagram. There were a lot of ads. Did everyone get this many ads or was it only those of us who had been tracked clicking on them and buying stuff?

This, I realized with what felt like a rock dropping into my stomach, was a perfect microcosm of what had happened.

Where and how I'd gone so very wrong.

As soon as I started making my own money, earning my

own way in the world, I had tried to purchase what I considered the life of the grown-up that I wanted to be. Tried to surround myself with things both beautiful and interesting, things that would delight guests and make my friends envious.

Things that would make everyone say, "She is so *interesting!* I could wander through her house for days."

The optical-illusion black-and-white "hole in the floor" rug came to mind. It was rolled up in my closet now, waiting for a trip to Goodwill. The little moon night-light that had to be charged for two days and stayed lit for seven minutes, which was just enough time to lose the charging cord forever. Oh, how about the "sustainable source" (plastic) ankle boots in oxblood (purple) that some anonymous internet source I apparently trusted implicitly declared, "The most comfortable things I've ever worn!" They were not. Instead of Cinderella skipping around, I was Anastasia or Drizella, trying to wedge Jurassic feet into Barbie shoes.

It wasn't that hard to see where I'd gone wrong. It was far, far harder to see how to make it right. The brutal truth was I wasn't sure it was possible. And when a future isn't possible, then what do you do?

Really. When you're out of money, out of pride, out of energy, and out of ideas, and the world doesn't just stop turning and giving you the break from dystopia, what then? What the hell do you do then? How many times can you keep getting up before you just stay down?

Chapter Four

Thirteen Years Ago

Stop!" she said firmly and pushed herself out of his arms. Her foot wobbled on something on the floor and she fell straight on her ass. As she scrambled to get up, she noticed it was a skeleton of some sort. A possum's, maybe. She shrieked and jumped away from it.

He caught her. "Calm down. Do you want someone to hear you?" His voice was a little harder now. Not quite so persuasive.

"There are *bones* there!" She pointed with a shaking hand. Then: "Oh my God, I don't feel good."

"Sit down," he commanded.

"No, thanks." She headed for the door, but two steps out, her legs went weak. "Something's wrong."

"You had too much of Sharps' Special," he said with a laugh. "That's what's wrong. That shit will make anyone feel like hell."

She remembered the taste of it on his tongue. "Do you?"

He hesitated. "I didn't have much."

"I did."

He laughed. "I see that."

This was stupid; she shouldn't have come. She'd been kind of tired tonight. She remembered telling her sister on the way that she wasn't sure she was up for it. Her sister had made a joke about bringing a tent and a sleeping bag and sleeping through the party, just being the designated driver.

That had gone out the window pretty fast. There was no way she could drive right now, that was for sure.

"You look better," he said, bringing her attention back to him. "A little less pale."

"I feel better," she lied, and turned for the door. "I think I'm going to go back out and get some fresh air—"

"Not so fast." He clutched her forearm, turned her back around. "Just one more kiss." Before she could object, he pushed his tongue into her mouth, and once again she tasted the maple and spices, a warm contrast to the fear she was beginning to feel.

"*No.*" She shoved him and he stumbled back a step.

She ran for the door, but in two quick strides he was upon her again, and she felt herself jerked back by her sweater. She almost fell but he caught her, then pulled the sweater off in one surprisingly smooth move.

"*Yes,*" he countered in a mocking tone.

The barn was spinning. She couldn't figure out where the party was. She could hear it but suddenly had no concept of how far they'd walked or why. "What are you doing?"

"Just having a little fun." It was amazing how he could change his tone from demanding to coercing and back. "You want it too, you know you do. *I* know you do."

What she wanted was just a moment to collect herself, get a little strength back. She was just *so tired*. This was the last thing in the world she wanted to deal with right now.

He kissed her and she just let him. She closed her eyes and half dozed through it. It felt so good to just let go and sink into the darkness.

"Get down on the floor," he said.

She couldn't object to that. She needed to lie down for just a moment. Half a moment.

Her exhaustion numbed her to the point that she barely felt him tugging at her shoes, then her jeans and her bra. She was vaguely aware of being chilly until he put his hot weight on her.

This wasn't right. She knew that. This wasn't okay.

"Don't," she said with as much force as she could. "Please."

He ignored her.

"Tyler, *don't*. I don't want to."

"It will just take a minute," he assured her. "Come on, stop complaining. It's not like it's the first time. You're being such a whiner."

"I'm not a whiner." She winced as he pressed into her. It felt like the wrong end of a screwdriver wrapped in sandpaper pushing in. Yes, she'd had sex before, willingly, but not like this. This was pain.

This was torture.

"This is rape," she said out loud.

The slap across her cheek came fast and hard. "Don't you dare fucking say that."

Those were the last words she heard before the darkness took over.

Chapter Five

Frances

The audition sucked and when I carried myself with as much dignity as I could muster out to the car, it was gone. I'd missed the No Parking deadline by three minutes and they worked that fast; it had already been towed to an impound lot five miles away. That might not sound like much until you consider that five miles in LA can take an hour or more to travel, so my heart sank.

A little investigation told me that if I didn't get it by five, they'd tag on another four hundred and fifty bucks for "storage." It was infuriating. That was criminal and I didn't have time to pay the ransom before the brunch was over. Did I take the risk and try and get the car and go to Jill's or get a ride and get my car later?

It was Fletcher Hall. I couldn't blow that chance.

So I ordered a Lyft and waited for what seemed like forever, watching the little car on the app wind around everywhere but where I was. Finally I walked to the main thoroughfare and texted my new location. It still took longer than it should have and I got in the back seat of the Toyota Corolla annoyed and disheveled. This wasn't a great start. Everyone said you should never go to an audition in a bad mood, and this was definitely an audition.

I closed my eyes and concentrated on a mantra meditation. My father swore by this technique and he used to make Crosby and me do it every afternoon at four for twenty minutes. Naturally we'd both come to resent the whole thing but it was hard to argue with his easygoing nature and happy disposition.

Nam myoho renge kyo, I repeated silently to myself. I didn't know what it meant but my dad said that was the point. It would make my life sublime without bogging me down with associative thoughts.

It worked a little. God knows I had enough time to get into it. I finally got to Jill's street at one thirty, half an hour before she expected her guests to leave. I know she didn't like it when there were stragglers after a party, so I really hesitated to go in so late. But not showing up at all seemed potentially ruder and, come on, when would I ever get the chance to meet Fletcher Hall again? If he was even still there.

This was stupid. I was way overthinking it. Jill had invited me for a reason, so I was going for it. And she would understand why I was late.

I opened the door and went in with the familiarity that came with my regular trips to the house, as if it were just another day and I was there to cook another meal. Then I tried to pepper in a bit of the zest and energy of the girl I was trying desperately—oh yes, I know it was desperate—to become.

The speakers were humming a Fleetwood Mac song and there was a strong scent of Christian Dior's Poison hanging in the air. That meant Abbey Van Werner was here. She *always* had just a bit too much of it on.

"Frances!" Jill grabbed a glass of wine from a server's tray and hurried over to me, nearly tripping on her caftan. "These damn things," she muttered when she got to me. "Hides a lot of sins but every time I sit down in it, it slips back and strangles me." She handed me the wine. "I'm going to go like Isadora Duncan yet."

I laughed as I took it. It gave me a small thrill to feel like a guest—as if it were normal to walk into the house and be handed rosé. "Sorry I'm so late. There was . . . a lot." I raised the glass to her and took a long swig. It was way too sweet. It went down like medicine.

"As luck would have it, Fletcher just arrived. And as *always*, he's in a hurry. Let me introduce you before he disappears." She took me by the arm and led me across the room, past so many not-quite-the-same TV faces from my childhood. When we got to Fletcher, I was struck by how short he was. This is not unusual in Hollywood, but sometimes it can be really startling.

"Fletch, my love, *this* is Frances Turner, the actress I've been telling you about. She's named for Ol' Blue Eyes, isn't that just *charming*? Her father is a musician and penned "Happily Never After," you remember that song, don't you, darling?"

Fletcher's face broke into the smile I'd seen frozen in print a million times. "I loved that song. Hey, how are you? Fletcher Hall." He put out his hand. He sounded easy, breezy, so comfortable with who he was. And with good reason. He might be short, but he emanated power and cool.

I resisted the urge to bow and kiss his ring and instead shook his hand like a normal human being. A normal human being with enough confidence to stay totally chill. "So nice to meet you. I'm such a fan." Lord, how unoriginal. Like he hadn't heard that a million times in his life. I reached for a reference to something obscure that he'd done. "Believe it or not, I did a paper on *Booster Shot* in school. You probably hear that kind of thing a lot."

If it sounded unbelievable to him, he didn't show it. "Wow, blast from the past."

He laughed, and so we did too.

"Darling, tell her about the show." Jill gestured, sending a waft of Chanel No. 5 my way.

And of course, I sneezed, reflexively raising my hand and spilling my wine on Jill. "Oh, *shit*." I took my cocktail napkin and dabbed uselessly at her. She flashed me a look and stepped back.

"Not a problem! I've been dying to change out of this damn thing anyway. Wasn't I just saying? Excuse me you two, will you?" Before I could say anything else, she hurried toward her room. It had been only a little wine, since I had guzzled quite a bit, but it was still mortifying.

I turned back to Fletcher, red-faced. "I'm an idiot."

He laughed. "Life. Shit happens."

I thought of my car, languishing in some shit parking lot across LA for more than I'd ever paid for a hotel room. "It really does."

"So here's the thing, I'm looking at doing a series of independent-story hours, and I want a base cast to appear on a regular basis."

"Oh, like *American Horror Story?*"

"Not quite. I just want the background to remain consistent." He was gesturing broadly so I was careful to draw my wineglass back out of his radius. "So I'm looking for people to play very small rotating parts on an ongoing basis. The kind of thing where you're familiar but people don't quite know why."

In other words, what most working-but-not-famous actors called *life*. "I see. Sounds *fascinating.*" That was overplayed. "Essentially, the people become the set."

He snapped a finger gun at me. "Precisely."

"Cool! Wow, that's sounds great!" I feared I sounded manic but I couldn't help it.

"Jill was right," he went on, "you have the perfect look for a background character."

"Oh. Huh." I smiled faintly, like that wasn't the fear I was constantly trying to squash. "Thank you?"

"You could be in every episode and people would say, 'Where have I seen her before?'" He laughed and shook his head like this was the greatest opportunity an actor could have.

With complete sincerity, I said, "I do get that sort of thing a lot." It wasn't impossible that in three days I'd run into him at a gas station and get it from him.

He went on, driving the point in like a spike. "In fact, I may have seen you before right here in this house, cooking, and not realized it."

I was pretty sure I would have noticed *him* if he'd been here before but it seemed better not to mention that. "Assuming the food was good, it may well have been me." I gave a weak laugh.

"Yes." He was nodding, clearly agreeing with himself and not with my quip.

Meanwhile, I was trying to avoid an onslaught of negative thoughts. Had Jill bragged that her cook was perfectly bland? That I could be forgotten in just about any role, so that made me perfect for this? On the one hand, it was so kind that she'd thought of me and recommended me, but on the other hand, it was completely disheartening. No one ever became a film icon because of how *forgettable* they were.

Nam myoho renge kyo.

"Well—" I started.

"Tell you what." He took his wallet out. It looked a hundred years old. A bad joke about *old money* came to mind. He dug through and produced a card. "This is my assistant's number. Give him a call and tell him I said to set up an audition for the teacher." He nodded again and, I'm pretty sure, gave me a small wink. "He'll take care of it from there."

"Thank you so much." I took the card as if it were a diamond ring. No matter what, this was better than anything that had happened thus far in my career. If I had to be forgettable to become successful, so be it. I guess.

And that wink—was that an assurance? Or was it *This ain't happening, sugar, but good luck with it all.*

"Good to meet you." He reached out his hand to shake again and I did. "Gotta run." As he walked away, I saw him take a small tube of hand sanitizer from his pocket and, with an embarrassing wet sound, squeeze some into his palm.

Well, that was just prudent, I told myself. In this day and age, that was just how it was. It wasn't because he thought I was gross.

Jill emerged on the other side of the room in a bright blue jumpsuit. It was the same color as her eyes and much more flattering than the caftan, though I was sure she'd disagree because it hugged her hips in a way the dress had not. She was in her mid-sixties and she looked fabulous—I would have bought forty if I didn't know better—so her constant worry about aging and expanding was exasperating and unnecessary.

"How did it go?" she asked conspiratorially. "He looked like he was really paying attention to what you were saying."

"Did he?" I shrugged. "He gave me his card. Told me to call his assistant to set something up."

She clapped her hands. "Well, that's *marvelous!* Oh, I'm so glad to hear it. I'm *certain* you'll get the part."

"Really? It sounds like it might be . . . small." Did that sound spoiled? I didn't want to sound spoiled. "Not that I mind small. Small is great. I would love small."

She chuckled and put a hand on my forearm. "Small stinks and we all know it, but it's a start. And it's a living." She pulled me closer. "And it's Fletcher Hall."

I knew what a regular job like that would pay. If I stayed in the background, it wasn't exactly a lot. "Thank God I have a real job," I said with a smile.

Her expression darkened. "You . . . do. It's true. As a matter of fact, I wanted to talk to you about that."

My chest froze. Was she firing me? "Are you firing me?"

"No!" The word exploded from her so quickly that it drew the attention of people around us. "Never. But the thing is, I'm really not working much anymore. There's no need for me to be rattling around in this house in town. Mortgage, taxes, insurance—it's a lot."

I could imagine. I looked it up on Zillow now and then because I'm a nosy ghoul, and the place was valued in the low millions. More than once I had thought it was a lot for one person, but she'd been there so long I never thought she'd leave. Of all the things I worried about—and there were many—that was not one of them. "Are you saying you'd leave LA?"

She nodded. "I've always loved the desert. So peaceful. None of this damn traffic."

"So—Palm Springs." Common wisdom was that Palm Springs was two hours away because it was originally colonized by movie stars so they could get some R and R while being only a couple of hours from LA if they needed to come back on set. As the years passed and traffic got worse, though, that time could easily stretch to three hours or even more.

Which worked for movie stars who *might* need to come back and film a scene or two now and then. It didn't work as a daily commute for a cook.

I must have looked crushed because Jill rushed to add, "You haven't heard the best part, though. Not only do I want to keep you on *but* there's a beautiful poolside casita where you can stay. Here, let me show you the whole place." She took her phone out and started clicking.

She handed me the phone. The house was gorgeous—high ceilings, pocket doors that opened the entire back of the house, a huge curved pool with a tile-roofed casita nestled in landscaping so lush, it looked like a Hawaiian hideaway. I flipped through and saw that even the quarters she proposed to be mine had a state-of-the-art kitchen with a gas Viking range.

It was stunning.

"Don't answer yet," she said. "I want you to give it some real thought. I'll forward the listing to you so you can picture yourself there. With a ten percent raise and the income from renting your LA place if you wanted, you could really make a killing!"

It was all too much to take in right now. A shock, really.

Yet her offer was a good one. Generous. "I'll definitely think about it. When are you're going to move?"

"Closing won't be for at least a month." She looked thoughtful. "You know, I'm just not sure. It's been so long since I sold a house."

"Closing? You sold the house already?"

"Actually, yes. To Mona." She gestured vaguely in the direction of the woman who owned several top restaurants. "This little do was sort of an introduction to local friends and neighbors for her."

And the last thing in the world Mona would need was a private chef.

A great big cartoon clock materialized in my imagination. *Tick-tick-tick*—time was almost up.

What was I going to do? Restaurant jobs seldom paid well enough to live on, especially if they were part-time, as any job would have to be in order to accommodate my potential audition schedule. But it was getting harder to find people who wanted a full-time private chef. People found it easier and cheaper to order Grubhub or DoorDash and not have anyone working in their home.

Really, it was a blessing that she was willing to keep me on, and at such excellent terms. Something told me I was going to angst about this for too long and then take the job. Nevertheless, I wasn't ready to commit to it yet.

"Let's see if anything wonderful happens with Fletcher," she said as if reading my mind.

I nodded. "Here's hoping."

Someone across the room caught Jill's attention; her face lit up and she waved. "Excuse me, dear," she said. "We'll talk about this later. It will all be *fine*. I promise. No—better than fine. It will be *great!*" She clearly believed it. She wouldn't have said all this to me this way if she'd had any idea how alarmed I would be.

Maybe, for once, I *shouldn't* panic. Maybe I should have faith in what she, the professional actress and friend of Fletcher Hall, thought would happen next. I took a deep breath.

Nam myoho renge kyo.

"Excuse me." I heard a female voice and felt a hand on my right shoulder. I turned to see none other than Mardie Mariano, the former teen pop star. The once-upon-a-time music sensation whose flipped, chunky-highlighted locks had determined the *look* of my and all my friends' early teenage years. When she went from sweet to sexy, we thought we should too. When she made an anthem for being boyfriend-less, we all used it as an excuse for our singlehood. When she chopped all her hair off and stopped wearing makeup and still managed to look pretty, well, let me just say, too many of her followers thought such drastic choices would work well for them.

It was uncanny, like I was looking straight into a 3D version of the autographed picture my dad had brought home from the studio for me when I was thirteen. Her eyes—now the eyes of a nearly forty-year-old woman—were circled a bit too heavily in kohl, and she was wearing a cropped peasant blouse with jean shorts and kitten heels. It was pitifully out of date and yet so on brand for her twenty years ago that I couldn't tell if it was a bad choice.

I have to admit it gave me a thrill.

But all I could think of was that I had to get out of there. I didn't have time to indulge in a conversation I could lord over Crosby's head later, tempting as the prospect was.

"Do you know where the bathroom is?" She grimaced charmingly. "I've been looking but I keep finding bedrooms."

"The last door down the hall, facing out." I pointed.

"I thought that was a closet."

I had to laugh. I'd thought the same thing the first time I was here, pumped up with Red Bull and coffee so I'd make a bright impression. "That's just the design. It's a closet first, but if you go in a couple feet it should be obvious."

She looked grateful. "Thank you. I'm about thirty seconds away from totally peeing myself." She hurried off and I watched her go. She moved exactly like you'd expect, just like I'd seen countless times on TV and in the two movies she'd done. Though I knew that in the human race, there was tons of crossover in traits, I found it amazing that she could be quite as . . . well, *her*, as I had anticipated. The pretty-but-raspy voice, the mannerisms, the walk.

I didn't even know I remembered her that well.

As long as I'd worked for Jill, I'd never gotten used to seeing these people in person. I always felt a combination of thrill and disillusionment. Somewhere deep inside, I wanted icons to be distant, untouchable. As many times as my dad had *almost* been able to introduce me to Paul McCartney, somehow it had never panned out, and deep down I was glad. If I'd met him, he'd become a mere mortal and though the compulsion was still there, the truth was I really didn't want that.

I turned on my phone and ordered a Lyft. Thirty-two minutes. My God, why was LA so busy today? I realized there weren't a lot of drivers hanging out in the hills but I could get from here to the center of town in less time than that. I frequently had.

With nothing else to do and feeling self-conscious about standing there with my empty wineglass, I went to the kitchen to help clean up. I wasn't there five minutes before Jill showed up.

"Frances Turner, you are *not* working today!"

"I am now."

"I'm not paying you!"

"I'm not stopping."

She sighed and reached for my arm. "You're a *guest*. If you start scrubbing my kitchen, I'm going to take it personally."

I laughed and let her manipulate me away from the sink. "I'm just waiting for my ride."

"If you have a ride coming, you should definitely have another glass of wine!"

"I'm fine. Really."

"Hi again."

We both turned to see Mardie wandering in, looking as lost as she had when she'd asked me where the bathroom was. I got the feeling she always looked like that. The little doe-eyed face contrasted with her sexy confident onstage presence had been her thing in her heyday. She probably wasn't lost at all, just snooping.

"Oh, Mardie, have you met Frances? She's my wonderful and talented chef, but she is *not working today.*"

She mimed choking me, and I felt humiliated but smiled anyway. "Hi, yes, we met a moment ago. You found it okay?"

"Yep," said Mardie.

Here she was, out of the pages of *Teen Vogue* and four feet in front of me, basically hearing me ask if she'd *managed not to pee herself.*

"Jill," Mardie said. "This is the . . . I think you said"—she lowered her voice, as if that would make it so Jill could hear her but I, next to her, couldn't—"*her sister* was going to be here?"

"Who? What?" Jill asked in the same tone.

Mardie looked at me, clearly irritated that I was there. "The *writer.*"

"The—oh! Yes, this is her sister." Jill gestured at me as if I were a prize on *The Price Is Right.* Not a good prize, though. Not a boat. A living-room set in oxblood Naugahyde that no one could actually want.

Wow. Really? How had Crosby managed to show up in this conversation, and how was she showing up as preferable to me?

"My sister is the writer. I'm the—chef."

"You're Crosby Turner's sister?" Mardie asked me in that scratchy, forever-Lolita tone.

"I . . . am." I felt like I was a pale imitation of my younger sister, even though she was famous as a writer and not a model or anything. Most people wouldn't know what she looked like, so I couldn't *really* take it personally when the implication was that I wasn't living up to the ideal.

"Is there any way you can help me get in touch with her?" She leaned toward me and said quietly, "Confidentially speaking, I need a writer, and I'd just be so honored if she'd do it. I loved her book."

Ugh, the humiliation. Here I'd been thinking I might have a chance to taunt Crosby with meeting her and it turned out she wanted to *get in touch with* her herself. I felt like she was stepping on me in an effort to look, above me, for my sister.

I actually gave a little shocked shake of the head. Neither of them noticed.

"Mardie has been contracted to do an autobiography," Jill supplied helpfully.

"And I can't write a sentence that makes sense by myself, so I need to hire someone to do the actual, you know, the *words*."

"Right." I nodded. "Crosby has a lot of those." I hoped they couldn't hear the bitterness in my voice. I heard it and hated it. "She's a very good writer," I added, which was true but still hard to admit.

Mardie obviously didn't give a damn what I had to say. "So . . . can you give me her number? Or give her mine? Maybe she'd be more comfortable with that."

Implied agreement seemed cooler than eagerly telling her

the famous Crosby Turner's number. I took out my phone. "Sure. What's your number?"

Mardie hesitated, and I felt weird and creepy until finally she gave it to me and then added, "Please put in a good word for me. I know you don't know me but I'm nice, honest. I'd just be seriously happy if she did this for me."

And the golden goose of life dropped another golden egg in Crosby's lap. I closed my phone. "I'll let her know tonight," I said, annoyed at the gratitude on her face. She was a fan. Mardie was a Crosby Turner *fan*. Thirteen-year-old me seethed while thirty-five-year-old me tried to be a gracious grown-up. "I'm sure she'd love to talk to you about it."

And I was sure of that. I gave what might have been a smile.

My car arrived, and I left, carrying with me the weirdness of Mardie Mariano being a Crosby Turner fan. I sat in awful traffic, headed for the awful and expensive ordeal of getting my car out of an impound lot.

I was shaking. I hated how mad this stuff made me. But today, a day that should have been an opportunity for me . . . *this*.

I work hard. All the time. I get a chance for an audition, but it's just a bad sitcom and I'm unlikely to get it. I get the chance to meet Fletcher Hall and he tells me I'd probably be perfect, and what I'm perfect for is to blend into the background. Then I meet an icon and she's just looking for Crosby. Crosby, who's probably ordering another bottle of champagne at brunch in Manhattan across the country, and way out here, where I'm trying desperately to be okay, the universe is arranging itself around her.

We'd been in traffic for half an hour when my nerves started to relax a little. Obviously Crosby wasn't going to want to write Mardie's book. She'd been struggling to come up with a new one of her own, so writing someone else's memoir—especially if it was to be ghostwritten—would be, I don't know, counterproductive. This was going to go down in the history of Crosby as one more cool offer she got.

Meanwhile, I was in gridlock, just hoping to get to the impound lot in time.

Chapter Six

Crosby

The days passed slowly. I got nowhere with new book ideas, as I hadn't for a couple of years now, and I'd begun checking Indeed for high-paying, low-time-commitment jobs I could do that would still allow me to joust at the word windmills that could really take me out of this nightmare.

I even got a couple of interviews, but the problem that cropped up in each of them was the time between my last proper job and now. No one was as impressed by my writing history as I hoped they'd be. It was all the reward my impostor syndrome had ever needed.

No one gave a shit what cool stuff I'd done before if I hadn't mastered whatever technology went with the job in question.

It was after a particularly disheartening interview to be a social secretary for a family name everyone on earth would recognize that I came home and poured myself an uncharacteristic shot of tequila. Then another. Then just one more.

They tasted like shit, but I have to admit, it took the edge off.

Until the phone rang.

The caller ID was hidden behind cracks in the screen from me constantly dropping the phone. You would have thought it was made of wet soap. But I could see the readout: *Frances*.

Frances rarely called. When she did, it tended to be out of some obligation to remember she had a sister or to tell me she was worried about our parents active social life and I should go by and make sure they were not *overdoing it*.

Frances, like everyone else, was under the misapprehension that since a writer worked at home she could interrupt her life at any time day or night to do something else. She seemed to think the creative process was something that could be turned on and off, like a movie on the DVR. Or a sitcom.

Admittedly, I was not in the midst of a creative burst. It was worse. I was in the midst of a total life failure.

If I answered, no matter how hard I tried to disguise that fact, she'd hear it in my voice. Then she'd ask *questions*.

I wasn't up for questions.

I hit Decline.

Somehow I'd thought that a bestselling book would keep paying on and on like a hit song, but that wasn't the case. A hit song became an *oldie* and had just as much life on that side as the first. A bestselling book, if it wasn't the Bible, eventually became passé.

Too bad I hadn't had a hit song. I couldn't believe how much money Dad made off "Happily Never After." I saw the statement once, and he had laughed.

"Don't start mentally spending it yet, missy, we're still here, alive and kickin'."

"I'm not mentally spending it!" I objected, hands planted on hips. It would devastate me if anything happened to either one of my parents. "I'm just thinking I should have gotten the lobster tail tonight."

"Oh, was the filet not good enough for you, princess?" My mother, the famous vegetarian cookbook author, had smiled.

"No. I meant *also*." I smiled at her and gazed up at the halo appearing over my head.

"Please," she said.

But my dad had laughed, enchanted by me as always, even when I said obnoxious things like that. Being around them always regressed me, but in a way that seemed to make us all happy.

I knew if worse came to worst, as it appeared to be, they would say I could move back in with them.

That, more than anything else, motivated me to do something—*anything*—to get myself out of this hole. Not that I wouldn't have loved moving back in with them. I would have. They're delightful people and my mother is a supreme cook who loves to nurture her loved ones. I could be fat and happy living there for the rest of my life.

Except for the small fact that they were young sixty-somethings looking at the golden years directly in front of them and the last thing in the world they needed was their thirty-three-year-old spendthrift of a daughter moving in with them because she'd failed at adulting.

Nope, nope, nope, I'd rather live in a cardboard box in the street than turn their glorious retirement years into day care and therapy for their adult daughter.

Maybe I could chronicle my search for meaning after success. Success after success. Changing careers in the netherworld that is one's thirties—not quite young, not quite middle-aged. A time when you were supposed to be firmly ensconced in some profession that either would or wouldn't turn out to be your passion. I couldn't be the only one having a crisis like this. Maybe I could write the book for myself and help a lot of other people in the process. I could see it now, in all its glory: *Book3new.docx*.

The phone rang again.

It was her again and this time I answered it because the sister never rings twice. Maybe it was an emergency. Immediately my nervous system went into high gear. "Is everything all right?" I asked instead of the usual greeting.

"What? Yes, what are you talking about?"

"I was afraid something was wrong because—"

"Because you declined my call before?"

"I was tied up."

"I *knew* it. I knew you hit Decline. You're lucky I even tried again, honestly."

I glanced around and heard the ticking clocks in my empty house. "Sorry, I'm just busy at the moment."

"If you were really busy, you wouldn't have been declining so quickly."

I sighed and fell backward. "Foiled again."

"Listen, I'll get to the point. I've got a potential gig for you."

"*Gig?*" I had to laugh. "Since when do you say that? You *hate* that word. All those times Dad's musician friends would say that and you'd—"

"Look, it's a word out here. *Forgive me.* A job." She sounded irritated. "I have a potential job for you. Of course you're not going to want it, but I thought you'd get a kick out of hearing about it."

A job? I wondered how bad it would have to be for me to refuse it. Birthday clown? I did enjoy makeup.

"Ready?" she asked, then didn't wait for my answer. "Mardie Mariano asked me to give you her number."

"Who's Marty Mariano?"

"Mar*die. D.* What's wrong with you?"

"Oh, Mardie *Mariano.* I get it." I laughed. Mardie, the anthem-scribe of our teenage years. Sure. "Cool, well, Brad Pitt texted me and was wondering if you're free Saturday. I told him you've got plans."

"I'm serious."

"I'm sure."

There was a long pause. "So you really don't want to know why she's asking for your number?"

"Oh, come on, Franny." I couldn't live with myself if I acted like she was serious and found out it was a drawn-out misfire of a joke. "Why would she want my number? Advice on repurposing crop tops? Because I got rid of all mine twenty years ago when the school principal said they were indecent and threatened to suspend me."

She would probably read my tone is cavalier, but on the off chance this was a prank, I would not be made a fool of by way of my enthusiasm.

She made an impatient sound that only I, as her sister, could identify as such. "Look, I'm completely serious. She has a book deal for a memoir, but she can't write, so she needs a writer. She wanted to know if you'd write it—isn't that the wildest thing ever?"

There was a silence, during which I narrowed my eyes, and I knew she was probably doing the hand thing that meant she was feeling invisible.

"Hello?"

"Is this for real?" I asked.

"Do you think I made this whole thing up out of the blue?" Her tone was impatient. She was serious.

"Oh my God, you're telling the truth." I sat up. "She wants to hire me to write her memoir?"

"I could not have made this up."

"Well . . . I mean, that's not a bad plot for, like, a nineties movie. Freddie Prinze Jr. and, like . . . Mandy Moore. They were never in anything together, were they?"

I heard her sigh. "I'm not the writer, remember?"

It probably sounded like I didn't care at all, but in fact, even the gust of hope had been enough to bring back my pleasantness. "How much does it pay? The ghostwriting thing, I mean. This is ghostwriting, right?"

Desperation. Dire need to pay my bills.

"Oh, yeah, I actually have all that written up, we had a

meeting that lasted all afternoon, you should have seen the agent I got you, she negotiated quite a deal for you."

I was silent, trying to figure out if—

"I have no idea how much it pays, you dummy, why would I know that? She just knew I was your"—a frustrated pause—"sister. She asked where the bathroom was and then she asked if she could get in touch with you. That's the extent of our interaction. I figured you'd get a kick out of it but—are you saying you're interested?"

I tried to sound casual. "I could be, I don't know."

There was a pause before she said, "Okay, then, seriously I have her number, want to write it down?"

I looked around for a pen, my silence surely reading as indecision. "Yeah, hold on. So she was just like, *Where's the bathroom and can you give your sister my number?* Just like that?"

I took my phone from my ear and put her on speaker, opening the notes app. There were only three items there.

To do.
TO DO
MONDAY TO DO.

"Go on," I said.

"Okay—"

"Wait." I sank into a horrid posture and held my phone to my mouth like a Real Housewife in a driving scene. "Is this seriously for real?"

"Crosby."

"Because it wouldn't be funny as a joke."

"I know." Her voice softened. "It wouldn't. It's not a joke."

"It would just be cruel." The words sounded positively medieval for me and I shut my eyes, knowing she'd know that. "If you're still holding a grudge against *me* about—"

"Stop it! If nothing else, this is another super-cool thing to put in your own memoir someday. Don't make me beg to do you a favor."

"You're right. I'm sorry."

She hesitated, then said, "Hang on, what's wrong?"

"Nothing's wrong." Everything was wrong.

Another pause, like she was analyzing the silence on the line. "I don't believe you."

"Everything. Is. Fine." And in that moment, apparently I gave it away.

"Something's wrong," she said definitely.

I sighed. "Define *wrong*."

"You're the writer, not me."

"Not *I*."

"God, you're the worst." She made a noise of exasperation. "Wait a minute. Would you actually, really, honestly take this job?"

"Why wouldn't I?"

"No glory. No credit. Flat fee. This is the kind of thing artists tend to hate."

I shrugged even though she couldn't see me. "I'm open to anything. It's writing. I just want to write."

I just want not to go broke. I could ghostwrite. Sure. Why not? I was sure I could do a better job than half the hacks out there.

Plus, I had liked Mardie. Not as much as Frances had. Admittedly, I found her music a little boring, especially through the thin wall between my room and Frances's. But Mardie was cool for a while. She was such all-American, girl-next-door plastic glamour. Golden blond, California tan, pearly white smile. I remember she was funny on a couple of *Saturday Night Live* appearances.

Maybe there was more to Mardie than anyone knew. Maybe I could write the book that redeemed her from her child-star-and-nothing-else reputation. The book that would bring her back, better than ever. And everyone would say it was because of that great book.

My heart started to lift as I began to believe in the phone call. "I want this more than I've wanted anything ever," I said, suddenly sounding like I was lying, even though it was true.

"Oh my God," Frances said.

And I knew. She'd seen me.

"You're broke, aren't you?"

I felt myself make the face I always made when she called me out. "I'm—wow, that's, like, incredibly rude."

"When did this happen?"

"I—it's . . ." I sighed, giving in. "I don't even know. How did you know—"

"How did you go through all of that money? You had so much effing money."

"You don't know how much money I had. And when they pay it out over increments, it's really not *that* much." I frowned. "Did you say *effing?*"

"I'm at Whole Foods."

"Oh, yes, don't let the keto-dieters hear you swear."

"There was a kid by the apple samples—can you stop deflecting?"

"I'm not deflecting." I untied the lace on my slipper. "Are you still seeing that guy?" I deflected.

"Crosby, I swear to God." A pause. "And no, he called his mom three times a day. *In secret.*"

"Ew."

"I know, I know. But seriously, what the hell? Were you robbed or something? Did you hire some seedy investment broker? Please don't tell me it's the clichéd dishonest accountant who took off for some island nation."

I thought about whether or not that would make me come off better but decided, reluctantly, on the truth. Things— I—needed to change and I needed to change now. "No, Frances, I'm proud to say I did this *all by myself.*"

"Are you joking?"

"And you thought I'd never make it on my own."

"Listen, I'm just really shocked."

"*Listen,*" I mocked angrily. "I don't need you lecturing me about how shocking this is, how irresponsible you think I am, when you don't know *anything* about my life or what I've been going through or doing or—or—"

I got a flash suddenly of the last fling I had when the guy

was always alluding to the fact that I *didn't even know* what all he was *going through*, which, at the end of the day had been a manipulation tactic to keep me from digging deep enough to find out about his unfortunate tendency to meet up with degenerates from the personals on Craigslist whenever he went to Vegas.

Now I sounded like him.

I did not want to be a liar.

"It's just not your business what I do with my money," I said, in closing. "I'm struggling enough without you being a Grand Canyon echo of my daily self-flogging."

"I'm sorry, I didn't mean it to sound that way."

"Well, it did."

"Sorry—" Her voice went distant. "Oh, excuse me, can I just grab some ginger? No, no, you're fine! Thanks, yours are cute too! So festive—are those pumpkins on the toe?"

I rolled my eyes like I had better stuff to do. She was always getting into nice little interactions with strangers while she was on the phone with me.

When she finally came back on, she said, "Okay, I just sent you her contact."

I looked at my texts. She had sent the contact. She had saved her as MARDIE M WTF.

I laughed, but she probably didn't hear it. "Got it. Well. Thanks. I appreciate it."

It sounded so lame, but I couldn't find more gratitude. I was too embarrassed.

"No prob. Bye."

She'd always been the type to hang up the second she said bye. I thought she'd probably missed a thousand *I love you*s.

I spent the next twenty minutes composing a text.

I landed on: Hey, this is Crosby Turner. My sister said you needed help on a project. This is my contact, I look forward to hearing from you!

I must have deleted that exclamation point ten times, replacing it with a period every time but one, when I typed in an ellipsis and then panic-backspaced over it. I double- and then triple-checked to make sure I hadn't written I look forward to hearing from.!.

Satisfied that it looked fine, I set my phone down and started thinking about how big the fee might be. Embarrassingly, I wasn't thinking about my bills, I was thinking about whether I could finally get that outdoor set that—

My phone was ringing.

Not just ringing.

FaceTime ringing.

What the *hell* kind of monster FaceTimes without a week's notice?

Mardie.

MARDIE M WTF, to be exact.

My hand went to my hair. I hadn't used my now-cherished water to shower in over two days. I had no makeup on. I wasn't even wearing a shirt, just a bra. I couldn't answer like this.

But I couldn't miss the call either.

I declined and quickly texted that I was at the grocery

store, I'd call right back when I got home. A stupid panic-lie. What if I'd missed my chance?

I screamed a bunch of words unsuitable for Whole Foods and cursed the invention of FaceTime.

Why did she need to *see* me? Why, why, why? Why did people *ever* prefer FaceTime? Did the rest of the world walk around FaceTime-ready while I alone looked like something the cat had dragged in? My face was puffy and undefined, my hair was sarcastic, my shirt was . . . nonexistent.

I decided I would pretend I had sent the text and then walked away from the phone, like people with lives must do. She wouldn't need to know that I had then bathed, blown out my hair, curled it, and done my makeup with the precision and waste worthy only of a glamorous—I don't know—New Year's Eve on Leonardo DiCaprio's yacht or something.

I put on my most flattering casual look, slapped on some strategically placed bronzer, and FaceTimed her back.

And . . . nothing.

No answer.

All dressed up and nowhere to go, and literally nothing to do. For the next hour, I cycled through Netflix, trying to find something to watch while I waited for her to call me back.

* * *

SHORT OF THE alarm going off at seven a.m. for school, there is no more upsetting sound that I can imagine than a FaceTime call from a massive celebrity at a barely civilized nine a.m. after you had a late night of psyching yourself up for that person's call until finally falling into a deep sleep.

"Hi!" I answered too enthusiastically, wishing I could delete *that* exclamation point. "Good to hear from you."

"I'm sorry," she said, her voice like chamomile and sandpaper, but in a good way. "Did I wake you up?"

"No, no, I was just—" I observed myself. I looked like two a.m. "I've been up for hours."

She had a neon-pink headband in her icy blond hair. Dark roots, just like always, but I had to admit, it was her look. It suited her. She was tan and flushed, like she'd just finished a tough spin class. The whites of her eyes practically glowed, and the blue of her irises was piercing. How did *anyone* look like that on FaceTime?

This was so surreal, to see her on my phone, talking to me.

"Did Francesca tell you why I wanted to talk to you?"

Francesca? Is that what she had LA calling her? I made a mental note to mention it every day for the next year. "You need help writing a memoir?"

She nodded, her ponytail flopping. "I'm hopeless. I need someone to help and I loved your book. Seriously, told all my friends about it."

All. Her. Friends. All her friends? All *her* friends? All her *friends*? *All* her friends?

Who *were* her friends, anyway? The tabloids said she didn't speak with Trey anymore. I didn't know who else she knew.

"I know you're probably at work on another bestseller," she said.

Yeah, the great American novel *Booktwoforrealdecfinal4.docx*.

"I totally understand if you're too busy to help with mine."

"No, no, as it happens, I'm sort of"—I looked helplessly at the screen of my computer beside me, the screensaver repeating a line of text over and over, a kid at the chalkboard: *You can do it, you can do it, write the book, you can do it.* "I'm on a hiatus from my current project. I'd love to help." Then, afraid I'd sound unprofessional or, worse, free, I added, "I really enjoy taking ghostwriting projects every now and then. Gives the right brain a rest and . . . sharpens the writing reflexes."

It was not true; I had never done any ghostwriting before. But hey, it was the perfect lie.

"Oh, I don't know about that," she said bashfully. I thought of the "Don't Let Me Say Sorry" video that had come out in the sophomore era of her career in which she had employed the same demure look. "Right brain, wrong brain, I just like the way you put words together. I don't think my career or life makes any sense, so you may have to help glue those things together a little."

I liked that. The conversation flowed a little more easily from then on. Just when I felt at my fanciest, my most surely directed toward success, my most elite and above all my former peers, she said, "I like you." My ego was about to carry me away when she popped it with a simple "You're kind of a mess, like me."

"Oh. Thanks?"

"I mean, you're easy to talk to."

She said it so apologetically, so nicely, that I couldn't even really feel offended. Worse, I felt seen.

"So I'll have my manager call you. Money-wise, I don't know, do we have to go through an agent?"

I breathed a sigh of relief. There was a *money-wise*.

We waded through the muddy nature of the logistics before ultimately deciding to talk to our respective in-charge people, her manager and my literary agent, like two tenth-graders who want to go on a date but need a ride.

"Well, this sounds great," I said after the business was done. "I'm just dying to dig in and get started."

"Me too. So when can you come?" she asked.

"Come?"

"To California? So we can write it?"

"I live in New York."

Doubt took over her tone. "Ohhh. I really wanted someone local. You know, so we could talk about everything in person."

"Oh, of course." My heart leaped. I pictured myself nestled away in a Beverly Hills casita, forging a friendship with scandalous, divisive Mardie. Under the stars, surrounded by stars. Maybe I'd meet some unattached French director or something and be engaged and in a new life within the year. "That's not a problem. In fact, my sister lives there. As you know."

"So you *can* come?"

"Anytime!" I heard myself say. "I'm ready."

At the time it felt like a six- to eight-week try and a supplemental income but deep down I knew it was my only shot at a meaningful change in my life.

Chapter Seven

Thirteen Years Ago

Sisters are supposed to be able to trust each other more than anyone else in the world.

Not the Turner sisters, though.

Despite the best parents anyone could ask for and a childhood that would have looked like idyllic fiction if you read it in a book, the Turner sisters managed to be the exception to the rule.

Previously, they'd overcome their squabbles with each other, usually fairly fast. A borrowed and ruined sweater was annoying but not catastrophic. Music played too loud could be shouted over. DVR recordings deleted in favor of someone else's favorite made for the inconvenience of streaming but little else. These disputes were evidence of taking advantage of each other, maybe not respecting boundaries as well as they could or should.

But the uncrossable line was that they should be able to trust each other.

And while they'd each come very close to crossing that line in the past, neither had ever actually done it.

Until now.

So when she saw her *sister* sneaking off to the barn with her boyfriend and then staying there for what seemed like hours, it was pretty devastating. The kind of thing that could—and would, she was sure—affect their relationship for a lifetime.

The lie was just so ugly. Other people had seen them go in there too. It wasn't like they'd been super-subtle about it. So other people now thought she was a fool for trusting both her boyfriend *and* her sister.

"Hey, don't go in the barn," Rex Stuckey had actually said to her with a laugh. "Unless you want a *big* surprise."

"I know what you're trying to imply, but we broke up. He can do whatever he wants to."

"It looks like he wants to do her."

"Well, *she* can do whatever she wants to too. I don't care."

Pia Markley had been a little more gentle, though there was no mistaking the subtle note of gossiping glee when she said, "You're not looking for Tyler and your sister, are you?"

"No."

"Good, because they're"—she looked right and left, then lowered her voice—"*in the barn together.* And I don't think they're cleaning stalls."

"Tyler and I broke up, so I don't care what he's doing or where *or* with who." Lies, all lies. She hadn't been planning to break up with him at all, though it wasn't like she thought they were going to get married or anything. They'd been together for only a few months but long enough for everyone in town under the age of twenty-five to know about them.

It was humiliating.

And why would she do it? He wasn't the only guy at the party. He wasn't even the best-looking! Or the smartest. In other words, the *only* reason she would have done it was on purpose. Maybe revenge for some imagined slight?

It had seemed like all their lives, there had been an undercurrent of competition between them. Well, maybe not *all* their lives, but ever since middle school. As different as they were, they didn't actually *look* that different from each other, and with only two years between them, their ages mattered less and less as time went on. So any guy that chose one of them over the other was demonstrating a preference that could *only* be taken personally.

She looked at the barn. There was no light on in it, but the moon was bright and she knew what it looked like shining in those windows. It made it bright enough.

It wasn't like they needed lights.

She was tempted to just march down there and throw open the door and catch them in the middle of whatever they were doing. Their expressions would surely make it worth it. At least for a moment.

But then she'd have to come back and face the rest of the party. See the looks of pity or amusement or probably some gross combination of the two. The town wasn't exactly known for its humanitarian interests. Politicians were elected for how much money they'd save the rich people, not what policies they'd put in place to help the needy or save the farms.

No, it was better to stick with the story that they'd broken up and she didn't give a fig what he was doing or with whom. It was basically true, after all. Tyler just didn't know it yet.

A technicality.

She had to make herself look away from the scene of the crime. It was otherwise a beautiful, starry night. The smell of late-autumn hay from the last cutting hung in the crisp air, mingling with the burning wood and leaves in the bonfire. Some people had made long twigs into kebab sticks and were toasting marshmallows over the flame. She wasn't a big marshmallow fan in general, but it smelled wonderful.

A lot better than this crappy beer someone had made. The best that could be said for it was that it was successfully alcoholic. It tasted like the sugar-free flavor syrups you could buy for coffee—artificial and sickly sweet. When she was a kid and didn't realize that what she thought of as cinnamon was actually cinnamon mixed with a lot of sugar, she'd topped a piece of buttered bread with pure Vietnamese ground cinnamon, took a bite, and nearly choked to death. The scent had stayed in her nose and throat for what seemed like days.

That's what this beer reminded her of.

All in all, the night was a bust, unless you considered finding out your sister would betray you at the most base level a worthwhile lesson.

It was. Better to learn this now than when the guy was her husband.

The thought was angry but the emotion was pure sadness. Once upon a time the two of them had shared so much. They'd played with the same toys, counted on the same parents, eaten from the same popcorn bucket while watching *The Lion King*, begged for the same bedtime stories, and stayed up in the same room whispering and giggling as the moon crossed the sky outside their window.

Sisters were supposed to be able to trust each other more than anyone else in the world.

Not the Turner sisters, though.

Chapter Eight

Frances

Crosby was coming to LA.

And I was terrified.

That sounds like a big word, I know, but I really was. I was still working to build my life out here and, to be brutally and embarrassingly honest, I was terrified that she was going to sweep in and outdo in six weeks everything I'd done in six years. If anyone could do it, it was her.

One summer three and a half years ago, while I worked my ass off to get a role as a blurry background barista in an antidepressant commercial, she hit it so big as an author, it was breathtaking. TV interviews, magazine coverage; it looked like she'd be on top of the world forever. The money rolled in—I know it did because I saw the home she bought and the trips she took and the champagne she drank.

Who wouldn't envy that? Believe me, I was ashamed of how jealous I was. I constantly reminded myself I was being idiotic because I'd never even tried to write a book; it made no sense to tell myself that her being a winner in that realm was a sign of my being a loser in every other, but it felt like that.

Now she was coming to my turf, and I was already afraid her light was going to dim mine in my own, self-created territory.

My mind raced with nothing but terrible scenarios. What if she embarrassed me in front of someone who mattered? Not by acting like a fool—one of Crosby's greatest gifts was making other people think she was charm's gift to earth—but what if she made *me* look like a fool by comparison? What if, as had happened so many times in the past, I was the easy butt of her jokes?

If I was upset about something it was: *Oh my God, don't have a Franic attack, I was kidding. Of course you're not losing your hair. Obviously. It was a rabbit-and-tortoise joke, get it?*

If I went to her room to look for a missing sweater, it was: *Looky here, Francy Drew has come to sleuth out the ark of the covenant! Check on top of the dryer.*

Even good news was *Frantastic!* and it would make my face hot just to hear it.

She had a seemingly endless number of puns on my name and everyone else thought they were delightful but they got right under my skin.

I'd worked hard to create a new identity for myself, and it was not the clown she seemed to think I was. It wasn't perfected yet, I wasn't quite *there* with it, but I was trying and, as difficult as this is to admit, I didn't want to be shown up by my little sister. Again.

Even to my own ear, that sounded incredibly petty, so I took a breath and tried to rationalize this back to earth. She was coming for a job. People traveled for work all the time. It wasn't a big life-altering thing for anyone.

In fact, she wasn't even going to be staying that close to me. Initially she'd made noise about staying in the Hollywood Hills and commuting to Mardie's place in the Valley every day. She said it was "only twelve miles," as if that could be traveled at the same speed here as it was back east. There was traffic there, sure, but it was nothing like here.

She'd emphasized that she was concerned about money, and the prices of rentals in the hills were out of her budget. She ended up with a place in Tarzana, about three miles from Mardie's house. It wasn't glamorous, she said, but it was practical and conveniently close to where she needed to be. And it was easily half an hour from my place, forty-five minutes from Jill's. Our acquaintances would never overlap.

I was waiting semi-anxiously for the phone to ring the day she was due to arrive. She was supposed to call me from the plane before she landed so I would have enough time to put whatever I was doing on hold and go pick her up. As it happened, I was preparing pork and scallion purse dumplings for a small dinner party Jill was having the next day, a task that couldn't easily be put on hold, when the doorbell rang.

I wondered if I'd ordered something because people never,

ever came to the door unexpectedly unless they were trying to cold-sell something, like pest control or religion.

Before I could get far with my musing, the bell rang again, followed immediately by pounding and some muffled yelling of what I realized was my name. The rest of the words were indistinct but the tone was unmistakable. It was Crosby.

I put a damp cloth over my dough and wiped my hands on my apron as I walked over to the door, bracing myself for a visit that could go any number of ways.

The minute I opened the door, she spilled in, like water on the *Titanic*. "Close the door! Quick! Lock it!"

"What? Why?"

"He's following me."

"What are you talking about?" I looked out over the sunny parking lot at the familiar courtyard. "Who's following you?" She reached behind me and pushed the door shut.

"Darren Neville."

I *had* to have misheard. "What are you *talking* about?"

"I swear I'm being followed by Darren Neville."

No, I hadn't misheard. Every syllable was enunciated clearly. "Darren Neville. The actor. Probably the next James Bond. You think *Darren Neville* is following you."

"No," she said carefully, "I *know* Darren Neville is following me. I had a little trouble parking and I think maybe that pissed him off because as soon as I got out of the car, he started yelling something, no doubt about how I'm just a stupid tourist who can't drive, and I just hightailed it in here."

"You think the notoriously charming actor Darren Neville cussed you out for being a bad driver and then chased you to my door? To—what? Cuss you out some more? Slap your face?"

"Weird, right?" There was no question that she looked rattled.

"This is the stupidest thing I've ever heard. And I was there when Dad decided to take up riding the unicycle."

The doorbell rang.

She looked at me, panicked. "It's him!"

"It's *not* him," I said, "and I swear to God, you are the only person in the world who would come to California and imagine terrible celebrity encounters. Most people would be thrilled just to see someone who looks vaguely like the ugly Jonas brother or the nanny Jude Law slept with or something—what's wrong with you?"

She was positively wide-eyed. "I'm not making this up. You wouldn't think he had that much lung power, but he sounded really, really mad."

I had to laugh. Who comes to La-La Land and imagines the *stars* are looking at *them*?

The bell rang again, raising all the same questions it had the first time, and I looked through the peephole. I couldn't believe it. The door creaking was all I could hear as I pulled it open and stood, agape.

"I'm sorry to bother you," Darren Neville said, scrutinizing me. "But I think you—" He glanced behind me, his eyes alighting on Crosby. "No, *you*. You dropped this when you got out of your car." He held out a phone in a Chanel case.

Crosby lurched forward like a defective robot. "Oh, shit, I'm so sorry. When you started yelling, I thought—well, I don't know what I thought."

He shook his head. "Just trying to return your phone to you."

"That is so nice." She took the phone from him, pushing me aside. "Thank you so much. I would have been absolutely screwed without this. I didn't even hear it hit the ground! God, I'm so embarrassed."

"No need to be. It's a drag to have to cancel your cards and all." He gave an adorable Darren Neville smile. "Anyway. I hope you enjoy your time here and I'm sorry to have alarmed you."

"This is so nice." She smiled and looked, as usual, adorable. Golden-haired with eyes that could be described as twinkling blue. All she needed were dimples and the *ding* on a triangle. "What a great introduction to LA."

He gave a nod, turned, and left.

"Isn't that so nice," she mused, closing the door after him. "Just so nice."

"How is this happening?" I looked through the peephole, but he was gone. But he'd been here. Right here on my doorstep. Looking like, well, like himself and smelling like fresh laundry. How did Crosby *always* seem to attract such weird and wonderful things? Even when it started with something bad—losing her phone—she came out of it golden.

Oops, I was doing it. Gravitating immediately toward the negative. "You are really lucky. There's no denying it."

She tucked the phone into her purse and closed the zipper top. "I really have to be more careful."

"Yeah," I agreed, leading her toward the kitchen. "You wouldn't want Bradley Cooper to have to buff out a scratch on your bumper or Donald Glover to have to remove a splinter." I wasn't even sure I was kidding.

She sighed and shook her head happily. "For a minute, I thought this place was more unsavory than I'd ever heard, but this is actually a pretty good welcome to town."

"I'll say."

Finally our eyes met. "Well." She smiled awkwardly. "It's good to see you!" She came to me and gave me a quick hug. "I can't believe I'm actually here."

I hated the way I stiffened up whenever someone tried to be affectionate. "Me neither."

"And it's all thanks to you."

"Glad to help. Do you want something to eat? Drink?"

"You relax, I'll get it." She made her way to the fridge. Within three seconds she'd pulled out a bottle of Rombauer chardonnay I'd been saving. "Mind if I open this?"

"No, sure, go ahead," I said automatically, wishing she'd chosen the Trader Joe's Blanc de Blancs next to it.

"Boy, I need this after all those hours traveling. Ugh. No wonder I haven't been to this coast in twenty years."

"It's not *that* bad."

"Torture. Pure torture." She went straight to the utensil drawer and pulled out a wine key before I could answer. "Funny how we instinctively keep things in the same place in the kitchen, isn't it? I bet I could find just about anything I needed in the first or second shot." She stopped short of taking the foil off and looked at me, hand poised over the bottle. "Is it really okay?"

I nodded. "Go ahead." I could use it, and it was true, she'd spent hours on several flights; I really should have offered it myself. "The wineglasses are—"

"Don't tell me!" She started for the wrong cabinet, stopped, and, without me saying a word, went to the right one. I watched, amazed, as she opened it and clapped her hands. "Ta-da!" She took two of the glasses out.

They were the two remaining Waterford ones I had; I'd lost the other four from the set to tipsy guests. I flinched as she spun one in her hand before setting it down.

She must have seen me or heard my sharp intake of breath because she said, "Don't worry, I'm not going to break it." She expertly uncorked the wine and poured it evenly into the two glasses. Then she handed me one and tapped the other to it. "To California."

"Welcome."

"I know I keep saying it, but I just can't believe I'm here."

I took a sip. "Me neither. I'll keep saying that too."

She smiled. "Funny how you can say that like there's an audience who's in on the joke."

She was exactly right; I'd felt it myself. A chirpy *I can't believe I'm here!* followed by a glum *Me neither.*

"No!" I objected, probably too loud and too fast. "It's just—I don't think I've had someone over in literally weeks, and boom! It's you, of all people. It blows me away." That was true.

"I can't believe it either."

I gestured toward the stools by the counter. "Have a seat, tell me everything while I finish making these apps." I went back to my place, and Crosby settled on a barstool, pulled an apple from the bowl on the counter, and watched me start my assembly up again.

"You're so much like Mom," she said, a bit wistfully.

"I wish!"

"You *are!* It's not just the cooking, it's your whole sort of Zen energy while you're doing it. You really go somewhere when you're in the kitchen."

I smiled without looking up. "I can't think of a nicer compliment than to be told I'm like her."

"You've always been her favorite."

I gave a half shrug. "Not true."

She rolled her eyes. "By rights, I should be Dad's favorite, but Dad doesn't have favorites. I know this because I studied him for years, hoping for signs that I was it. Every time I thought I had the edge on you, I'd find out you two had gone off on some adventure without me. Like that time you went roller-skating the night the rink closed for good."

I closed my eyes, remembering. He'd been friends with the

owner. They'd sold it to make way for a small community of large houses. To this day, even though that was maybe twenty years ago, I think of them as *the new houses*. Dad knew I had loved going there and racing around in circle after circle after circle, listening to Christina Aguilera, NSYNC, Backstreet Boys, Mardie Mariano, and the rest of the hits of the day over scratchy thin speakers that would have sounded better playing the first hits of Muddy Waters or Billie Holiday.

The night it closed, after the last group had left and the last Three Musketeers had been sold, he produced a key and took me in. The lights were on and there was still the smell of stale popcorn hanging in the air. He pushed a button and all of my favorite songs played as we did our last laps around the familiar rink.

"That's true," I said. "He did that. It was one of the best nights I can remember."

"You loved that place."

"I'm still mad it's gone." To this day I can picture the broken wood in the far right corner and the view of the generator and the woods beyond out the left end. I'd spent so many hours there, dreaming of so many futures for myself. The one where I stayed in town and got married and had kids just like my parents, maybe even lived on the same street. The one where I was a famous figure skater like Michelle Kwan or Tara Lipinski. And of course the one where I was a movie star living in a big house with a pool and when I went to work I got to kiss Brad Pitt all day long for my role as his girlfriend.

Back then, I think the one where I stayed in New York in a

pretty old Colonial house with a view of the apple trees from the window over the sink was my favorite.

I was still fond of it today, though it was far, far out of reach.

That was the thing about our father. He knew how to make special memories that showed us who *we* were. Both our parents did. They gave us room to come up with our own dreams, even if they took us far away, as mine had.

But you're never really that far away from anywhere in this world, are you?

Two weeks ago, Crosby had been thousands of miles away, literally and figuratively, and now here she was in front of me.

"What's your favorite memory with him?" I asked her. "Just the two of you."

She smiled. "Easy. When I was eight he took me to a miniature-horse farm where you could ride the horses or be pulled in a cart around a track. They had a show with a huge Clydesdale and a little miniature guy that looked like him, and they could add simple numbers and prance around. And they sold those plastic horses and riders and saddles and stuff from England in the shop there."

"Oh, I remember those. You *loved* those." I could picture the stamp on their bellies: *Made in Great Britain*. "See, I didn't even know about that excursion. Maybe you *were* his favorite."

She shrugged. "You're probably right."

I probably was. "So how's your rental place?" I asked, picturing some sweet little house with a pool and a diving board. Maybe an inflatable flamingo floating around, pink on blue.

"It's—it's great." She took a bite of the apple and added, "A little smaller than I expected, but that's fine. Interesting fact: Did you know Tarzana was named that because it was once a huge ranch owned by Edgar Rice Burroughs, who wrote *Tarzan*?"

"Yup."

"And it's convenient." She nodded and took another bite. "Right off the highway."

"Freeway."

"Right, the *freeway*. So it's super-handy."

I tried to think of the area of Tarzana near the 101. There were a lot of strip malls and apartment buildings. I'd had a friend who lived near there in a cute old house, but for the most part, the area was pretty busy. "So you see what I mean about the traffic here."

"It's a nightmare." She nodded enthusiastically. "Way worse than home. Probably worse than Manhattan. But it's nice having so many restaurants around. And I'm right by a grocery store that's open twenty-four hours. And if things get desperate, the guy with the balcony under mine seems to use his patio as a pantry so I could send a wire hanger down and fish up a bag of flour or sugar or pancake mix or just about any dry goods you can think of. Canned too, but I'd need more of a grabber contraption for that."

"The guy in the apartment below you uses his *patio* for *food* storage?"

She nodded. "Huge bags, like twenty-five pounds. Maybe he owns a restaurant."

"Holy shit, that's unsanitary."

"I know, right? It's gross." She took a sip of wine and added, "But if I keep the door closed, the smell doesn't really get in."

"It *smells*?" I couldn't help but imagine what unholy germs or rodents could make their way up to her abode. Rats climb, you know.

She nodded ruefully. "But if I keep the sliding glass door to the outside and the bathroom door inside closed, it's okay."

"What's wrong with the bathroom?"

Her face colored slightly. "I've only been here a few hours so I'm not sure, but it looked like the tub wasn't completely draining, so it was sort of mildew-smelling."

This place sounded awful. "Did you call the owner?"

"Well, actually, I already had because of the toilet seat, so I figured I'd tell him when he came to check that out."

Oh my God, I was going to have to have her stay with me, wasn't I? "What's wrong with the toilet seat?"

She took another sip of wine, another bite of apple. "I guess it was cracked because when I sat down to pee, it pinched me, so *of course* I reflexively jumped up but it must have been pretty loose because it broke off the hinge and the seat went *flying* like a skateboard on a hill."

"The whole seat?"

Another nod. "It was already broken off the other hinge so it wasn't like it was super-secure to begin with."

I tried to assimilate what I knew so far. "So you're saying this place has a rat hotel underneath you, no toilet seat, a shower tub that won't drain, and it smells foul, and they're *charging* you to stay there?"

"To be fair, I haven't actually *seen* a rat."

I rolled my eyes. "Does it have a bed or just a sleeping bag on the floor?" I had to do something. I had to help her find a new place; this sounded dangerous. If my place weren't so small, I'd offer to let her stay, but . . .

"Oh, it has a bed. It's almost like new, in fact."

Some small measure of relief trickled through me. "Well, *that's* good, at least."

"Or keeping that thick plastic on it really gives that impression," she went on. "But it also makes it really stiff and hot. I tried to take a nap on it earlier and I woke up covered in sweat." She saw the look on my face and quickly added, "Which would have been *fine* if there was an air conditioner. That reminds me, is there a Target or something around here where I can get a fan?"

"That's it," I said, knowing I might very well regret this. I hadn't even said it yet and I regretted it. "You're just going to have to stay here. Damn it. You knew I'd say that."

"Nice. But no." She laughed. "Don't be ridiculous, you don't have room!" She frowned and looked around, but since we were in the kitchen/living room, she couldn't really tell the extent of the place. She looked at the sofa, considering. "That probably is about the same size as the bed, though."

"I have two bedrooms," I blurted out.

She jerked back to me. "You do?"

"Yes, and two baths." That was when I remembered hedging about that previously. I never told people I had room here because I didn't want them to overestimate the size of the place and plan long visits. I know, I know, that makes me sound like such a jerk, but the main bedroom is small and the guest bedroom would be small for a closet back home. Plus I'm used to having my privacy, and taking on guests was really stressful for me. But what else could I do? *"Technically. But not big enough for me to have offered this as a reasonable accommodation. It's not big enough for me to have a real roommate, but it's big enough for you to stay here instead of there. My God, the street would probably be a better option."*

"I had no idea you had so much room," she said. "I thought you were in basically the same boat as me in Tarzana. Except, you know, you have nice decor, a good kitchen, and a neighborhood that Darren Neville apparently visits."

"He lives here," I said quietly.

"What? He *lives* here? In, like, a *third* bedroom?" She smiled devilishly.

"No, obviously I don't have three bedrooms." She was looking at me incredulously. "And obviously I don't know . . ." This was stupid. "I don't know him, I'm just saying, he lives near here. In a house, obviously, but it's a nice neighborhood. This is, you know, a safe place. Basically. As safe as LA can be, anyhow. And we're around the corner from some really nice areas."

She took another bite and nodded. "I noticed the bars on all the windows."

"If you don't have a gate and a guard, you have bars." A fleeting mental picture of a sunny garden and sparkling pool crossed my mind.

"They look nice." She must have thought that I looked insulted because she quickly added, "Seriously. Some of the ironwork is really fancy. It looks like leaded windows. I was thinking I should do that to my place in New York. If I keep it."

"Why wouldn't you?"

She rubbed her fingers together to indicate *money*. "I might have been a bit, how do you say, financially optimistic when I bought it. Though I rented it out on VRBO while I'm here and it went fast, so I don't know, maybe it's not such a bad investment."

"Yeah, if you don't need to actually live in it." Rental income and no overhead wasn't a bad deal.

"That's the problem." She got up and started to wander around, wine in hand. "So you're saying you have, what, stairs and a second floor somewhere here or what?"

"No, I'm just saying that technically I have two bedrooms down that tiny hall there." I gestured in the direction of it.

"Oh! I thought that was a pantry."

I nodded soberly. "You see why I don't generally tell people I have two bedrooms. I use the other room as an office because it's so tiny." I realized I was overexplaining; this was, in fact, something I was working on in therapy. I didn't need to overexplain myself. I didn't need to explain myself at all. This was my life and I was living it the way I wanted to and if I wanted to have an office, a sewing room, and a wrapping-paper room and say I had no place for guests, that was my prerogative.

But at the same time, if I was living my life in a way that was meant to make me happy—and that was the goal—then I had to also follow the instinct that was telling me if I left Crosby in that hellhole in Tarzana, I was going to be worried about her every moment she was in California.

Big-sister habits die hard.

The room I was offering wasn't good enough; it was literally the size of a closet in our old house, but it was better than what she was dealing with.

She looked around. And I know the kitchen is pretty big. When I'd bought the house, I'd had a wall taken out to get rid of the useless dining-room area and expand the kitchen. So it was pretty nice, and the sitting area on the other side seemed generous, owing to the fact that there were no borders, though in fact it was fairly small, square-footage-wise. Maybe the size of one of our childhood bedrooms, possibly a tiny bit bigger. Certainly not the arching "great rooms" of the newer condos.

"This *is* a lot nicer than where I'm staying."

"I hope so. I have to warn you, this is the biggest area of it. But there are no rats."

She looked at me. "And roaches. I don't know how much

to worry about that, but it's pretty gross. I was a little worried. Rats climb, you know."

"I do know."

"Yuck."

"I can't even imagine. It just sounds like you've been"—I searched for a word sufficient to express it but came up short—"ripped off. It happens with a whole bunch of websites, preying on people coming in from out of town who don't know better."

"There were pictures. It didn't look so bad." Her expression hardened. "You know what? It's *not* so bad. I'm fine there, really. You should come over for wine and cheese and I'll show you. We can play foosball!"

"There's a foosball machine?"

"There was. Technically, now it's the coffee table," she explained. "It rattles, so I guess the ball is in there somewhere."

"It . . . rattles?"

"You know, if you put your feet up or something. It's uneven, so it rocks. Someone cut the legs down so it would be low enough to go in front of the couch."

"Oh, well, then, it sounds glorious. Forget I offered. You're on the concierge level of the Tarzana Ritz with food available for the grabbing and drinks twenty-four hours with a siphon." I threw my hands up. "My mistake. When you said *mildew*, I thought you meant it negatively."

"No, no, it's *fabulous*."

We were silent for a few minutes, her eating her apple thoughtfully, washing it down with wine, and me preparing dumplings: systematically filling them one by one, then clamping the edges shut, along with my jaw. A big part of me was relieved she'd refused my offer but a bigger part of me felt like a raging asshole for feeling that way.

Why did it always go this way with us?

"I hate it," she said finally. "It's awful. It's sticky, it's hot, and the front door lock feels about as secure as a bathroom stall at a public park."

I knew it. And I couldn't let her be stuck with that. I couldn't. I'd been in shitty LA and it was awful. There was no way I could let her go through the exact same hard lessons I did when I moved here. If nothing else, our parents would be horrified. They'd taught me better than this. "Then stay here."

She looked at me cautiously. "Only until I find another place."

"Perfect."

"And I'd insist on paying you."

I nodded. "Fine."

She looked surprised. "Really?"

I shrugged. "If you're going to be like a roommate, you're going to pay like a roommate."

She smiled behind her apple before taking the last bite. "Remember when we used to talk about growing up and getting a place together?"

I searched my memory. "No," I said, suddenly guilty. "Did we? Are you sure?"

She laughed outright. "No, I'm kidding. Obviously. We

never talked about that. You were always way too mean for that." Something unsaid hung in the air for a moment. "But maybe we should have. Most sisters have that kind of shared memory, don't they?"

There were other things in our past that family *wouldn't* do, so I couldn't say it was that hard to imagine us being different. Or at least that I didn't know what happy families did. "Do they?"

"Who the hell knows?" She stood up and picked up the remainder of her wine, considered it, then set it down unfinished. "Better not if I'm going to drive."

"You're leaving already?"

She gave a sly smile. "I've got to pack." She reached into her purse and pulled out three, then another one, hundred-dollar bills. "First week's rent," she said. "Is that enough?"

I considered. "The wine bill's bound to be pretty high."

"I didn't even finish one glass!"

"I meant mine."

"Ah. Good one." She shot a finger gun at me. "Tell your fancy friends I'm looking for a guesthouse so I can get out of your hair."

I smiled. "I'll spread the word."

"Perfect." She slung her purse over her shoulder. "Dad said he'd help if there's an emergency, so . . ."

Typical Dad. Mom too. We were so lucky to have them. That was probably one thing we could really agree on.

"You might pick up some groceries too," I said as she gathered her things. "I don't have much here. At least, not much you'd like. I usually taste as I work so I don't have a ton to prepare at home."

"Already planning on it," she said. "How many Twinkies do you have left in the freezer?"

"What? None! God, I forgot you do that. So gross."

"It is not! You just don't know how good it is!" She did a chef's kiss. "This is going to be a match made in heaven."

I rolled my eyes. "How long are you staying in town?"

"Six weeks is the plan, though I rented my place out for eight. If I end up with time left over, I'll hang out on one side of the country or the other until the renters are gone."

"It pays well?" I asked.

"Well enough to get me here and into a rattrap in the wrong part of town." She laughed. "I hate to brag."

I tried to laugh but failed. "I wish I had something better than the office to offer."

She shrugged. "Maybe there's good work juju in there." But she looked a little doubtful. I don't know if that was because of her work juju or what she assumed to be mine.

I couldn't remember the last time I'd stepped foot in there, much less tried to do anything creative there, work or otherwise. It had become more of a storage place for things I didn't know what else to do with. "I'm sure there is."

"So I'll see you tomorrow?"

"You can stay tonight if you want."

"No, I have to get my stuff. But thanks. I'll be here in the morning. Probably earlier than you think."

I nodded, continuing to assemble the dumplings. "I'll give you a key then, is that okay? I'll have to get one made."

"Sounds good." She started for the door then stopped and turned back. "Fran?"

I looked up. "Hmm?"

"Thank you. Seriously."

I felt the heat rise in my face. "No problem." I tried to sound casual but even I could hear the strain behind it, all the thoughts that went up and down and up again.

She looked at me for a long moment before turning to go. "It'll be fun," she said over her shoulder.

I had a fleeting memory of Scrabble boards and Pictionary clues and laughter. Pity the memory wasn't my own. "Yes," I said, my voice a bit hollow. "Fun."

Chapter Nine

Crosby

I let the door shut on my rental, and the framed poster on the wall rattled. The frame was cheap plastic, coming apart in the corners, and the poster was for *The Endless Summer*. The retro stylization and the colors were far warmer than the place it was attempting to adorn.

Now that I was leaving, I could truly admit how god-*awful* this place was. Some show, I can't remember which one, coined the term *graduation goggles* to describe the warm, nostalgic feeling you get when an era is ending, no matter how terrible or shitty the era was. There were no graduation goggles for this dump.

Thank *God* Frances had offered to have me.

I have to admit that at first, when I told her I was coming out, I was a little hurt that she hadn't said, *Come! Stay with me! Of course, it's not a problem!* But we hadn't been super-close for a very long time and it had become pretty obvious years ago that she didn't particularly like me. It's hard to have guests you're not that comfortable with even if you live in a palace, but she also had gotten used to her space and even I could tell when I was there that her essence really *filled* it. It's hard to explain but I knew I'd be intruding at least somewhat, no matter how many hours I spent out of the house.

It was my intention to find another place as soon as possible but that wasn't a promise I wanted to make out loud until I had some luck. Wine was cheaper in LA than in New York, thank goodness, but everything else was more, it seemed. Even the cheapest rental homes cost a lot, particularly when you added taxes and fees. The cleaning fees alone on some of these places were totally outrageous.

The truth was, I was a little embarrassed that the apartment was so bad. Did I used to be better at finding places, or did I simply have lower standards once? Seriously, it's not like a ton of comparison shopping went into picking a place in Fort Myers for spring break. That rental was actually legit, though. There weren't cockroaches, and the last tenant had left behind a bag of weed that delighted the six friends who were staying in that two-bedroom. I guess it spoke to the level of cleaning between tenants, but overall the place had been nice. It seriously hadn't been *horrifying*.

Really, though, how had I gotten this so wrong?

LA was an absolute mystery to me; I had no idea what the neighborhoods were like or where they were in relation to one another. I knew it wasn't like other major cities, like New York or Chicago, in its walkability. But that's something everyone knows.

For example, it didn't occur to me that the place I rented might not have parking *anywhere close*, in which case I'd end up having to feed a meter miles away every few hours all day and night.

I don't know how great a place would have to be to make that worth it, but it probably didn't exist. So a monthly contract with a parking garage, even just for two months, was a huge add-on to the costs I'd already calculated.

I wish walking into Frances's place felt like home. Like my parents' house did. As soon as I walked into their house, I relaxed. I could time-travel to almost any age I could remember and feel nurtured and taken care of. It was something I valued a whole lot and consequently constantly worried about losing. I'd calculate my parents' ages, factor in their good health, and try to reassure myself that I didn't have to worry about losing them for a long, long time. But still, I worried. More than you'd think. More than a normal person would.

Life was never hopeless as long as I could go home. And my parents were, to me, home.

Did their place feel like that to Frances? Did we have that in common, at least? How odd that we both had the exact same parents and so many of the same childhood memories yet we felt so much like strangers in the ways that mattered most. We never even talked about our shared childhood or holidays or memories.

Why did it feel so cold around her?

Gah. Better not to think too much about it. I'd just keep on being the clown, my apparent role in the family, and she could keep on judging me and being superior. Practical. Confident. That was her role.

The truth was, ever since I stepped foot in California, I had felt lost, small, foolish, and hopeless. Small, especially, and not in the good way. I felt backward and positively rural, though one could hardly describe where I lived as anything close to that. But something about being here, not knowing the city's secrets or being able to hear the rhythm, made me feel dumb.

I didn't know which apps were best for ordering food, what the local grocery stores were called, and I couldn't even remember to call it a freeway.

I wouldn't have wanted to admit that to Frances. I would just like for her to have, I don't know, imagined what I must be feeling. It is this kind of demand for mind reading that has consistently negatively affected most of my relationships.

Basically, as much as I didn't want to admit it—and especially not to her—I wanted and needed her help. I couldn't have lived in that place for six weeks. I spent an entire night awake here, hiding from two flies that kept landing on me like they were doing some demented, middle-of-the-night mating dance that was in some way enhanced by my presence. I imagined the guy downstairs had any number of dead rodents in his piles of stinking food, and their little fly feet had probably landed on all kinds of horrifying rot.

Anyway, Frances had saved me, at least for the moment, and I was relieved. And grateful, though there was more than a little guilt.

I threw down the rental key chain, a ring loaded with keys to things that were not mine, and sat down on the towel I had laid out on the mysteriously sticky couch.

The cockroaches, who had just realized I was there, scattered quickly like spilled Skittles.

I went to the bedroom and started packing. It was unlikely to take long, as I had wanted to isolate my things from the questionable environment. Usually I was the type to unpack completely. I put clothes in drawers in hotels, even if it was just for a few days. I enjoyed feeling like I lived wherever I was and didn't mind the process of packing or unpacking nearly as much as I disliked the feeling of rifling through a suitcase every time something was needed.

I'd packed a lot into this suitcase, because on top of everything else, I'd seriously misjudged the October weather in Southern California, so I'd brought a bunch of light shirts and shorts. (Easy to pack a ton when it's small clothes. I went to Michigan for Christmas once, and my optimistic little suitcase was full after two sweaters and one pair of over-the-knee boots.) I had hung things, feeling that they're being suspended in air was a safer bet than anything else. As I removed things, several of the plastic hangers snapped. It was a fitting *Fuck you* from a place that didn't seem to like me any more than I liked it.

My phone rang just after I'd dropped the last of my sandals into my bag. "Hey, Dad!" I zipped the bag and went over to sit on the bed, feeling I deserved the break already. The plastic squeaked under my weight.

"Hey there! Are you with your sister?"

"No, actually, I just left her. I'm packing up to go back, though. She suggested I stay with her so"—I took a moment to be glad my dad didn't use FaceTime so he couldn't see the dive I was in—"I just figured, why not?"

"Wonderful! Just like old times."

"Oh God, I hope not." My first thought of "old times" was middle school and high school and . . . let's just say we both had challenging teen years. With each other and with everyone else. Doesn't everyone?

"What's that?"

"Nothing, I just hope we get along."

"You're sisters. You find a way to get along." His voice was stern, but I knew he understood that we had never exactly been two peas in a pod.

"We will, we will."

"How's the weather there?" Classic Dad, skipping away from the tension. I knew where I'd gotten that. "Is it sunny?"

"Isn't it always?"

"That's what they say. It never rains in Southern California." He paused and then quoted the old song: "*It pours, man, it pours.*" He had it on a 45. He still listened to them.

I stepped out onto the balcony and looked at the impossibly blue sky. "No pouring today." There really is something to the quality of light here. I don't know if it's the whole

West Coast or just Los Angeles, but the blue of the sky could be so deep, and somehow the sun blasted all the imperfections out of the concrete walls of the adjacent building so even that looked pretty. "It's super-sunny and bright, but the sun is already starting to go down."

There was a shuffling beneath me and I looked down to see my neighbor, shirtless but so hairy I thought for a second he was wearing a textured tube top. He began to pick through his groceries, like a rat picking through trash. I backed in and closed the door. I locked it.

"Boy, I remember those sunsets on Lookout Mountain," he said. Lookout Mountain was somewhere near where I was now, in Laurel Canyon, where all the great hippie rockers used to live and record. "The sun would go down like someone dropping a ball," he said. "But the nights were so beautiful. Like children's book illustrations. Do you remember that place, Cros?"

"Only a little," I said. "I mostly remember being afraid of someone who I now think was David Crosby. He had wild hair, like a lion."

Dad laughed heartily. "That he did. But those were some good times, pumpkin. You were lucky to spend time amid all that talent, whether you remember it well or not. We all were."

"Why didn't we just move here?" I asked, wondering how it was that Frances was the first to make the commitment.

"You know, Gran and Grandpa were here and your mom

didn't want to go too far away from them. By the time they were gone, we didn't want to uproot you two. Life gets away from you that way."

I didn't want life to get away from me that way. Already too much time had passed with me just going through the motions. "It's never too late," I said.

He chuckled. "Oh, it would do my heart good to be there, that's for sure. Meanwhile, I'm glad my girls are. Now you need to make sure you get out in that magic California sunshine for at least half an hour a day. It does wonders for your mood."

"And her immune system!" I heard my mother call in the background. "Tell her traveling is stressful and she needs to take care of her immune system so she doesn't get sick. Eat some oranges! And *drink water*."

"Your mother says—"

I smiled to myself. "I heard her. Tell her I will." I wondered if Frances's complex had a pool. It had to, right? The weather was only in the seventies, but the sun was strong and I could use the vitamin D.

Then again, I'd be spending a lot of time at Mardie's— surely she had a pool on her . . . what would it be? An estate? Yes, there was probably a pool right next to the guesthouse I'd been privately hoping she'd invite me to stay in. No such luck. But if we hit it off and she knew I wouldn't be loud or crazy or whatever else one might fear in that situation, maybe she'd still invite me. She had said she'd ask around to see if any of her friends had a guesthouse they wanted to rent but then she'd never mentioned it again and I sure as hell wasn't going to bring it up.

"And what about the star, have you met her yet? Maddie?"

"Mardie. I meet her tomorrow. She's no David Crosby, of course, but still I'm kind of nervous," I confessed, wishing I could sink down on the sofa next to him, be enveloped in the scent of his Blue Waters cologne. "What if we don't hit it off?"

"You have your mother's charm; you hit it off with everyone. She's going to love you. Come on."

I hoped he was right. I couldn't afford for her to decide we weren't a good fit and fire me. I had *just* enough money to sustain myself for six weeks. Truth was, we'd agreed on a payment that was only a fraction of what I used to make from the book, and it began with an upon-signing amount that was less than I used to spend in a month. The next payment would come when she turned the book in. It was due December 1, so with luck, I'd get paid more by the end of the year.

There was no sense in thinking what I'd do if that didn't work out. It just had to. I'd been stupid with money and had nothing to fall back on. I'd sooner beg on the street where no one knew me than ask my parents for another loan. Every time I did, it launched them into Worryville. It was as if the loan were actually just a product, and the cost was the intense inspection of my life. They unturned every stone, and half the time they found something I didn't know was there, and then I *was* depressed.

No. It wasn't worth it. Even though they had it to spare.

Crazy old hippies though they were, they'd invested smartly. The song royalties were hefty, but my dad had invested in Apple in the 1980s when it was just starting out and everyone was gonzo for Windows. And, of course, his investment grew and grew.

You'd think I would have learned something from him. His wisdom or his risky luck.

If I ever have money again, I will not make the same mistake.

But first I have to have money again.

And maybe ghostwriting could be a *way in* to celebrity biography or something. God knows there were a lot of people out there making a lot of noise in that arena. It seemed to me that if Mardie and I worked as well together as I hoped, I might be able to talk her into giving me a byline on the book. *As told to* or *With*—that would make the meager fee I'd agreed to completely worth it.

"Are you there?" my father asked.

"Oh. Yes, sorry. What did you say?"

"I was saying you should get Mardie to make a comeback by covering 'Happily Never After.'"

I laughed. "That's not quite her style. As a matter of fact, I don't even think she sings anymore. There was a rumor that she'd be a judge on *The Voice* but that's not happening either. Her stage mom is trying to push her younger sister as the new Mardie now, I think, but it's not getting much traction."

"Your mom said she heard one of her songs playing while

she was picking out produce the other day. She took it as a good omen for you."

It was never a good omen for a singer or band who still hoped to be relevant to be playing on the grocery store sound system. "Here's hoping." I raised an imaginary toast to myself.

"What's going on with your place here? Do you need me to go check on it for you?"

I was so lucky to have him. "I rented it out to some people who are looking for property there. I might need to stay at your place for a bit if I get back before they're ready to leave."

"Perfect! We'd love it! And I'm proud of you, that's using really good business sense."

"I'm trying." It had, at least, paid for my ticket out to LA and then some. And it served to prevent me from chickening out or otherwise giving up and running back home with my tail between my legs. "Look, Dad, I'd better go, I've got tons of stuff to do."

"Okay, honey. Get yourself some dinner—do you still have my card on your phone wallet . . . thing?"

He was so anti-tech that I was amazed he remembered that he'd given me his Amex for my Apple wallet once when I was picking up some stuff for him at Best Buy. "Yes."

"Well, dinner is on me. Anything you want, and for Fran too, if she's around. I think they even deliver booze there. Get some champagne for you and Frances. Raise a glass to the old folks."

I felt the flush of embarrassment I always got in response

to generosity. I missed him suddenly. Homesick for my parents and the safety found there. "Thanks, Dad. I'll do that. That's so nice of you."

After we hung up, I sat quietly for a moment, looking around the room. It was dark, even with the curtains drawn all the way open. The sun was going down, casting the room in a dismal light through the dingy glass.

This was exactly the kind of view that would have had the Mamas and the Papas California-dreaming and tickled some vague early memories of mine when we used to come and see Dad's musician friends when they were still cooking out, toking, and jamming freely in Laurel Canyon.

This apartment, though. This was not California-dreaming material at all. The walls were nondescript beige but there were a few fine cracks running down. It was bound to happen to cheap construction in the land of earthquakes. There was a floor lamp lacking a bulb, its cord trailing away like a rat's tail, not plugged into anything. I'd already stepped on the hard plug several times in my bare feet.

This really was a shithole.

I opened my phone and scrolled through the options on Yelp. I only had one meal on Dad, and I was going to make it a good one. Not lobster and filet mignon or anything, just *good*. That's what I needed, I decided. Maybe I would feel better if I could live how I might have a year ago. Dressed up, not worried about the price. Though, a year ago, I had a boyfriend and a group of friends. Now I didn't. I was across the country from my life.

I pulled out a few options and went with the Leith dress that hugged in all the right places and a suede jacket that perfectly matched my favorite pair of suede heels. I spent an hour getting ready and listening to my pump-up playlist, which was mostly stuff from the early 2000s. Britney. Beyoncé. Mardie was even on there. Anything up-tempo that I knew every word to.

I looked my best; I snapped a picture, then put it on my Insta story.

In a fit of self-pity, I nearly started crying, but I stopped after one sob, refusing to mess up my makeup. I took a deep breath and shook my head. Why the tears? I needed to get it together. Things weren't so bad.

I stared at my phone, my thumb hovering over Frances's contact info. I could call her and invite her out to eat. How nice that could be, in theory. What a nice, normal way for us to behave—in fact, why hadn't she thought to ask me out to dinner upon my arrival in LA? If she was coming to New York, I would have asked her. Well, actually, it was impossible to say, since our parents would pay for that for all of us.

But in theory.

Screw that, I thought, *she hadn't thought of it or didn't want to. Or hell, I mean, she* is *a chef, she could have made me dinner.*

I rolled my eyes at myself. I was doing it again. Writing the script for how people ought to act around me, inevitably asking them to go above and beyond, even when I never have.

I tapped her name and it rang once, then half a ring, then to voice mail. A telltale sign of an ignored call.

I laughed once and waited a second for the potential following text that explained. Something like Other line, or One sec, or Talking to my neighbor, what's up?

But nothing. Just a blatantly ignored call.

This was so typical. I always felt like it was impossible to get a meeting or a call with her. Always had. She was so *busy*, and, I'd always thought, so cool. Right now she was probably having drinks with some Hollywood heavyweight. I didn't need to bother her during that.

I was all dressed up, fine with going out by myself, but now uncertain about going to her house after.

I slipped on my flip-flops, took everything down to the car, went back up, and bade adieu to the apartment from hell by tossing the keys on the counter and locking the knob from the inside, as the landlord told me to.

I had to be on to better things.

I found a place to eat in Fran's neighborhood so that I could have a drink or two if I wanted, but I decided to drive around and take the long way and see some sights. It was too early to sit at the bar and meet normal people.

I didn't care too much about seeing the sights you're *supposed* to see, and I cared even less about visiting tourist traps like Ripley's Believe It or Not or Madame Tussauds. In fact, it always stunned me that people were willing to wait in such crazy-long lines.

I cared more about the drive-by experience that equated to the real-life establishing shots from *Real Housewives*. I saw the Walk of Fame and the characters dressed up as Superman and Marilyn Monroe. It was just more of Times Square—another place I had never cared about. I geeked out a little at the restaurants from *Vanderpump Rules*. The Griffith Observatory brought me a little thrill because of *La La Land* and not because it was, you know, famous on its own.

Whatever, no shame. I was as happy watching the vapidity unfold on Bravo as I was watching William Holden floating in a pool off Sunset Boulevard. Old Hollywood, new Hollywood, it was all entertaining to me.

Frances lived north of Wilshire, not far from the OJ Simpson murder scene. I drove by and gawked at that, like a monster.

I rounded a crest on the 405 and saw the *sign* for Sunset Boulevard. The real thing. My heart did a little leap. I knew it existed, knew it was real, obviously. Yet something about seeing the sign for it, knowing that people took that exit and lived on that famous road, just thrilled me. It was cooler than meeting half the celebrities who lived in the area.

The town suddenly spread out before me, Universal Studios high on a hill to the left (a quick glance and I could see the spires of Hogwarts pointing skyward) and the round Capital Records building on the right. My father had signed his first contract with Capital Records five decades ago. Just like the Beatles, though, admittedly, the Beatles had made it a *little* bigger.

I had to force myself to keep my eyes on the road because the landmarks just kept coming. Finally I took an exit to take the slow route into town and one minute I was looking at a bridge underpass with a lot of garbage spread across the road, and then, one left turn and thirty feet later, I was smack-dab in front of a view of the Hollywood sign high on a hill.

Fortunately, the light was red, so I could stop and just gaze at it. This was another landmark I'd known was real and I had no business feeling like fantasy had bloomed to life, but this was Hollywood. It *was* larger than life. Larger than *my* life, anyway.

One could argue that every big city is like this. Like each city has its own bucket-list items. And maybe that's true, and I just care less about most of them.

But Hollywood. LA. It had so much history!

I drove on, eventually coming to a beautiful neighborhood stretching into the hills. The huge gate pillars announced that this was Bel Air. My grandmother used to smoke Belair cigarettes. The package depicted a blue sky scattered with light, puffy clouds. That was how it looked right now. Minus the smoke, of course. I wound through the roads, passing tall hedges and wrought-iron gates, occasionally glimpsing a huge home through the gaps. This one Mediterranean, that one Spanish-style, yet another bungalow on a large plot of land.

It was breathtakingly gorgeous.

I wondered if Mardie's house would be on a scale like this. I didn't know much about Encino, but it was an old town too, older than Beverly Hills, though not quite as over the top. I'd done enough research to know that it had been home to plenty of luminaries as well.

I drove on, passing iconic iron signs for Beverly Hills, along wide streets lined with tall palms. I rolled the windows down and breathed in the air. It was the exact temperature and breeziness of an ideal East Coast autumn day. The difference was, California wasn't careening toward a cold gray winter the way home was. This was about as "bad" as it got. No wonder Frances had come out here and stayed. It was her little secret bliss. She never talked about being blissfully happy here or compared it to home, which always seemed more pointed than bragging.

I put the radio on a '90s station just as Christina Aguilera finished up "Genie in a Bottle." Next up—you guessed it—Mardie Mariano's first big hit, "Double Dare."

God, I could remember Frances playing this over and over again, singing along and imitating the dance steps from the video, and, most humiliatingly, re-creating them with her friends and filming it on our shared Canon PowerShot (a Christmas gift from "Santa" for us both). It was always loaded with tons of pictures of Frances and her friends doing that sort of thing.

I remembered one fateful night when they tied their T-shirts into midriff shirts and did a version of Britney Spears's "Oops, I Did It Again." They couldn't stop laughing in the video and I remember standing off screen just absolutely bewildered. Bewildered as people always are when they're not in on the joke.

I barely even used the camera. It probably had some tragically emo-looking photos of me and a high-school boyfriend at, like, the park or something. Before selfies were a thing, they were a thing.

Or maybe I had deleted them all.

Wherever that camera was, I hoped it was dead, not just lurking in a box at my parents' house one charge away from revealing cringeworthy evidence. Same goes for the brick-size hard drive I knew stored a thousand of overly confident memories and indulgent teenage narcissism.

I finally got to the restaurant and pulled up to one of the metered spots. The sun had set, and the place looked just busy enough to make it a nice solo night out and not just sad.

I slid into my wedges, clicked the car locked, and walked through the door, which was thrown open to the street.

The bartender asked if I would like sparkling or still water.

"My dad is paying for his adult daughter to take herself out to dinner, so"—I patted the counter—"let's go sparkling, baby."

The bartender laughed and nodded. "You an actress?"

Yes, at the moment I was acting the part of a writer. "Isn't everyone?" I responded.

He poured me a glass of wine. "This one's on the house. One for good luck."

I needed it. The wine and the luck. "Thanks." I took a sip. It was bad stuff. Probably a couple of bucks a bottle.

It would do just fine.

Chapter Ten

Thirteen Years Ago

It was a month and a half after that horrible night, almost time to go back to school, when she realized the consequences of it all.

She wasn't a virgin, it wasn't as if she were an innocent child who didn't know what was happening, or threatening to happen. She knew right from wrong, and she understood her measure of culpability and that she'd have to deal with this like a grown-up.

She'd been such a fool. How had she kept drinking beer after beer, thinking she was fine? That was the mistake of a kid, a mistake she'd actually made as a kid; she never should have let herself be so foolish. She had all but begged for trouble.

Well, that wasn't really the point now. Because now she had to get a pregnancy test and try not to freak the fuck out about the possible results until she had them. Now was not the time to be flogging herself for her mistakes and questioning whether she was somehow *paying* for them, like it was justice for her sins.

She headed to a drugstore in the next town so as not to start the gossip about her purchase in her own. It was a longer drive, but she welcomed the highway hypnosis of the extra ten miles. It helped her relax and put things into perspective. She was about to go back to school. She was nervous about her new roommate, her new dorm room, her upcoming classes after a summer of reading by the pool. There was a lot going on in her head and that translated quickly to her body; it always had. When she was nervous, it always manifested in her stomach. There was every reason to believe that overarching stress like this would affect her cycle.

As she drove, she thought back to that night. Damn, she wished she could remember more. It was all so foggy. And she'd been so *tired*. That was the strongest impression she had when she thought about it. She'd never wanted sleep so badly in her life.

Apparently, to the point where she'd passed out on the floor of that dirty old barn, near the possum skeleton and God knew what else. Spiders had probably strung down and played in her hair while she slept. There had been dirt on her mouth when she woke. Dirt everywhere, actually. At first she'd wondered if she'd just conked out and rolled around there for an hour, but then she felt the soreness between her legs and all of her muscles and she realized what must have happened.

Since it wasn't her first time, it wasn't as if there was

blood or tearing or anything. No, the soreness she felt was from force. From hard thrusting against her pelvis and inner thighs. The ache in her arms could have been from either pushing him away or trying to pull him closer.

She wasn't entirely sure which it was.

But the lingering niggle of doubt in her said it was from fighting. Because she never would have done that—slipped a few yards away with *him* and done the deed in a filthy rodent graveyard on the floor?—if she hadn't been nearly blackout drunk.

She pulled up outside the Rite Aid and grabbed her purse from the seat next to her. After a moment of hesitation, she decided to pull her hair back and leave her sunglasses on. It was a lousy disguise, but better than nothing, just on the off chance that someone who knew her would see her shopping in the feminine-hygiene aisle for pregnancy tests.

There were a lot to choose from and she had no idea if any one was better than the others. Certainly some were a lot more expensive. After about ten minutes perusing them, she settled on a brand name, figuring the company had a reputation to live up to. It was surprisingly expensive. She hoped that meant it was good.

The drive home felt a lot longer than the drive there had.

When she got back, she shoved the paper bag from the drugstore into her purse and went in to get it over with.

"Well, hey, lovebug, where you been?" her dad asked as she passed his study.

She thought fast. "I couldn't stop thinking about Egg Mc-Muffins. I had to go get one."

"Ah. I can relate." He chuckled. "Come on in and listen to this new song I'm working on. I want to know what you think of it." He gestured to the comfy chair where she always sat when he played his music for her. "I'm thinking I can have a hit for myself every forty years and establish a whole new category: the two-hit wonder."

She wanted to join him. She wanted it to be like it used to when she was young and he was working on commercial jingles and came up with words to make them laugh. She had had more laughs in front of his guitar than most people had in a lifetime.

Then she thought of the bag in her purse.

"Can I join you in a couple of hours?" she asked, then patted her stomach. "I pigged out and now I'm ready for a nap, you know?"

He smiled. Was it her imagination that he was seeing through her? "Sure, sure. I'll be here all day. I'll put you on the list—mention your name at the door and you can get in free."

She laughed. "Will do!"

The Diet Pepsi she'd picked up with the pregnancy test was starting to kick in, fortunately, and she had to pee. She hurried up the stairs and into the bathroom, locking the door behind her.

She ripped the box open and pulled out the stick. A quick

glance at the directions told her what she already knew—
uncap, pee on the exposed end, and wait. Read results in the
window.

It was science, but not rocket science.

She sat down and peed on the stick, relieved and apprehensive at the same time. Then she put the cap back on and
set it on the counter next to her. She stayed on the toilet,
looking across the room at her gaunt face in the mirror.

Was this the face of a pregnant person? A pregnant *her*?
Did she look any different? Would she really see it if she did?
At this point it was easy to imagine anything. Fear was strong
and a great creator of illusions.

She stood up, pulled up her pants, washed her hands, and
tried to resist peeking until the whole five minutes had passed.

She sank down on the floor next to the tub and watched
the time tick down.

Finally it was time. Shaking so hard she wondered if she
was doing her body harm, she stood up and looked at the test
on the corner of the counter.

One line.

Negative.

But where she had expected intense relief, she found
tears. Not because she wasn't pregnant—God knew, *that* was
a miracle. But the emotion came from all the torture she'd
put herself through worrying about it. The way the world
had gone dark as she drove the familiar roads to get a test,
wondering all the while if by afternoon she was going to be a
different person, one who'd never feel happiness again.

She knew that if it was positive, she would be alienated from her friends, her family, the life she had spent twenty years building. That she wasn't going to have to pay for it forever wasn't the point. The point was she'd put herself in a position where she might have to.

She was never, ever going to let that happen again.

From now on, she was going to be careful. She was going to create a new life for herself and it was *not* going to have the shadows of this on or in it anywhere.

And she was going to appreciate going away to college more than ever and avoid the duds and the town-bound assholes who would try to ruin her that way.

She was at the bottom of the pits, as low as a person could get, and her own sister had ignored it and even snapped at her for taking so long to be ready to leave the party. She'd given her shit for drinking too much too, even though she was sober as a judge and totally able to drive.

Everyone had let her down.

She washed her face with cold water, slapped some makeup on her flushed cheeks, and went down the stairs to listen to her father's new song. She would never talk about this—no, she would never even *think* about this again if she could help it.

Chapter Eleven

Frances

I'm not like anyone else in my family. I'm a worrier. Constantly rattled. Out of the four of us, I'm the only one. It was always like that—if Dad was late coming home, I figured it was a car accident. If Mom was out longer than expected, I was sure she'd been murdered. I can't tell you how many times I was sure Crosby had been kidnapped. I worried like it was my fucking job.

A job I couldn't quit.

While I've been wrong in my premonitions every time, thank God, I recognize that the rest of my family seem to get by fine without forever fretting about the future, but it's that very fact that makes me feel even more strongly about my role as a kite string for them.

Maybe I've saved all their lives with my extra precautions and they just don't realize it.

I stretched the bamboo sheets over the soft, expensive

daybed mattress in my office and tucked in the fitted sheet. I spritzed a little Lavender Vanilla sleep spray onto them.

I was saving Crosby's life.

Well, okay, that was a bit of an exaggeration, but I was definitely making myself uncomfortable for the benefit of someone else, so it felt like I was doing the right thing.

It occurred to me that maybe I should have a talk with her about adulting. As great as our parents are, that's one thing they missed in their often do-your-own-thing hippie upbringing of us—they hadn't taught us that much about living in the real world.

Witness Crosby losing all her money.

She hadn't meant to be reckless, I knew that. Though I felt irked with her for doing it to herself, I could also see exactly how it had happened. Our upbringing had been modest. Not a lot of big, glittery luxuries. But Crosby was a magpie, and she loved big, glittery luxuries. So when she got paid a huge amount for her book and everyone around her was telling her how great she was and how she'd have a career that stretched happily into her dotage, she must have decided it was safe to buy some pretty things she didn't need. Take some trips that weren't necessary.

Who wouldn't want all that?

It was probably when I left Tompkins County and came to LA to look for a place to live that I realized that scrimping and saving were going to be necessary. Especially if I was going to be an actress. *Everyone* knows that's an uncertain business, even people who would never, ever entertain the idea of getting into it. So I figured out early on that I had to earn as much as I could while I could and be smart with it.

And here I was, up against the "while I could" part of that. Losing the job that supported me without any solid prospects to replace it.

They say you should have enough money in your account to cover at least three months' worth of expenses in case of financial catastrophe. I have six months' worth of savings. And for a long time I felt really good about that, like I'd be safe from whatever befell me because I had savings and skills. I could always get a new job. In theory.

But now that the befalling had begun, I wasn't comfortable at all. I guess I'd talked myself into thinking that enough money to cover six months was good, but the minute I had to dig into that I'd have less than enough for six months, and *that* was *not* okay. Five and a half months? No good. Five months? Worse. And so on.

In short, with just weeks before Jill left, the walls were closing in. She was going to move to Palm Springs, and while I knew I could pick up work with her now and then, at least until she found someone out there, there was no practical way to keep it going. The drive there took two hours, at best. At worst, it was much more than that. And you could never tell when *at worst* was going to happen, because the 10 was always under construction and half the drivers on it were always idiots. So for all intents and purposes, my job with Jill was ending.

It made me so sad.

And a little mad.

I fluffed the feather pillows a bit aggressively and then smoothed the pillowcases and set them on the bed.

It wasn't just that I needed the money. I definitely did, don't get me wrong, but there was an added element of difficulty because I was really going to miss Jill. I was going to miss cooking in that bright kitchen, looking at the boxwood-bordered yard and the old kidney-shaped pool. I was going to miss hearing her sing along with Seals and Croft and the Beatles and Judy Collins off in the far reaches of the house. Pandora was always set to play the hits of the '60s and '70s. It was so nice. Really. It was like spying on a happy person's private life, even though I was obviously there, obviously part of it, and keeping her from being alone. My impression was that she was utterly content with where she was in life and with what she had.

For that reason, the move made sense. It would cost her less money to live there and give her even more sunshine, less smog, less traffic. On the rare occasion she did a role, it would be easy for her to come to town, but I could honestly see why she wanted to move. I almost couldn't understand why she hadn't done it sooner.

But I was very glad she hadn't.

I folded the puffy all-season comforter in its linen cover at the end of the bed.

I went into the kitchen to handwash the decorative pillowcase for the throw pillow. I filled a utility Cambro with gentle detergent and started kneading it. My phone rang.

Crosby.

My hands drenched in soap and water, I tried to answer with my elbow, but I accidentally declined. Damn it. I tried to tell the phone to call her back, but the voice activation never worked for me. Everyone else could whisper at the phone from across the room and find out what temperature it was outside or how many lengths Secretariat won the Belmont by, but even if I was standing over my phone enunciating clearly, it remained dark.

With my hands still in the soapy water, I stared at it for a moment, thinking she'd call back if it really mattered. She didn't. And she didn't leave a message.

I went back to cleaning the pillowcase. It was ridiculous to care so much about getting it clean before she arrived, but it had gotten woefully covered in dust, and also it was one of the few things in the house that didn't come from the internet. I would love it if she noticed it and I could tell her that it came from some of *my* own life's adventures.

Plus, I know she sneezes around tons of dust.

I tossed the pillowcase in my tiny dryer on low.

I lit a blue Paddywax candle on the chestnut credenza I'd found on a curb when I first got out here. I dusted off the record player and moved *Evita* off the top, choosing Fiona Apple as the display record. Like I ever listened to records.

I threw open the window and a cool breeze came in to waft the scent of a chai-latte-and-vanilla-bean candle on the sill.

I checked the oven, where the snickerdoodles were probably almost ready. Little longer, I decided.

No, she likes them gooey.

I took them out and let them cool on the stove for a few minutes before putting them on a cooling rack.

Lord, I had turned right into Mom.

I looked around. The house looked so . . . alive. I had all these candles I rarely lit, but it's the sort of thing women who do not know you well and whom you do not know well can reliably gift in any circumstance, so in the few relationships I have out here, there has been a lot of candle giving and receiving.

I had the door to my room and the office thrown open, the blinds raised on both, letting in the pale blue light of evening. It smelled like candles, cleaning spray, cookies, dryer sheets. I had music on, which I never did. Just some mix involving Father John Misty and Alabama Shakes that had been recommended to me on Spotify. I liked it, but I really could hardly remember the last time I'd listened to any music at all. Record player or not.

Even the sound of the dryer tumbling was nice. It felt like a life was lived here. This was my own version of that age-old dream of re-creating my parents' domesticity. Whenever I went home, which was pretty infrequently these days, there was always food cooking, drinks being shaken or chilled, noise.

Noise.

Every time I come home now, it's dark and empty. Still. Calm. I usually tell myself that's a good thing, but I also never look forward to coming home. Almost never. Unless I am merely looking forward to sleep.

The one place that should have felt like an escape—home—didn't.

It's not that I hadn't tried. I'd gone to great lengths to strike the right mood. I'd tried cozy but it made me feel claustrophobic. Airy felt too cold. Modern felt impersonal, while retro felt like Disneyland. And it wasn't just about decor, I knew that. It was about *my* identity and expressing it in my environment.

That was what I couldn't find.

I'd been living alone for a long time, almost ten years without a roommate of any sort, though I'd moved a lot. I'd been in this condo for a little over two years, since just before I started working for Jill (when I still had a regular W-2 to qualify for a mortgage), and it was the first time I'd owned my own place. It was a drag to pay the mortgage but it was bliss every time I hung something on the wall and knew I wasn't going to have to fill the hole and paint over it in a few months in order to move yet again. It wasn't big, it wasn't fancy, and I can't pretend there weren't times when I wished there weren't always loud city sounds outside the window, but it was mine.

***

WHILE I KNEW Crosby was planning to find another place to rent, I also knew it was going to be harder than she expected. A recent housing boom coupled with increasingly restrictive laws about short-term rentals had started to turn this back into a hotel town. It was possible she was going to have to stay with me the whole time she was here.

A month and a half was a long time to have a guest in an apartment that felt small after three hours with another person in it.

I knew that noise was something that came with Crosby. But what if it was all too much?

All signs pointed toward it being *a lot* when she eventually arrived.

It sounded like a battering ram on the door. I had just poured a glass of wine and sat down to relax when I heard a repeated slamming sound and then the door opened and I got up to see Crosby coming in with three suitcases and a shopping bag from a local dispensary and a bottle of champagne poking out of—was that a *Burberry bag*?

"I got some stuff," she said, nodding at her things, while one of her suitcases slammed hard against the front door, undoubtedly leaving a scuff if not a scar. "Can you get the door?"

I got up and went to close it. "How do you manage to make *everything* you do so loud?" This had always annoyed me. She was just naturally loud. It wasn't even just when she talked or laughed, though our parents *had* had her hearing tested when she was little just to make sure. It was just like she had invisible cans tied to her ankles and every movement she made was a ruckus.

"You're right. Sorry, I probably should have made more than one trip. Almost got through clear but I thought I saw something behind me and it startled me."

I had to make an effort not to roll my eyes. "Who did you see this time, Meryl Streep?"

She did roll her eyes. "No, a swarm of wasps."

"Oh, well, of course. If they were chasing you like Darren Neville was, that was definitely worth beating the hell out of the door for."

"Come on, my suitcases are soft. The door is fine. And Darren Neville *was* chasing me; I just didn't know he was being nice." She stopped and set her stuff down. "You don't need to Franic, I'll be more careful now that I know how much it matters to you."

"I'm not *Franicking*." I was, though. I just resented the term . . . and how well it fit. "What are you wearing?"

"A dress. I figured you could use some extra time so I went out to dinner." Reading my mind, she supplied, "I sold some crypto so I'd have some money for incidentals. And this other guy picked up the bill anyway."

"What other guy?" I thought about it. "And you buy crypto?"

"Just some guy at the bar. He was fine." She shrugged. "And only a few hundred dollars' worth. I have an app for it. Anyway, he started talking to me and then his friend got there and then we all chatted. It was fun; we actually all did a shot with the bartender and the chef came out because it turned out that guy was like . . . some sort of big deal, I don't know."

"I see."

"Are you still Franicking?"

"No, God, stop."

"Yes, you are. Good thing I went to Med Men." She brought the red bag over to me. It looked like a gift bag from a fancy department store but it did indeed say MED MEN on it, with a logo of a cannabis leaf. "I got you some stuff."

"I hate weed."

"That's true, you do, but *you* hate the psychoactive effects." She looked triumphant. "I got you some CBD oil to relax you without any THC to make you high. They said there are no *psychoactives*."

I did not believe in CBD oil any more than I believed in homeopathy. I worked with edible things all day every day, and if it takes a quarter cup of basil to make a pot of tomato bisque taste right, I don't believe the *imprint* of a flower cell is going to cure cancer. "Does it actually *say* 'for entertainment purposes only' on it?"

"Very funny. For your information, this stuff really works! And it's a good alternative to wine." She nodded at my glass with a wry look. "You don't want to have too much of that, you know. It's *terrible* for you. Is there more?"

"In the fridge."

"I'll replace it, I swear." She dropped the bag on the kitchen table and rooted through it. "Look, I know this is not your dream situation, having me here. I know you've been living alone for a long time and you've always kept to yourself, so this is going to be an adjustment."

I started to object but she held up a finger.

"*Even though* I'm only here *temporarily*." She smiled but I thought it held a tinge of sadness. "Don't worry, we're on the same page there. I promise I will try to find a new place fast."

"You don't need to—"

"Yes, I do." She took something out of the bag and came over to the sofa. "Now, look. I'm not trying to goad you, I really just thought this might be something you like. I know you get anxious and the person helping me at the shop seemed really knowledgeable. This is brand-new and apparently it works really well." She handed me a small box that said AUNTIE ANXIETY on it, with a line drawing of a serene-expressioned, stylized fifties woman and the words *As soothing as a soft blanket and a nice hot toddy.*

I had to admit it was appealing. Just the kind of thing that would have caught my eye. "Thanks." My feelings toward her softened. "That is cute."

"Right?" She gave a confident nod and headed for the kitchen. "Need a refill?"

"Not yet."

She went to the cabinet, took out another expensive glass, and gave herself a hefty pour. "Okay, before I drink that, let me just go change really quick and then we can hang." She came over to me and grabbed her suitcases and dragged them over to the office. Out of sight, I heard her say, "Aw, this is so cute!"

She didn't shut the door, and I leaned against the butcher's block and watched her. She had a pleasant look on her face, even though she didn't know she was being watched. What must that be like? Every time I did a meditation that said to relax the muscles in my face, I realized I was doing an impression of a grumpy old man.

She was just made of different stuff than I was.

I sliced myself a piece of Brie from the cutting board, where I'd put out a few things.

"I love this pillow!" I heard her say.

When I looked, I saw that she had changed into a matching PJ set of soft-looking T-shirt and shorts in pale blush pink and heathered pink socks. She'd thrown her hair up into a ponytail and she was bending to take a picture of the nightstand-and-bed setup.

I popped a grape in my mouth.

Funny, when she arrived, it was like taking a silent room and unleashing five Chihuahuas.

My phone dinged. I looked and it was a text from Jill. It was a little late for her, so I looked at it with some concern. When I read what she'd written, my stomach clenched like a fist.

Incredible news: Fletcher just learned that your sister is the writer and he's interested in having her maybe guest-write a couple of the scripts for his new show! Wouldn't that be marvelous? You acting and her writing! He said to tell her to get in touch with him—you have the number!

And that right there felt like the end. I knew *exactly* how it went from here. Crosby was a proven commodity; her name on a written work would mean something. Even if I did the best acting of my life, that was no guarantee it would be to Fletcher Hall's taste. Or to the audience's, for that matter. Bringing Crosby into the project would create a subconscious feeling of *We only need one of them* and it would be her.

I'd lose any chance of getting the job. And that job, *amazing* as it would be, *life-changing* as it would be, was my last and only chance. This was it. I was up against the wall. In a month (more or less) I'd have to start living on my savings, and that was *very* finite. If I didn't take the job with Jill, I'd be in very uncertain territory and heaven only knew when the next audition would be or if I'd be right for it. Parts for a woman my age were hard to come by because I was in between ages, leaning ever closer to mother roles. There were always commercials, but TV and movie roles were thinning out.

And so far I'd effectively gotten nowhere.

Who was I kidding? Why was I even *thinking* about staying in LA instead of taking Jill up on her offer? If the Fletcher Hall project didn't work out, it was over for me. I would be a cook forevermore.

Crosby wasn't in that kind of trouble at all. Yes, she might have screwed up with the money she blew through, but that was just a matter of irresponsibility. Not coming up with a second book was a matter of laziness. But she could keep working on that forever; no one was ever going to say she was too old to write.

So this wasn't a matter of her or me. I wasn't saving myself and letting her drown. This wasn't the oxygen dropping in front of us both on a plane and her having no arms and needing me to help her before I helped myself. This was me getting on a plane to Idaho and the pilot asking if she'd like to come too when she'd never even talked about wanting to go to Idaho before.

"Who's texting you?" Crosby asked, startling me. My hand went reflexively over the screen. I knew I should tell her. I should tell her right away. But I also knew that if I did, I'd be almost certain to lose the part and she'd end up winning an Emmy for the script. I just couldn't take it. It would be the last nail in my career's coffin.

But it could make her career.

"Frances?"

My hesitation felt like it lasted years. Finally I found my voice. "It's nothing," I said. "One of those insulting spam texts advertising a weight-loss program. That reminds me, why did you call earlier? I had my hands full."

"Oh, it was nothing. I was wondering if you had Pop-Tarts but I decided to err on the side of caution."

"Meaning you bought Pop-Tarts."

She nodded. "They're still in the car."

"Good call. I don't have anything quick here."

"I figured. So delete that stupid weight-loss spam. Ew. You don't need that kind of energy in your life. And you definitely don't need to lose weight." She shook her head with disgust. "Swipe left and delete."

I did. I swiped left and deleted Jill's text. "Thanks."

"Of course. Bubble butts like yours are in these days."

I sighed. "Thanks."

"There," she said approvingly. "Feel better?"

Did I? "I guess," I said. "A little."

"Good. If anything else like that comes in, don't even read it, just delete on sight, okay?"

I looked at her and nodded. Panic grew in me. Had I just made a huge mistake? Was I a terrible person?

I was. I was a terrible person.

Even worse, I did nothing about it.

Chapter Twelve

Crosby

$\mathcal{H}$i, is Crosby Turner there? This is her tenant in New York calling."

My stomach clenched. What now? What hell was befalling me now? Had the place burned down? If so, was my insurance up to date? What would I do? Insanely, I had to fight an urge to just hang up or say it was a wrong number and stick to that story.

But these people were in my *home*. I couldn't ignore whatever they were calling about. "This is Crosby," I said, my voice tense and thin. "Is something wrong?"

"No," she said on the other line. "Well, yes, maybe. I don't know. There is a foreclosure notice taped to the door."

"Foreclosure?"

"Actually, it says *intent to foreclose*. So pre-foreclosure. Foreclosure Eve." She laughed, then caught herself.

It was *exactly* the kind of joke I would have made.

But it pissed me off.

"Good Lord, there's obviously some sort of mistake." This was not what I'd feared. This wasn't even in the neighborhood of what I'd feared. Yet. Relief flooded me. "Listen, can you take a picture and text it to me? I'll get to the bottom of this. Meanwhile, enjoy yourselves. I'm sorry you had this intrusion on your stay."

"No problem!" It sounded like she did have no problems. Not a care in the world. I was growing sensitive to that. "It's actually a little disappointing that it's not a foreclosure because we're looking for a place and we love this one." She laughed obnoxiously and didn't backtrack to explain how she wasn't exactly *disappointed* bad luck wasn't befalling me.

I was starting to hate her.

"Oh. Well, good luck with your search!" I chirped merrily, but it was quickly dawning on me that this was a pretty unusual mistake. Unless it had someone else's address on it, I was headed for a nightmare of research, calls, et cetera. "I'll just wait for your text," I reminded her before hanging up.

The text came about three minutes later.

It was definitely my address. There was a phone number to call, but I couldn't bear the idea of speaking to someone, so I logged into my mortgage company's website, where I had long ago set up autopay. *That* I was sure of.

I clicked around and found that I did indeed have autopay set up. That allowed me just a moment of relief before I saw that it was coming from my savings account instead of my checking account.

Now, once upon a time, that wouldn't have mattered because I had a very healthy amount of money in both, but when things began going south for me financially, I'd stopped distributing funds to my savings because there just wasn't enough to go around. At first I'd told myself that I'd be back to saving soon, but when it reached a more critical level of survival, I'd stopped thinking about savings altogether.

And I'd stopped thinking about that account, mistakenly believing that I'd transferred all of my regular monthly transactions to my checking account.

If I had, this wouldn't be happening. But as it was, I had believed my fluctuating checking balance to be correct as I went along, so now I was three months behind on mortgage payments with no immediate way to rectify the situation.

And to answer the unasked question, I'm sure they did send notices letting me know. I was getting so much junk mail from so many banks et cetera that I always set them aside for "later," whenever that was.

Plenty of people would have been more responsible. In fact, maybe *most* people would have been more responsible. Those are people who don't understand the psychology of circling the financial drain.

Why didn't you stop spending on non-necessities?

Why didn't you get another job?

Why didn't you get a cheaper phone plan, get rid of cable, et cetera, et cetera, et cetera?

God forbid Frances should find out about this; those are questions she'd ask. Questions that are inherently judgmental (maybe even justifiably judgmental) and completely irrelevant after the fact. The damage was done. It didn't need to be understood by anyone but me.

And I was the one who needed to fix it.

She didn't need to know the true depth of my financial devastation. I'd been on top, I'd been on the bottom, I'd spent most of my time in between, but I was determined to get on top again. No need to embarrass myself—or her—by confiding my desperation.

I called my friend Julie Powell back home. She was not only one of my oldest friends and the person I'd spent countless Saturdays shopping and lunching my funds away with; she was also a Realtor. A good enough one to probably still be shopping and lunching as much as she wanted.

"Hey, girlie!" she said, recognizing my number. "How's Hollywood life treating you?"

God, I wished I could answer the way she expected me to: *Everything's great! Mardie is a hoot! You should see the Jimmy Choos I got on Rodeo Drive, they looked so good I got every color!*

"Things are good," I hedged. "The weather is glorious! And it's absolutely wild seeing Hollywood landmarks when I'm just driving to Target. I swear if I look, I can see the Hollywood sign from just about every stoplight."

"That is so cool. Seen any stars?"

I told her about my encounter with Darren Neville and of course mentioned how Frances worked for Jill Cameron, which impressed Julie even more since she was a fan of the old glitzy nighttime soap Jill had been on.

"Do you remember that time we thought we saw Rufus Wainwright on the sidewalk outside the Book Nook?"

"Whoever it was, it wasn't Rufus." And whoever it was, we'd followed him for nearly a half hour, trying to get close enough to see without being so close we were seen.

"Sadly," she agreed. "So what's up? Why are you interrupting your turn at stardom to call boring old me? Not that I'm complaining."

"I'm thinking about selling my place there. Are you interested in taking it on?"

There was a moment's pause. "Are things going so well you're going to move there?"

"I don't know about *that*, but I do think it's time for a change."

She sighed. "That's sad for me to hear. I've missed you but I was looking forward to you coming back."

"Oh, I'll be back, I just—I need to sell."

She didn't ask for details, though I think she heard the urgency in my voice. "You've picked a good time for it. The whole area is an advertisement for autumn. Even the worst places are given curb appeal by the foliage. What kind of time frame are you looking at?"

I swallowed. "Now? Ish?" I cleared my throat. "Now. I mean, I got it all cleaned up and nice for the renters—oh! That reminds me! The renters said they were interested in buying. I don't know if they meant it or not, but that might be a good place to start."

"Got it." I could tell she was jotting down notes. "I can

approach them, no problem. I also have another client who might be perfect. Now, let's talk price."

The conversation lasted another half hour, with Julie laying out exactly what I stood to make on the sale. In the end, I'd had to admit that I was behind on the payments, so my takeaway was going to have a big chunk of interest added onto it, but there would be enough left over to get me on my feet and even be a down payment on a modestly priced place somewhere else.

At least buying my house had been a good use of my money, unlike so many other things I'd spent it on.

I came away from the conversation feeling quite a bit more optimistic. It wasn't how I'd intended for things to go but I was going to be okay. And if I looked at it the right way, it was really a great opportunity to start a new adventure. I could stay in the same town if I wanted to, but maybe it was time for me to stretch my wings.

It wasn't as if my parents needed me nearby. If anything, I'd benefited from the proximity more than they had. Delicious meals courtesy of Mom, Dad always running over to fix little things around my place when I couldn't figure them out. In the past year alone he'd added a dead bolt to my front door, replaced my dryer vent, and fixed a kitchen cabinet door that kept dropping off the top. To say nothing of the countless fuses he'd replaced over the years and the two times he'd come to change a tire for me.

None of those emergencies had freaked me out because I always enjoyed the chance to have a laugh and a drink or meal with him afterward. Between those times with him and the hour or so I spent on the phone with my mom a couple times a week, just gabbing about life, I'd been pretty comfortable but maybe not quite the adult they'd expected me to be by age thirty-two.

Maybe this was a good thing. A nudge—no, a *shove*—in the right direction.

I opened a spreadsheet in Excel and put down some hard, true numbers: bank balance, IRA balance, meager Crypto .com balance versus monthly debt, including way too much credit.

When I finished putting down the solid numbers I saw that I was . . . okay. Not great and not for long, though. It would be ideal if I could blow through Mardie's book and get paid for it but that was going to depend on her schedule. I had zero control over that.

My friend Kurt worked for an online magazine based in Manhattan, and he'd told me a thousand times he wanted me to freelance for him and, as he put it, "try and pull this lackluster pony ahead of the rest and win the race." I called him.

"You're not going to believe what I did!" he said when he answered.

I was thrown. "What?"

"I quit!" he trilled. "They were so ticked, they didn't even ask for notice. I'm outta here, baby, on my way to Colorado!"

"Since when?" How long had I been gone? I knew he'd been wanting to go on a ski vacation this winter because he was texting with a guy in Colorado who seemed interesting to him, but I'd had *no idea* he was anywhere near exploding his life. Which was cool, if that's what he wanted. I was happy for him.

"I quit Monday. Packing up my place now."

"*Wow.*"

"I know, right? How about you?" His voice was all but singsong. "What's going on in La-La Land?"

Unlike Julie, he didn't want the rundown right now. He was on cloud nine about his new relationship and undoubtedly overwhelmed with quitting and packing up. There would be time to talk when he got back down to earth. He definitely didn't need me begging him to find me freelance work right now. "Everything's good so far," I said. "It's really weird how you can run into stars anywhere and everywhere." I told him the Darren Neville story because I knew he'd get a kick out of it, and he did.

"Only you would run away from a movie star," Kurt said.

"I like to think that was refreshing for him."

"It probably was." He laughed. "Look, I've got a shit-ton to do here and no time to do it. Can I give you a ding from the road in a few days?"

"Oh, sure, take your time. I'll be around."

"Cool, cool. Catch ya later, kitty cat!"

We hung up and I looked through my text messages to see who I might be forgetting about that might have a lead on some extra work I could get. Once, people had been full of offers—technical writing, smoothing out the wording on websites, et cetera. Even first-person accounts of getting published and hitting it big. Back then I didn't need the smaller dollar amounts; it didn't feel like the most effective use of my time or my writing energy.

Now I needed anything I could get. Pride was no longer part of the equation. Unfortunately, neither were job offers.

This was really getting me down.

With no other obvious supplemental ideas, I had to count on the Mardie book to get me my fastest income. It was worrisome that I hadn't heard from her since I left New York, even though she had my itinerary and knew I was here specifically to work for her. And she knew my time here was finite. I was usually overcautious about being a pest, but in this case I didn't have the luxury of being polite. I opened up a text.

Hi, Mardie! It's, Crosby! I'm in town now, ready to get to work on your book. Can't wait to meet you and write the blockbuster memoir I know this will be. Please give me a call or text at your earliest convenience so we can get started ASAP.

I paused, then hit Send. Then paused again before adding:

I'm only here for a month and a half so we should take advantage of all the time we can to work together. I'm really looking forward to it!!

Send.

There were so many exclamation points in there I looked

like a total weirdo but I didn't care. Wasn't Mardie one of the perkiest, most energetic pop stars of the '90s? I was just showing her that I could keep up with her perk, stride for stride, giggle for giggle.

But, God, I was exhausted.

It's amazing how emotional stress can wipe you out. And until I had some money coming in, I was going to remain stressed. So on top of all that, I was going to have to try and hide it from Frances.

Chapter Thirteen

Frances

What is lunch without cheese? That's my philosophy. Fortunately, Jill feels the same. And today she was having one of her former costars, Ingrid Rockwell, who happened to be vegetarian, over for a light lunch by the pool and had requested my "famous grilled cheese and supreme cream of tomato soup."

The grilled cheese wasn't famous but it should have been, if I do say so myself. It began with thick slices of San Francisco–style sourdough, painted on both sides with butter and just the slightest bit of mayonnaise. It's an old diner trick and a lot of people know it, but that is what gives you a really beautiful buttery golden crunch on the outside of the bread, leaving the inside tender and not soaked in oil. You give it a quick sear, almost like a steak.

Any good cheese will work—that's a personal flavor choice—but the ones *I* liked best were nutty Swiss Gruyère, some paper-thin slices of Fromager d'Affinois (note: put it in the freezer for a few minutes so it doesn't just collapse in a creamy pile when you go to slice it, and use a sharp knife), and some Morbier if you can find it. A little grating of nutmeg and sugar and wine-caramelized sweet onions make it into something that tastes like French onion soup, especially if you put au jus on the side, but since we were staying veg, I added a whisper-thin slice of heirloom tomato and the lightest grating of tangy Granny Smith apple.

A mulligatawny soup would have been a nice side too, picking up the apple notes, but it's hard to go wrong with a good cream of tomato. Brown-sugar-roasted tomato slices, stirred in with caramelized shallots with a bloom of allspice over the heat, then vegetable stock. Simmer it all for twenty minutes or so, puree, and finish with a kiss of cream and brandy. It makes me hungry for it all over again just thinking about it.

Was I obsessing over this a little too much?

Maybe. But I had to keep my mind occupied or else the telltale heart beating beneath the floorboards—in this case, the potential (and unlikely to appeal to her at *all*) job I hadn't told Crosby about—was going to haunt me until I screamed.

I know, I know, I *know* I shouldn't have done it. And it wasn't too late to tell her now. But more than feeling guilty about it, I was terrified that she was going to take over the one cool connection that might get me a life-changing job. She needed work but she wasn't seeing this as a *career*. It wasn't going to ruin her not to work in Hollywood when she was finished with Mardie's book. I, on the other hand, had worked my entire life for a career in acting. Dreamed about it, obsessed over it, prayed and prayed and prayed for it. Now I was at a crossroads where I could go full force on my acting or just give it all up and make a career of cooking. Because I couldn't keep serving two masters the way I had been. Working for Jill had been lovely; it (and she) had complemented my audition schedule, and, further, she'd been a great person to talk to about my aspirations. She had tips, connections, everything I needed. So it seemed like fate was really on my side when the Fletcher Hall thing had come up.

And damn it, I didn't want Crosby getting in the middle of it. How many times was she going to get between me and a person, place, or thing I liked or wanted? If there was a lesson in all this, maybe it was that I had to start being a little more selfish and taking what was due to me.

It was easy to see signs in everything.

At the last minute, Jill told me this wasn't lunch for two but for three; Ingrid's adult son was joining them. I made two more sandwiches and put them all in a warm oven to wait until Jill was ready to serve. As soon as that was done, I could leave. I wanted to get home and practice a few monologues.

"Why don't you join us for lunch?" Jill suggested when they arrived.

"Oh, no, thanks anyway. I've already eaten." Every time I cooked I ate my way through the process. "Quality-control testing" my father would jokingly call it. But today it was more that I couldn't resist cheese. Especially those whisper-thin slices of Gruyère that leave you wanting more. And the triple-crème fromage that just melts in your mouth.

Jill moved closer and said under her breath, "I think it would be good for you to get to know Vince."

Vince was Ingrid Rockwell's son. I glanced behind Jill and saw him talking with his mother. He was a tall, muscular guy with a wide smile, tawny skin, and curly black hair. I would have bet money that his was the male version of his mother's original nose (which I'd never actually seen). Wide to begin with and wider still when he smiled. Ingrid had Italian roots—not just in her hair—but had never been Italian enough to follow the Sophia Loren blueprint, despite her labored Italian affectations, so she'd become famous for playing the bombshell who stole rich men from their wives. She'd played opposite Jill as that exact character.

Jill was standing next to me as they came in and I whispered, "If this is your attempt at a setup, I'm really not interested in dating anyone right now."

Jill frowned. "What? I wasn't thinking *that*. Although . . ." She glanced at him. "He's not . . . *bad*-looking."

He kind of was, but I liked to think I was the kind of person who didn't care about that sort of thing.

"Anyway, he's available!" Jill gave me a wink and turned to summon her guests to the table. I plated the food and served them each, marveling, as always, at the way the sun filled the room and made it feel like summer every single day of the year. It wasn't quite pool weather, but there was very little to complain about in terms of temperature in a Southern California winter.

It would be warmer in the desert, I thought. Usually a good twenty degrees or so. It was pool weather there.

"Frances, this is Vince Carmel, Ingrid's son," Jill said as I set the food down.

"I know it's a cliché, but I've heard so much about you," he said to me. "You have a lot of fans here."

It was rare that Ingrid ever had more than a bite of anything but she did tend to try everything. I smiled. "That's kind of you."

"Francesca," Ingrid said (she was so desperate to be the modern Sophia Loren that she had adopted an Italian persona), "I have something extremely important to propose to you. I wonder if you'd mind having a seat for a moment and talking with us?"

Jill stared at me from behind her big tortoiseshell Gucci sunglasses.

"Sure," I said, feeling apprehensive. She was going to offer me a job cooking for her and I was going to have to accept. It was a foregone conclusion and I wasn't sure I liked it. I'd wanted to move on by now. To cook for fun, not for a living.

"I'm going to get right to the point," Ingrid said, then didn't. "Because I am so excited I can barely think straight."

She seemed to be waiting for me to say something but I didn't know what, so I just smiled and said, "Okay . . ."

"I've had an idea," she said. "Now, you can ask Jill, here, my ideas are legendary. I'm the one who suggested shoulder pads to Nolan Miller, and where would *Dynasty* have been without that fashion touch?"

Oh, boy. I shook my head and shrugged. "It was a big part of the eighties."

"You *bet* it was. And that's how I am—I can see a trend coming a mile away and jump right on before anyone else."

My brain automatically tried to untangle the logic of that. If she saw the trend when it was a mile away, didn't that mean she was already at least a mile behind on it? It was just semantics, but still, it didn't make sense.

"Do get to the point," Jill said to her friend.

Ingrid flashed her a look and then said to me, "What do you know about me?"

I glanced uncertainly from her to Jill to Vince and back. "I'm not good at pop quizzes. I'm not sure what in particular you're asking me."

"Oh, for Pete's sake, Ingrid, *get to the point*." Jill was losing her patience as fast as I was.

"All right!" Ingrid snapped, then quickly arranged her face into practiced pleasantry. "As you are probably aware, dear Francesca, my love story with Vince's father was one for the ages. Why, back in the day, we were the couple *du jour* for so long, they had to make us the couple *du siècle*." I must have looked confused because she added, "It means 'of the century.'"

"Ah." I nodded. I had definitely never heard that about Ingrid Rockwell and her husband.

"And I want to tell our story for all those fans who have been begging to hear it for decades. I want to produce a mini-series called *Ingrid 'n' Jack*."

"Oh!" I felt Jill looking at me and glanced in her direction to see her hiding her smile with her hand.

"You haven't heard the best part yet." Ingrid looked at me expectantly.

I glanced at her son, wondering what part he had in this and what he thought about whatever the hell was coming, but his face was stonelike, no readable expression whatsoever.

I flattened my hands on the tabletop and took a breath, demonstrating how very seriously I was taking this. "I'm ready."

Ingrid looked like she could barely contain her glee. "I want *you* to play the role of *me!*" She laughed and clapped her hands together rapidly. "Now, don't go thanking me just yet, I want you to know this is not a favor, it's just that you're *perfect* for the part. Why, you look so much like me when I was younger that it takes my breath away. I said that to Jill the first time I saw you, didn't I, Jill?"

"It's true," Jill said with a nod.

"And what with your job here ending in a couple of weeks, the timing could not be better!" She clapped again.

"I don't know what to say," I said sincerely. Had someone actually *bought* this idea? *Who?* And no matter who it was,

was there any way it could be interesting enough to make this a step forward for me instead of a forgotten role in a show that flopped?

"It gets better," Ingrid went on. "As if casting you isn't brilliant enough, I want my Vince here to play his father. He's a dead ringer for him, though of course he comes by it honestly."

I suddenly felt a strong urge to Google Ingrid Rockwell and see what she and her husband had looked like when they were young and find out if they were, in fact, that captivating to the world. I had never heard of them, and I knew a lot about the pop culture of generations before me, thanks to my parents, but I couldn't pretend I knew it all.

"This is very flattering," I said to Ingrid because I knew she'd intended it to be. "If you want to give me the information about casting I can pass it along to my agent to set something up, or . . ." My voice trailed off because I didn't have an *or* to follow up with. I looked at her son, wondering why on earth he wasn't saying anything, though he did look at me and give me a polite smile. I think. With those teeth, it was difficult to be sure if it was a smile or a grimace.

"That might be the most exciting part." Ingrid gave a dramatic pause. "I am financing a spec pilot. We are going to move forward and show the networks what we have to offer. Now, that *will* mean your pay might be a little less than I'd like, though still scale, of course. No one is here to rip anyone off."

So I'd be paid scale to work on a single pilot episode of

a series or miniseries that almost certainly wasn't going to sell. I weighed the options rapidly in my head. It was certain money, although not a ton of it. And work in my chosen field, so a credit on my résumé. But if it was as terrible as I feared it might be, it could damage my reputation as an actor with discrimination and taste.

Then again, how many actors had dud projects in their pasts? Probably all of them. Jennifer Lawrence had been in the flop *The Beaver*; Jennifer Aniston had done an early horror flick called *Leprechaun* and still gone on to greatness. Hell, even Robert De Niro had voiced a character in *Rocky and Bullwinkle*. A stupid role wasn't necessarily a career killer.

"I did have Vince draw up a contract, just in case you said yes," she said. "It's standard, almost boilerplate. I'm sure your agent won't have a problem with it."

"Wait, you had *Vince* draw up a contract?"

Finally he spoke. "I'm a contract lawyer," he explained.

"For now." Ingrid was positively glowing. "But he is *such* a talent, just *wait until you see*. The good thing is he can review his own contracts when the roles start pouring in."

"I think I'd get an entertainment lawyer to do that," he told her.

"There is one problem," Jill interjected, speaking at last. "And I have tried to tell Ingrid it's a big one."

Ingrid's face went a little pink and she waved away Jill's words. "It's a common clause."

Jill looked at me. "You have to commit to the production until it's completed or until such time as they're ready to release you from your contract. In other words, the audition for Fletcher is off the table."

My heart sank. I needed the money. I *really* needed credits on my résumé. I needed the legitimacy of having acted myself, not just handed miniature Brie tarts to people who had.

But I couldn't give up the biggest audition I'd ever been offered in order to take a sure thing that was also sure to fail. I'd already taken drastic measures to protect that chance. I thought of Crosby and hoped to God Jill didn't mention that before I left. Given that Fletcher Hall was the biggest potential payoff that I could possibly have at this point in my career—even though there was a good chance that would go nowhere—I just couldn't give it up.

I was tired of settling for the bird in the hand.

Ingrid was so excited I couldn't tell her that now, so I stood up and gave her what I hoped looked like a sincere smile combined with gratitude. "I cannot tell you how much I appreciate this chance," I said. "If you or"—I turned to Vince—"*you*, I guess, could send that contract and the details to my agent, I'll discuss it with him and see what he advises."

"Consider it done," Ingrid said. "Dear, get her details before she leaves."

"I have her agent's card," Jill said, giving me a sly wink. "You know you have to send the offer to him before she can answer you, Ingrid. Don't try and take advantage of my girl."

"Certainly not!" Ingrid raked her gaze over me, obviously assessing me. I was braced for her to say I'd have to lose a couple pounds, but instead she said, "I look forward to your answer, Francesca. I think this is the opportunity of a life-time for you."

"Thank you again." I glanced at Jill. "And thank *you* for arranging this."

She nodded. "Options are always important, I know that. And I feel just beastly that I'm leaving you in the lurch by moving. Let me walk you out, dear." She got up and waited while I over-thanked Ingrid and assured Vince it had been a pleasure to meet him.

Before I could promise them my firstborn, Jill slipped her arm through mine and guided me to the door.

"Don't feel obligated to take that role," she said when we were safely outside. "It could be a hoot, and the money's as real as what you'd make anywhere, but I know you have been hopeful about Fletch."

"Yes. Yes, I have."

"And Ingrid can be a bit of an egotist."

I couldn't stop myself. "You think?"

Fortunately, Jill laughed. "Okay, she *is* an egotist. And a showboat to boot. But she means well and with all the nostalgia in entertainment now, it's not impossible the show will sell and be a hit. You just never know."

"You never do."

"To make this up to you, I want you—and your sister, please!—to come to a party at Paragon tomorrow. A huge party, lots of people." She lowered her chin. "Fletch will be there, as well as a *lot* of other people you should meet. It's a charity event but we all know it's a schmooze-fest."

My heart leaped. *This* was the kind of opportunity I needed. *This* was the kind of life I wanted.

"Do be sure to bring your sister too," she repeated.

I felt my face go pale. "I—I—okay."

"Hopefully she has talked to Fletcher by now, but I told myself I was going to stay out of this one. If I push him to hire everyone, he's not going to hire *any*one."

"Good Lord, we don't want that," I said before I could stop myself.

She smiled. "I have a good feeling for you, Frances. A real good feeling. Come to that party. I'll see you there."

Chapter Fourteen

Crosby

It was five minutes to eleven when I got to the address Mardie had texted me *just that morning*.

Honest to God, it kind of felt like she thought this book was a side gig for me when it was my whole purpose in being out here.

It was five minutes past eleven when I realized I'd passed the wrought-iron gate that was nearly entirely hidden by ivy multiple times. There was no mailbox outside, at least not that I could see. And anything beyond the ivy couldn't be seen from the road. Pretty much anyone would have missed it the first time.

Any of my friends could tell you that I'm not exactly a stickler for showing up on time, but any former *boss* could tell you that my punctuality is one of my best qualities. I would never be late for a job. Not until I wanted to quit. For day one, especially, I would never. Day one of a job I hoped would catapult me into a new career? Absolutely not. Five minutes could be a dealbreaker. You never know how people are going to be.

I should have Googled the property first, and I'd even freaking *thought* of doing that, but the truth was I had decided it would be more fun to wait and surprise myself with it.

I pulled up in front of the gate and puzzled over what to do. There was no guard, no button as far as I could see. I didn't want to start our relationship by being a pain, but I didn't see any other option than to call her.

No answer.

I called again.

Still no answer.

Now *she* was starting our relationship by being a pain. Surely she knew how nerve-racking it was for someone to be coming into this situation from so far away (literally and figuratively).

I sat. Well, what the hell was I supposed to do now? Had she changed her mind about using me for her book? Forgotten the deal entirely? It hadn't occurred to me that that could be a possibility but now it seemed like it was *obviously* possible; she was famously flaky.

Was it possible that she'd just hired someone else instead? We had signed a contract, but I knew *nothing* about that sort of thing. But people in her position had lawyers to get them out of contracts if they wanted. It might have meant nothing to her to sign it.

I tried her phone one more time.

"Yes?" She sounded exasperated.

My face went hot with humiliation even though she was supposed to be expecting me, so I wasn't in the wrong. I was a professional here to *help* her. I had to keep that in mind. "Hey, it's Crosby Turner," I said, trying to sound as breezy and confident as possible. "I'm at the gate but I'm not sure—"

"Oh, shit!"

It literally startled me. "I'm sorry?"

"I forgot. Hang on, I'll open it." I heard something fall over and hit the floor on her end. "Come on in. Shit, I've got to get dressed."

My impulse was to say, *Oh, no, you're fine, don't worry about getting dressed*, but considering I didn't know just how not-dressed she was, I didn't.

There was a creaking sound in front of me and the wall of green pulled up and out to the sides, exposing a long, tree-lined asphalt drive to a white two-story house. It looked like the one from *Father of the Bride*: pristine landscaping, glossy black shutters on a couple dozen windows. The garage—it looked like it was for four cars—was to the left of the house, and there was a circular driveway in front. I followed the line and parked between the door and the garage, behind a gold Porsche Cayenne.

When I got out of the car, I was struck by the silence on the property. There was birdsong, and a light wind rustled the trees, but just a moment ago I'd been in the LA traffic, and this was a comparative Shangri-la.

I went to the door, took a light bracing breath, and rang

the bell. It was important, I decided, to act as if this were no big deal to me, like I was the celebrity here, helping her out. Ha. I didn't believe that for one second but it seemed like the best way to get her respect up front.

The breeze rose again while I waited and I could have sworn there was perfume on it. I wasn't good with identifying plants to begin with, and I was definitely bad at West Coast flowers that bloomed in the fall, but the scent was dreamy and old fashioned—it must be bliss to be able to open your windows to that anytime you want.

The door opened and a good-looking guy who appeared to be about thirty started coming out. Tall, with a good build, the kind that looks great in old jeans and a flannel shirt over a white T-shirt, which was exactly what he was wearing. His light brown hair was wavy and mussed; his skin tan. He struck me as outdoorsy, with easy, confident movements.

A boyfriend? A younger man—that would be an interesting twist for her. Forget the relationship with Trey Simons a thousand years ago; Mardie was not pining away for that, she had this hot young stud. He looked startled to see me.

"Hi." I smiled, expecting to be expected.

He looked confused. "Hey."

"I'm Crosby. Crosby Turner." His expression remained blank. I glanced at the number over the door. "I'm here for Mardie. She's expecting me."

He hesitated and glanced behind me, as if there were a camera crew from that old show *Punk'd* hiding somewhere. "She's . . . expecting you?"

Suddenly I wondered if she'd told anyone else about the book she was writing. Having never ghostwritten before, I didn't know how far I should go with discretion, but I figured I shouldn't say anything until I heard from her about it. "I just spoke with her. She . . . she opened the gate for me?"

His eyebrows furrowed over his light blue eyes, and I started planning how I could deal with this if it became a weird misunderstanding telephone game.

"Ohhhh." Realization broke across his face, and he smiled. The gentle smile lines around his eyes were completely unsurprising. "I think she did say she was having you over. Favorite writer, right?"

Relief flowed through me, cool and refreshing. "Well, I don't know about *that*, but she did say she liked my book."

"I'm so sorry, I'm just not really up on everything. She's a little hard to . . ." His voice trailed off. "Anyway, I'm Conor. Mariano. Her brother." He gestured toward the house. "I was just leaving. She's—well, go on in. She's on the phone but I guess she's expecting you."

My face grew hot. This was not the reception I'd imagined at all. Which was fine—seriously, I didn't need a grand celebration to commence our relationship—but I wasn't sure what to do with this feeling that I was imposing on everyone. I wasn't, I couldn't be; I'd been *hired*, for God's sake, but I still couldn't shake the feeling that I was a gawker.

Maybe because inside I kind of was. I'd grown up pretty comfortably thanks to my parents' hard-earned success. Met a few "celebrity" friends of my dad's, though they were all older musicians you'd know from elevator hits now. But we definitely hadn't seen this kind of grandeur in our lives. Even the nicest houses I'd been to in New York didn't have this extra zing that made you feel like some classic Hollywood types might be out back having drinks by the pool.

"I've got to run," Conor said. "Late for an appointment, but—" He gestured inward again. And with that, he left. I wasn't at all sure what to do with myself, but I knew I couldn't keep standing here on the front stoop, so I went on in, like I belonged.

The hallway was gleaming white marble with inlaid black and gold accents. A stairway went straight up the middle, leaving a wide empty space on each side that made me think of ice-skating. Rooms off to the left and right looked like catalog pictures: perfect colors, impeccable lines, items of furniture that each cost more than a car. I could have sworn I'd seen this place in an old movie, and maybe I had, or maybe it was just such classic Hollywood that it would look familiar no matter what.

There was a voice in the distance, behind the stairs. Mardie's. I would have recognized it even if it weren't logical.

I assumed the kitchen was that way and something of the echo told me that's where she was. I followed the sound through a wide hall into an expanse of light that was indeed the kitchen. The entire back wall was floor-to-ceiling windows, and light spilled in across pink-tinged granite and pale chrome. Everywhere. I'm not much of a cook—Fran got all those talents—but even *I* would be inspired to spend my days in here if it were my house. I *did* like to eat.

And then, suddenly . . .

Her.

"I know, I know," she was saying into her phone as she came in from the terrace. Beyond the terrace was a long, low sweep of green lawn and a jewel-blue pool that wound under a rock cave and waterfall. "I will, don't worry." The sun was behind her, so she was only a silhouette, but I saw her raise her hand to me. "My guest is here, I really have got to go."

Her guest. I was her guest.

The person on the other end clearly didn't think the arrival of a guest was any reason to end the conversation. Mardie rolled her eyes at me and held up a finger apologetically.

I waved and made a face like, *No, no, obviously I wouldn't expect you to get off the phone, that would be crazy!*

She chatted on the phone for a few more minutes while I tried to figure out what to do with myself. I ended up just standing there awkwardly, my hands limp at my sides.

I thought about scrolling through Instagram like I might in a waiting room, but that seemed akin to taking an immediate smoke break upon arrival.

Finally she set her phone down and came over to me. "Hey! Crosby! It's so nice to finally meet you in person!" She was smaller than I'd imagined she'd be. Tiny, even. *Maybe* five feet tall and super-skinny. Just little all around. Her face was more lined than I had expected, probably because she hadn't been in the public eye for a long time and everything gets overly Photoshopped when it's put out by publicists. Time takes its toll on everyone, and she wouldn't look the same at forty as she had at twenty. "Sorry about that. My aunt. She's always trying to micromanage me to make sure I'm doing everything right. Everyone in my family does. You didn't see my brother outside, did you?"

"Conor? Yes."

Her eyes widened. "Did you tell him why you were here?"

"No . . ."

"Good! I don't want any of them to know I'm doing a book. I mean, I told him you're a writer but that, like, you're doing research for *your* book."

"That's pretty true."

"It *is*." She looked embarrassed. "It's not as weird or as big a deal as it sounds, it's just that he butts in way too much and has opinions about everything, what I can and can't do, and"—she shook her head fiercely, like a child—"it's my story, I'm not going to have him write a script."

"Okay," I said carefully, knowing that any truth she might be on the verge of telling would be valuable. "Hey, I get it, I have a sister. Sometimes family get way too involved." Actually, I couldn't relate, but there were stories in the press about Mardie's family trying to keep her from speaking her truth, whatever that might be, so I suspected her reaction now was just the tip of some iceberg I might or might not see the whole of and I wanted to make her as comfortable as I could.

She came over and gave me a hug. This was surreal.

Watching her on-screen had made her seem larger some-how, so looking at her in person was like looking at a Mardie Mariano doll. "Thank you for understanding. This is just be-tween us—this is *our* project."

"Right."

"So, please, have a seat," she said, indicating the long pale wood table with pink-cushioned chairs. "Let's get this train going."

I put my bag on the table. It was Burberry, a purse that happened to fit my über-slim MacBook. The bag was one of the first (of many) insane purchases, and I'd rationalized that I needed it to *look the part*. It looked good. Jenna Lyons reminded us of the value of high-low in all appearances; I fig-ured I could get away with things like stockings from Target if I also wore Surratt concealer.

Like *anyone* would notice, but whatever.

I pulled out a side chair to sit when she stopped me.

"Oh, that's my place," she said.

"Oh! I'm sorry. I . . ." I what? Obviously, I had no idea what her routine was. Did she mean the chair was where she normally sat or the table was hers alone?

The chair made more sense, so I stepped over to the end seat. There was something presumptuous about sitting at the head of the table, even if that wasn't *her place*, so I went over to the side facing the pool and lawn. "Sorry about that."

"No, I know I'm weird about it," she said with a stiff laugh, confirming that she was, in fact, deadly serious about this. "I just . . . it's just, I always sit here."

"Of course. You need to be comfortable." My job, I guessed, was to coddle her and coax the good information out.

"So, should we sort of jump right in?" she asked. "I'm not sure what to do with you." She shrugged and looked awkward, like I had shown up unannounced.

"Totally!" I shifted my position and took my computer out. "I was hoping I could record our talks, is that okay?"

She didn't answer immediately so I glanced over at her.

She looked suspicious. "I . . . guess. Did you sign the non-disclosure thingy? Not that I don't trust you. My lawyer just made me swear up and down that I'd ask before anything else."

"I signed the paperwork your lawyer sent, yes." I should have read it more carefully. I'd been so excited that I hadn't bothered. But there was almost certainly an NDA in it.

"It's not that I don't trust you," she said again.

"You probably can't trust anyone. I mean, you *can* trust me, but I would think you have to be careful. But it's really important that we get *your* words, *your* tone, and the best way to ensure that is for me to tape it and be able to refer back to it."

"I . . . guess that makes sense."

My normal inclination is to bend over backward to make people comfortable, often at my own expense, so I had to squelch an impulse to say *Never mind*. I needed to tape her; there was no way I could take dictation fast enough to accurately record her own words. And for her autobiography, I needed her own words.

"Good," I said before she could change her mind. I'd purchased an app that was supposed to transcribe as well, so I opened that and set my phone on the table. "Where should we start?"

"Do you want something to drink?" she asked suddenly. "I need something to drink." She got up and went to the cooking area.

"I'm fine," I said. There was a Red Bull in my bag if my nerves settled down and I needed it.

She went to the watercooler in the corner and filled a paper cone.

"So," I started. "Where were you born?"

"Camilla, North Carolina. It's a little college town. My father was a professor. My mother's professor, actually." She frowned and touched her index finger to her cheek. "I don't know if you should put that in there, though. He was married when he was teaching and when they started . . . seeing each other. Dating."

Ew. "Oh. Okay. We'll figure that out later. It's whatever you want. How long did you live there?"

She crinkled her small nose. "I think it was a year? I'm not positive. When I was like nine months old, supposedly people were stopping my mom all the time to look at me. A woman at this store told my mom I should be a model. No, wait, maybe I was six months old. When do babies start walking? I was early." She tapped her chin. "Come to think of it, that might have been when we were in Arizona."

I was trying to type what she said as she went along, just

in case the app failed or the recording got lost or some other catastrophe took place, but we were off to a rough start.

Nine—backspace-backspace-backspace-backspace-backspace

Six—backspace-backspace-backspace

Look up walking and talking

Arizona

"I did ads there for the local department store, Lyman's, for their Christmas catalog. Then I got a Bounty paper towel commercial, which was national and huge. You might remember it—at the diner with Patsy?" She didn't wait for me to respond. "From there it really took off. My mother brought me out to California as soon as it was obvious I was getting every job."

"That turned out pretty lucky." Imagine what it was like to start getting that kind of work, starting such a glamorous career, before you even knew what you were doing. She'd essentially been born into luxury.

"Lucky," she repeated, looking down at her hands. "It was *her* dream. My mom's. I don't know, really, if she ever wanted it for herself, but it was certainly her biggest dream for it to happen to me. It came true *real* fast. She basically gave birth to her . . . like . . . what's that one fairy tale with the gold . . ."

"The golden goose?"

She shook her head and muttered, "No," as if I were a toddler myself, tossing up suggestions for what to use instead of canola oil. "Rapunzel. With the hair. Like mine."

"Oh," I said, now picturing a strange creepy baby with miles of blond hair. "Trapped in the tower."

"I don't remember it all that well."

"The prince climbed her hair." I couldn't remember it well either. Was that right? Why would he climb up her hair? Ouch. What did he do once he was up there? Didn't it get cut at some point?

"What?" She looked confused. I couldn't blame her.

"Sorry—did you mean you can't remember the jobs when you were really young?" I asked it with a laugh, but she just nodded solemnly.

"Right."

"That's okay, though it seems like a good place to start the book. The early days into the stuff you can remember. Childhood."

"It is when my career started," she agreed.

"Does your mom maybe have stories about those shoots? Maybe you could call her and ask."

"No," she answered firmly. "I lost her a couple of years ago."

Wow, I was really, really stepping in it. "Oh, I'm so sorry. I didn't know. That must be hard." How had I gotten that wrong? I'd had no idea her mother had died. I hadn't read that anywhere in my preliminary research.

She gave a strange little half shrug. "I don't know. We don't talk. She can't hear me, you know?"

Wait . . . was she dead? Or no? I tried to say something

that worked either way. "I don't know," I said vaguely. "I believe our loved ones can hear us even when we are apart like that."

She gave me a look. "Not that bitch. Excuse me, but"—she shrugged—"I mean it. She never heard me, and she still won't listen."

"I'm sorry." I had to just shut up. This was not something I could navigate instinctively. "I thought she was gone."

"She is."

"Oh."

"My brother still talks to her, so maybe he could ask."

"You mean he . . . he prays or . . ."

She looked at me like I was nuts. "What? I don't know if he prays." She sighed. "Anyhow, I don't know if she remembers anything more than I do but this is *my* story."

"Mardie." I hated to get off to an awkward start but if this basic fact wasn't clear, what was I going to do with the rest of it? "Is your mother alive?"

"What do you mean? Yes, she's alive."

"Ohhh, I thought you were saying . . ." I gave an awkward laugh. "I completely misunderstood everything."

She laughed. "She's in Santa Monica, she's not dead."

Whoa. "Jeez, what happened between you two?"

"We'll get there. Anyway, once we moved out here, she made it her full-time job to get me as much work as she could. I did commercials for Huggies, Charmin, Bounty, Singing Elmo, you name it. Right up to when they were casting for *Minus Four* on Nickelodeon."

That was the role everyone cited as her earliest. As big as *The New Mickey Mouse Club* but edgier, if that can be said about a show for little kids. Almost everyone on it had gone on to bigger and better things, even if only for a while.

"They said they wanted a tomboy type," she said. "So my mom took me to get a pixie cut, and I wore jeans and this, like, striped rugby shirt. One of the moms said, 'Look at that little boy's cool shirt,' and I cried and cried."

I thought we might share a laugh but no.

"But you got the role."

"Yup. But so did that mom's daughter. Kristi."

"Kristi Perkins?" My ears perked up. No pun intended. Kristi was still a big star today.

"Um, yeah. Anyways, my mom was right about that dress-for-the-role stuff. She always had me dress for the part and rehearse my lines with her first, even when I was really tiny."

I mentally skipped over her saying *anyways* and nodded. "Cool." I typed: *Mom, psycho stage mom, obsessed with daughter?*

"So," I said. "Kristi's mom—was she trying to rattle you or was that an honest mistake?"

"Oh, who knows?" She went and got another paper cone and filled it with water from the cooler.

"I think this is just a really good hook for us to open with. Was Trey at that audition?"

"I don't think so." She looked out the window thoughtfully. "The first time I remember noticing him was the first day of shooting." She looked at me. "I've loved him ever since."

This was juicy. "Ever since?"

"You know, for a while."

"Are you still in touch?"

"Nah." She looked regretful. "He never . . . it's just been a long time. I don't really want to talk about that."

Panic nudged at me. I'd expected her to *want* to tell her story. Maybe even to have pictures and memorabilia to illustrate her life and times. She'd been a huge success from a very early age. That was something to be proud of no matter who you were. I'd thought she'd be eager to share, but she kept clamming up.

Maybe my prompts were making her resistant.

I tried something else. "I have an idea," I said before it was fully formed.

She looked interested. "You do?"

"What if you just take a deep breath, relax, get into sort of a meditative state—"

"I love meditation!"

Aha! "Perfect. Then go to that Zen place and pull up whatever you want to talk about, starting from the earliest memories. That way we can put them down in order and decide what you want to keep and what you want to ditch later. If you want to elaborate or edit, we can do that too. Just, for now, speak from your heart." It sounded hokier than I wanted it to because I thought it might actually work for her.

She smiled and nodded. "Good idea." She closed her eyes, breathed in through her nose, let it out through her mouth. And I saw her whole body relax with that exhale.

"So what do you want to talk about?" I asked gently.

She shrugged. "I don't know."

Damn it. It was like pulling teeth to get anything out of her. Almost literally. Though I probably would have enjoyed pulling teeth more, even if they were my own. It was just so hard to get her to tell a story from start to finish, in order, with words that made sense. Time passed and I felt like I got nowhere.

When the sun began to go down, she started toward the watercooler for her millionth cup—there was a tree's worth of cones in the trash can—and looked at the clock over the sink. "We should probably wrap up for the day."

I looked at the clock like I was going to see something different from what she was seeing. It had been about four hours but my notes suggested it was more like one. "If you want . . . I don't mind going a bit longer, though, if you prefer."

She took out yet another new paper cone and filled it. She stood there and drank it, then crunched the cup and threw it in the wastebasket next to the cooler. It bounced off the rim but went in. "Score." She raised her hands. "Now you've got to go."

I felt immediately slapped. But it was day one; we had to go with her comfort, her pace. I didn't know her and had no business taking things personally. "All right. Maybe tomorrow we can talk about the evolution of the relationship with Trey?" *That* was what people wanted to hear about. Trey was still relevant, still out there, still a heartthrob even. There was only so much interest in Mardie's early paper towel commercials.

"We'll get to him eventually."

"Of course, of course. It's just—I'm only here a few weeks. I just want to make sure you tell me what you want to and I have time for it all. Obviously that's going to include the big points in your life and career but also the personal stuff. I think that's in your contract with the publisher."

"Right." She took on the posture of a kid who'd thought detention was over but just found out it wasn't.

I closed my computer, aware that the recorder was still going. It felt important to try and bridge the gap between us. "You know, I remember my sister used to watch *Minus Four*; she loved it. It's part of the background landscape of my consciousness from even before I started putting pieces together."

She looked at me. Clearly she didn't get what I was saying. "I think there are a lot of people like her out there who long to hear about those days." It was such an emblematic childhood marker. One that triggered other memories for me of the same time. Playing pretend in the backyard, taping big rings to the gutter and running past with my arm extended like I was jousting. Closing my eyes on the swing set so I couldn't see the suburban cookie-cutter houses all around and imagining I was flying. And I remembered my side of watching the episodes she recalled. What would it have been like for Mardie and the kids to go to a field of poppies with a scale model of Oz built right in the middle of it? Watching them on TV, it had looked incredible. Like they were really there.

"I'll see if I can find some of the old stuff my mom saved from the show," she offered, taking a few pointed steps in the direction of the front door.

"That would be great." I dropped the phone in my bag with my computer. "Same time tomorrow?"

"We'll see."

There. Right there. *That* was where I should have been a professional and kindly but firmly pinned her down. But I was terrified of spooking her. She seemed so volatile. For now, at least, I was going to follow her lead and do what she wanted when she wanted.

It was only the first day, after all.

I really needed to kick up my own charm. How many jobs had I gotten that I didn't really deserve? How many times had I scratched someone's car and managed to leave them laughing? How many times had I spilled my drink at a restaurant and wound up with an extra one because of the rapport I developed with the staff involved?

I could usually make people like me. I had to make her like me. And so far, she didn't.

"Hey," I said, tilting my head, raising an eyebrow, and smiling, "I know today was a little discombobulating, and this is new, and it's going to be a shit-ton of stuff to slog through and relive. But I promise, you can trust me, and this isn't always going to be hard." I laughed. "And when it is, we'll be doing it together. I know you don't know me yet, but trust me, I've got you."

The drawn look on her face started to pull upward as if by strings. Boom. Of course. This girl had been told what to do her whole life. I wasn't going to manipulate her, but I was going to tell her to calm down, settle in, and trust *me*.

"It's a little hard."

"Oh my God, I know." I smiled, doing a cringing face. "I'm sure you don't know what to say, what not to say, what is valuable to share with people. It's got to be hard."

"I mean that it's hard to have company for so long." She said it as though she were complaining about someone else who'd overstayed her welcome, not me.

This was going to be impossible. Writing this book was impossible. "Of course. We'll try to do things more efficiently from now on." Anything, absolutely anything necessary to get this damn book written so I could get paid.

"Okay, so maybe tomorrow." She frowned. "Or, no. The next day. That's better." She walked away while she said it.

"Okay," I said to her retreating figure. "I'll take this home and start putting the opening together." I tried to gather some false optimism. "I think it's going to be so good!"

"I didn't know it would be so tiring." She came out of the kitchen with another paper cone of water, downed it, and dropped the cone onto the table. At this rate, she'd destroy the equivalent of Sherwood Forest in a year. "I could go to sleep right now."

"Then you should do that." Ugh. I was so full of it. She needed to wake the fuck up and give me a good book. This was my last chance.

I went to the door and turned around. She was right there, making sure to boot me out and lock it behind me, I was sure. "This is going to be really good," I assured her again, reaching for the doorknob. "Your fans are going to just eat it up, I can tell already."

She scratched her head. "Maybe I should do another album."

"Great! It could be released at the same time."

She looked at me like she was surprised I was still there.

"Okay, so I'll go. Have a good night," I was being so chirpy I was even driving myself crazy. "See you soon."

I'm not sure if she answered before she closed the door behind me.

Chapter Fifteen

Frances

In all my time in California, I'd never been to a big fancy star-studded party as a guest. I'd worked a bunch of them—enough to wonder if anyone would see me at this one and ask for a canapé—but I'd never had to worry about what to wear beyond a server uniform and makeup.

Tonight was different.

And it was pretty foreign to me, I have to say. When I'd first come to LA I'd been anticipating some glamour just sprinkled about the streets like glitter and I'd been sorely mistaken, so it had been ages since I'd really tried to make a showing.

Somehow it figured that when it was finally happening, Crosby was going to be there, essentially competing with me. Not that she'd view it that way or that I'd *ever* admit *I* felt like that, but I did. Every single step of the way, I was afraid she was going to outdo me and that, despite my best efforts,

I was going to remain muddy and mousy in the shadow of her glow.

But what could I do? I'd already kept one *huge* thing from Crosby; my conscience wouldn't let me "forget" to tell her Jill had invited her to the party too. This was such a great opportunity. It would never happen back in Bumfuck, New York, and it would be selfish of me to keep it from her now.

My stomach twanged in reaction to that thought. Selfish wasn't just not telling her about a party. Selfish was not telling her about a majorly famous director and producer wanting to hire her to write a screenplay for the anthology he was getting ready to make.

But, man, I just couldn't bring myself to mention it to her. Not yet.

For now, I was taking her to a cool Hollywood party.

"Do you need any help getting ready?" she called to me from the other room.

"No, I'm good, thanks." I was not. I was inches from the mirror, attempting for the third time to apply the last corner of the Au Naturale Faux Luxe eyelashes. The name was laughably absent of accuracy; if anything, it demonstrated conflicting concepts. Faux? Definitely. Au Naturale? Not so much. But they were dark, not too comically long, and basically made me look like what I should have grown up to look like according to my baby pictures, when I had been a sooty-lashed, icy-irised toddler.

"Don't forget to get the back of your hair."

"I won't, I'm not an idiot." I was using Crosby's Beachy

Waves Curling Iron and Instrument of Torture to loosen up
my prison of straight blond hair. I actually liked the effect,
but the back *was* hard to do.

There was a clicking sound behind me and, unwilling to
move a muscle that wasn't ocular, I shifted my gaze to see
Crosby in all her underwear-clad glory. It took me a minute
to understand what exactly I was looking at.

The deep bronze of her tan was gorgeous. She had been
working on it daily for the past few days, either by getting
an hour in the sun, referencing a prescription for vitamin D
from our parents, or by using a mitt and spreading brown
coconut-scented foam over her body and asking me to reach
spots on her back she couldn't. She offered to do mine. I kept
telling her no, thanks, like I was too cool for such artifices,
and then doing it on my legs and shoulders when she left.

What she didn't know couldn't hurt her.

The bra she wore lifted her and sucked her in, and it pro-
vided another strap that went down to her waist that sucked
her in even further. Then she had on Spanx that went *up*
to her waist and increased her thigh gap and decreased the
circumference of her thighs by about a month of Prosecco.
It looked uncomfortable but worth it. Her perfume wafted
in (Clinique Happy Heart; I'd noticed it on the bathroom
counter); her hair was thick and curled in a modern take on
the sixties flip. She was in sparkling royal-blue satin shoes.

Her makeup was heavy but *shockingly* perfect: Squared-off
brows. Sculpted, contoured nose and cheekbones. Her jaw
looked chiseled. Her skin was dewy. She looked like she'd

gotten a syringe of Juvéderm in the other room. Actually, if anyone would sneak something like that in, it was she, but I knew she couldn't afford it. She had a healthy coral glow on her cheeks. The tan looked so good with her blue-red lipstick and bright white teeth.

Honestly, the girl could have been a professional makeup artist. Or a movie star.

There was only one thing missing.

"Hey, you forgot to get dressed," I said, not releasing my lashes because I wasn't sure the glue was dry. I'd already pulled the lash off and gotten it stuck to my thumb a bunch of times.

"Oh, shit, so you think Jill won't love me wearing support garments as *a look* tonight?"

"Nope."

"Well, I'd hate to embarrass you. As usual."

"Mmm," I said, trying to get the lashes to stick to my eye-lids and not my fingertips. Vanity was hell, it really was. "It's always the inner corners that betray you with these things. They peel off and it's like you have a spider on your face."

She shrugged. "It's still Halloween *season*. Sort of."

"If the first day of Halloween starts a two-week season, then, yeah, it is."

I released my eyelid and leaned back, blinking. "Now that I look at myself, though, it does seem like I'm in costume."

She cocked her head. "No, you look beautiful."

I glanced at her in the mirror. "I don't look like me."

"You look more like you than you think. All you see is

the artifices, but they're just little enhancements. You look great."

I didn't know what to say. "Eh. Compared to you, I look short. And over- and underdressed. I have to"—I turned around and squeezed past her—"finish getting ready. And so do you. I'm calling the car in literally five."

"Fine."

She clopped off to slither into her dress while I second-guessed my own. Jill had sent me a parting bonus. It was very, very generous. It had not only taken some pressure off the next few months, but made me feel obliged to show up in something good. Something nice. Something that showed her I was taking her constant advice to *treat myself*, to *give myself a little something*. I knew Jill well enough to understand that somewhere, consciously or not, she wanted me to do that. So I'd spent way more than I should have on a respectable designer-name dress, even though it had been on sale.

I put it on and adjusted it so everything was in the right place; I even applied some *fashion tape* that was definitely going to leave a mark or two. I slithered into some glossy stockings that worked with the dress. Stepped into the rhinestone-covered Badgley Mischka shoes I'd found at Nordstrom Rack that made me feel like Cinderella.

I moved in front of the floor-length mirror.

"Damn!"

I thought at first I'd said that out loud, but it was Crosby.

"You think?" I asked, glancing at her behind me.

"Money really does buy beauty."

"I don't think . . . there's a saying about that." Then I remembered seeing a picture of a famous actress before she hit it big and got some work done. The caption said, *You're not ugly, you're poor.*

"Turn?" Crosby tapped me on the shoulder.

I obeyed and laughed in spite of myself. "Ta-da."

"Wow, I feel like I'm Freddie Prinze Jr. in any nineties movie and you're literally any waifish star walking down the stairs. I'm stunned, you are stunning, you have *stunned* me."

"Please."

"Seriously. New Fran is all that." She made a puzzled face at her own words, then laughed. "I actually wasn't trying to make a *She's All That* joke, but now I am. Okay, so you're calling the car, right?"

I gave her a look but said, "Yes, yes, I am. New Fran?" She didn't answer, so I got on my phone, pulled up the app, and typed in Jill's address. "Ugh, surge pricing. Maybe we *should* just—"

"Frances M. Turner, you shut your stupid, stupid mouth."

My middle name was Katherine, and she damn well knew it, but she always used to call me Frances M. Turner when she wanted my attention. It was one of those arbitrary Crosby things (like Francypants and Francy Drew) that, I have to admit, I'd kind of missed. "Excuse me?"

"You are *not* designated-driving. Listen, for the past few weeks, you have been different. You're confident. You're calmer. You're worse in a few ways but in, like, a good way, in the ways that make you who you *are*." She ignored the expression on my face. "The things that defined you always. I can just tell you're poised for something. Tonight is a night, okay? It is a *night*. You can bid farewell to the Frances of before. You can close off that part of your life, in a good way, in a *great way*, and bid it adieu. You know? Theater girl? So long? Farewell? *Auf wiedersehen?* Goodbye?"

I opened my mouth, but she put a newly manicured index finger over my lips and shook her head.

"No," she said dramatically. "It's the end."

She removed her finger.

I stared at her a moment.

She nodded. Smiled. Self-satisfied.

"Actually," I said. "I was going to suggest that you drive."

All her calm left her. "Oh, hell no, this is my first Hollywood party, are you crazy? You must be crazy. Surge pricing be damned, let's go. Order up. Let's do shots. Tequila?"

I gave an enthusiastic *yes* but inside I felt just awful. She was being so nice, so supportive. And she was *right*—that was the kicker. I wanted so badly to believe we could be friends. The best of friends, like sisters are supposed to be, but even looking at her and knowing what I was keeping from her, everything that had ever been wrong with our relationship was still wrong. In spades. Now it was no longer some stupid high-school boyfriend at stake; it was everything I had ever wanted.

Literally.

And if history had taught me any lessons, I knew that there

was no such thing as both of us winning the same prize. There was always—*always*—a loser.

Crosby called a rideshare, then poured two half shots— a system she'd devised to have more drinks and fewer hangovers—and we did a cheers and went to wait on the street in the crisp night air.

As we stood there dressed to the nines, both of us really looking our best, teetering in heels and holding our clutches, I thought, *Is this what it might have been like? If we'd been friends? If we'd gone to school together or visited each other at school? If we'd, I don't know, been part of each other's lives at all?* Especially back in the days where it was common to do this. We had both gone out with friends with hair done, makeup done, tight dresses, maybe not even leaving the house until ten at night. What would life have been like if we'd been there together? Even a few of the times?

If things had been different then, would they possibly be different now?

Chapter Sixteen

Crosby

The party was ridiculous, like any good Hollywood party they show on the gossip shows or nighttime soaps on TV. I saw a few D-listers and reality stars the minute we walked in and pointed them out to Frances, who didn't care *at all*. It quickly became obvious they were easy to spot but there were bigger stars there too, talking to each other in flatteringly lit corners and shadows.

I had finally, over the past few weeks in Los Angeles, figured out my theory on celebrities and exactly just how interesting or not interesting they were. Because it cannot be denied that meeting a star is *different* than just meeting any old schlub off the street. It's cool. It's weird. Sometimes it's interesting, but only enough to go, *Oh, hey, look at that.*

Some celebrities are Toledo. Like, *Right, I have* heard *of it, but is it in Arkansas, Ottawa, or Ohio?*

Some celebrities who'd been around for a long time were

like Charleston or Savannah. Comfortable and nice to look at and definitely well known and highly regarded with a few deep-fried tasty moments, but not a place I thought about often.

Mardie was like Baltimore. A city loved by those who loved it and almost glamorous in places, but not enough to get universal respect.

Celebs. The sightings. It's like famous cities.

Then there were the celebrities you never see coming. The little dive city you've never heard of where you have the best night of your life—that's the micro-celebrity famous for something small. Maybe that was me.

Maybe that was Dad.

This party was like all the world balanced on the head of a pin.

The sky accommodatingly moved from gold to blush to dusty blue over the first two hours as a few rounds of sparkling wine and hors d'oeuvres were passed.

Privately, I felt like I was acting or in costume. Though that was a sore point with Frances, so after one brief mention I dropped it. She had taken it to mean I wanted to wear a costume and said if she saw anything resembling a costume in my things she was going to tell them at the door I was a party-crasher and that they should call the police.

The worst part was that then she kept thinking a lot of my *actual* things were costumes.

Anyway, no, I might love a good costume party, but, whoa, no, there's no part of me that would ever want to be the only person dressed in costume for any occasion. I still remember this one party we had in high school where I ended up saying I went as myself but dead, a bit of pale foundation and dark liner around my eyes that could have been *a look* anyway, because I hadn't dressed up. All because my insane teenage brain was convinced that no one else would dress up. I should have known better, since they were all theater kids who dressed up on Fridays. And Tuesdays. But whatever—if you're terrified of being humiliated you will humiliate yourself in the very act of avoidance.

So. The party was amazing. Pretty. Fancy. So *not* upstate New York, where it would have been rag-wool sweaters and chili-sauce-and-grape-jelly meatballs on toothpicks (which I love). No, this was so very California. Sushi on platters. Ceviche. A little jazzy lo-fi band in the grass with no shoes on. A virtual *Wait . . . Who's Who* of Hollywood.

But nothing really prepared me for the sighting of Trey Simons.

In fact, as I choked on soy nori and chased it with Moët, desperate to breathe, staring into the concerned eyes of my sister, I thought maybe I'd hallucinated him and it was just a server.

But when I swallowed the unraveling ribbon of raw fish, seaweed, and mango, he was still there.

I dug my brand-new, black-and-gold-reverse-French-manicured coffin-shaped fingernails into Frances's shoulders—she had totally been using my tanner; I could tell—and whispered his name.

"Holy what in the actual"—she followed my gaze to him
and then looked back at me and shook her head—"okay, just
be cool. For God's sake."

"I *am* being cool."

"You're not being cool at all, you're being a complete goon."

"Fran—"

"No time for that. Stand up straight, you're crouched over
like Rumpelstiltskin. *Stand up.*"

"You're the one who played Rumpelstiltskin on an actual
stage so maybe you shouldn't be throwing that particular insult in my face."

"Actually, that was the only role I ever quit." She took a
deep breath. "Even I had limits. And even then."

I couldn't help but laugh. "So funny, though. Remember
the prosthetic nose that went with the costume?"

"I remember." Frances did a double take in Trey's direction. "Is Jill walking him over here? Tell me Jill isn't—Jill!
Hello!"

I smiled. "Jill, it's so nice to finally meet you! I'm Crosby
Turner, Frances's sister."

Then, like it was a totally normal thing to take an hour
and a half to look at another human person brought over to
the group, I looked up at Trey.

Lordy.

So if meeting celebrities was like visiting a famous city, I
didn't know what city Trey was. I guess in my head before
that moment, he was something obvious, tacky maybe, that
I understood must have some depth that I didn't get and

that I knew had been through trauma. Like New Orleans. Right? That's a pretty good example. I've been to New Orleans only once, and someone threw up on my shoes and told me I looked like a man "in that dress," whatever the hell that means. I drank terrible beer and was too inexperienced to enjoy things like oysters, so I don't even know what I ate. I went for a bachelorette party for a bride who got married when she was twenty-two, so the bachelorette party was basically spring break, and the wedding was basically a church event planned by her aging family members.

But as soon as I looked at Trey, I knew I had it wrong. I'm not trying to make it weird. It just kind of *was* weird.

The lines around his eyes were subtle and I could tell they had made him more attractive, but I'd never studied him the way Frances had, so I couldn't say for sure. He had a sort of sideways smile when he waited for his turn to speak and a crocodile grin when he was about to laugh. His eyebrows were straight and went up like an apology every time that grin came around.

I noticed all these things without hearing a word he said.

And he'd been standing there for a solid few rounds of conversation that I definitely should have heard. I leaned over to Fran. "Did I miss anything?" I whispered. "I was staring at Trey Simons."

"Miss anything?" she whispered back. "What the hell—"

"Yeah, no, I literally wasn't listening."

"How is that poss—no, Jill is talking about her new house.

What is wrong—oh my God, just shut up! *Please* don't embarrass me this time."

She smiled and peeled away from me.

She really did look so pretty tonight. That dress, the makeup, the light in her eyes—it was all working.

I looked back at Trey and was unsettled—in a missed-a-step sort of way—to see that he was looking at me.

He had obviously been on my mind a lot. I'd looked at the old pictures and articles on him and Mardie back when they were teenagers. And I was familiar with his work as an adult, which felt completely separate from his younger days. So while I'd pictured him often in my mind lately, I really hadn't anticipated seeing him in real life.

And if I had, I don't think I would have imagined quite how attractive he was.

I actually laid a hand on my heart as it skipped a beat. I'd done coke once in high school—one of the biggest mistakes of my life, it had turned out, but that was a different story. It kind of felt like this. Awful.

I looked to the ground, then back up at Trey. He furrowed his brow and mouthed, *You okay?*

Who does that for someone they don't know? Who does that?

I smiled and took a deep breath. I was not going to let a panic attack get the better of me. This wasn't that time on a plane flying out of Colombia a few years ago when I'd felt lucky to leave with my life and limbs.

I nodded and pointed at his drink and mouthed, *Is that yours?*

It was a mojito with a pink umbrella.

His eyes narrowed. He nodded.

I took a sip of my champagne and looked away for the rest of the conversation. Even though every ounce of my concentration was still on Trey. And I was *positive* he could see the red that was burning in my cheeks.

I couldn't say exactly what was going on, but I knew one thing: there was a very attractive man flirting with me and I was going to go along with it as far as I could.

That he was famously the ex of the only employer I had right now—an employer I desperately needed—and that she seemed not to have gotten over their famous relationship was just a minor complication. A little flirting wasn't really going to hurt.

And she'd never find out anyway.

I could just consider it research.

Chapter Seventeen

Frances

I looked from Crosby to Trey and then back to Crosby.

What was *happening*?

Had they . . . had they somehow met already? Through Mardie or something? Would Crosby have forgotten to tell me that?

That seemed really unlikely.

I supposed there was a possibility they had, but I figured Crosby would have remembered to clue me in about something so huge. In fact, I was certain she would have.

That was a new one. I was a new one. I'd never said that about Crosby before. I had never been able to predict her movements, especially in relation to me.

Trey was straight up staring my sister down. Trey Simons. Trey Simons.

Trey Simons, who had looked down over my bedroom in high school from his yellow sunburst poster and stared at us both a thousand times, was here, now, staring at us in real life. Well, no; he was staring at Crosby.

This was absolutely consistent with the kind of luck she had, the kind of prizes she won. She could go to a carnival and win the huge stuffed bear on the top shelf that was covered in dust because he was all but impossible to win. But win the bear she did. Literally and metaphorically. Over and over.

Okay, so let me be absolutely clear on something: It wasn't that I wanted Trey staring at *me*. My days of being starstruck are long gone. I've served too many sloppy-drunk movie stars to care about celebrity anymore. So the old feeling of jealousy creeping up in me wasn't because I thought I was going to catch his eye, marry him, and live happily ever after. I think it was more that my first reaction was to wish my childhood crush could just stay my little childhood crush, deep in the recesses of my mind, and not become a flesh-and-blood person in my life via Crosby.

Psychology doesn't work in life the way it does in the movies. Identifying the source of your discontent doesn't automatically make it disappear. So I knew I'd had a lifetime of feeling afraid she would win everything.

In short, unfortunately, I did have the all-too-familiar twinge of resentment when I saw—or felt—the electricity arc between them. But more than that, I was curious. What would happen?

I looked to Jill, who disguised none of her interest in the developing situation between my sister and Trey Simons. I wondered if they knew it was that obvious to those of us on the outside.

We all stood around for nearly a half hour chatting, and it didn't even matter about what because it all seemed like it was a live-action memory surrounding the interaction between Trey and Crosby.

Gradually my jealousy melted away and I just observed the interaction between them.

It really started when she asked him, so casually, "So, what is it that you do?"

He smiled that famous smile and said, "Oh, me? I'm an ear, nose, and throat guy."

"Ugh, what a relief," she said. "Usually it's *I'm a boob guy* or *I'm an ass man.* It's nice to meet someone with other interests."

I braced myself for him to ask what she did. What was she going to say to that? *Oh, I'm writing your ex-girlfriend's life story. Well, yes, it almost certainly will include her relationship with you.*

But of course, that's just not how Crosby thinks. She was just a girl standing in front of a boy, as the saying goes.

And for once, I got it.

They went off into their own conversation enough for Jill to wall them out and talk to me. "I brought him over here thinking he might give her some scoop for the book. I didn't tell him anything, but . . . I don't know, do you see a love connection? I see a little . . ." She wiggled her finger.

I nodded. "That would be very Crosby. She never even fangirled over him, and boom, she falls right into it."

"Then she's his unicorn." Jill laughed. She tilted back her champagne flute and then traded it for a new one when a tray passed by. "Next we need to find yours."

"For now I'll settle for a job." I finished what was in my glass and traded for a new one too. Also grabbed a wedge of quiche, to be smart.

"It will come. You just can't give up."

"Mm," I said, mouth full, keeping my conversational foot in the door. "I'm doing my best." No denying that.

"What about your sister? How's her work?"

My stomach lurched.

"Is she enjoying working with Mardie?" she went on.

"Oh. I guess so. Apparently Mardie's a bit scattered, so it's not the easiest job."

Jill nodded. "Mardie is a unique bird. What about Crosby doing the—"

"Oh my *God*, I am not wrong!" Crosby's voice rose. "I mean, I guess you'd know," she said to me. When I looked her way, she said, "You know, that gross song about Skype sex." She snapped her free fingers.

"Skype sex?"

"Like from when we were kids!"

"*Oh!*"

"Yes!"

"Oh, oh, 'Digital Get Down'?"

"*Yes.*" She snapped again and pointed at Trey. "That wasn't you?"

Trey—Trey Simons—looked at me.

I smiled and shook my head. "I'm sorry. She's uncultured."

"I am—excuse me." She held up a finger. "I am not uncultured. I think you might be wrong about whether or not you wrote a song about Skype sex. Because I'm pretty sure you did." She said the last few words into her glass as she took a sip.

Trey stared at her in awe, but he was also clearly amused.

"Yeah, that was NSYNC and it was gross." I shrugged. "Catchy and a little hot, though."

It was kind of fascinating to watch them as they returned to their own flirtation. I'd met enough performers over the past five years to know that I didn't think I wanted to have a relationship with anyone who was grappling with fame and image. I wanted someone *normal*. So for that reason, I wasn't jealous of Crosby at all, even though we were talking about my childhood crush.

I might not have had a romantic interest in him but I was still eager to see how this show played out. But that was a foolish waste of my time at this party, given that it was filled with star power. Instead of watching the Crosby and Trey show, I should be schmoozing with the right people to get my *own* show. Or a part in one. Even a tiny part in one.

It seemed promising when a young but up-and-coming casting director who had just moved to Fox came and talked to me, but after a few minutes it turned out she was looking for a caterer. Not even a regular job as a chef, just a one-off caterer, which was something I wasn't equipped to do.

"Meet anyone interesting?"

I turned to find the voice belonged to Vince, Ingrid Rockwell's son and, if worse came to absolute worst, my future costar in the last nail in my coffin. "A few people. How are you?"

"Fine," he said, a little too loud.

"Oh . . . good."

"Maybe not *entirely* fine," he amended.

"No?"

"It's just . . ."

I waited a few moments before asking him, "Are you having a stroke?"

"No, no, it's just . . . I'm not sure I want to be an actor," he blurted out.

And just like that, even the worst wasn't available to me anymore. I almost had to laugh. "Well, then, it's a good thing you didn't spend your life working toward it."

He looked puzzled. "I spent a long time in law school."

"Oh, of course, I didn't mean—" I shook my head. "No disrespect, it's just that I've been trying to improve my craft, taking lessons and coaching between jobs to keep food on the table for years, and I'm as close to quitting as it sounds like you are."

"My mother really thinks that show of hers could take off."

I looked at him. "Do you?"

"Honestly, I don't know anything about TV or what works and what doesn't."

"Then why did you agree to do it in the first place?"

"Because it seemed like a way to throw a little respect to my late father. He's only known as a footnote on Wikipedia, Ingrid Rockwell's second husband."

"Second?"

He nodded. "The first one was her high-school sweetheart. My sister's father."

"Ooh."

"The world doesn't hear much about him either." He laughed. "Not like your dad. I hope it's okay, but Jill told us who he was. I collect vinyl and have his albums as well as the forty-five of 'Happily Never After.'"

"No kidding!" It tickled my heart to think of people having Dad's 45 in their houses, playing it, singing along. More than once I'd heard it in the grocery store, and people always hummed along with it.

"He was great. Seriously. It kills me that he's called a one-hit wonder when he wrote so many hits for other people."

"Yeah, well, people pay more attention to the performer than the writer behind the scenes. He doesn't mind. He was never thirsty for recognition; he just wanted to be able to do what he loved and take care of his family." I felt a sudden wave of homesickness. Not for New York so much but for my parents. The ease and comfort of having them around for small moments, not just during visits at Thanksgiving and Christmas, where we had to try and fit all of our big conversations into short times together.

How long would I keep trying to make it as an actor out

here before I finally gave up and accepted that I'd be a cook for the rest of my life? Would that be so bad? It felt like failure to think about it, so I guess it would be disappointing, but on the other hand, I could work wherever I wanted to, anywhere someone needed a chef. The restaurant scene in my hometown was growing rapidly; I could even go back there if I wanted to leave Los Angeles.

The thought of it made my heart sink.

I didn't want to give up. I just wanted—no, *needed*—a break.

"You know whose life story would be an interesting show?" Vince was saying. "Your parents'. Your whole family's."

"Lord, I don't think any of us could bear to have our lives out there like that." I realized he had said it as a compliment. "But thank you."

"I mean it. I didn't tell my mother I had a connection, but I actually did some contract work recently for a major production company that's looking for some retro family dramas."

"Really!"

"I can arrange a meeting if you have anything to pitch."

It had never occurred to me that maybe *I* could create a show. Even do screenwriting of my own. Admittedly, I wasn't the first in the family to write, but that didn't mean I couldn't do it. In fact, I'd be the last in the family to do it, so all indications were that this was a family talent.

After decades of keeping a diary, maybe it *was* time for me to try writing for profit.

We were interrupted at that moment by Crosby and Trey.

Crosby was alight with excitement. "What was the name of that TV show we used to watch about the garage band that solved mysteries? It was on for like two weeks when we were really young."

"Ohhhh." I remembered what it looked like so well: bright colors, choppy animation. Despite how cheap as it clearly was to produce, it hadn't managed to stay on the air. "I can picture it . . . but, listen, this is Vince—"

"*Crime Rockers*?" Vince suggested.

"Yes! That's it!" Crosby snapped her fingers. "Man, that was bad."

We mused on it together for a moment—apparently Trey had been too busy making a show people watched and had never seen it—before we all suddenly noticed that the party was thinning out.

"We should probably go," I said to Crosby, mindful of not being the last loser at a function like this. It was the worst kind of thirsty.

"Right." She smiled at Trey. "It was nice talking to you, Trey."

"It was nice talking to you too, Crosby." He looked absolutely smitten. I couldn't believe it.

I said my goodbyes and we were walking away when Trey called from behind us, "Hey, can I get your—"

Crosby turned and said, "Oh, please, you're rich. In this day and age, you can find me."

She didn't even see his face, another look of delighted surprise and confusion, because she was too busy pushing me away from Jill, whom she had not acknowledged at all. I knew Crosby. She had not acknowledged her just in case she was the assailant. And in a way, she was. But in a messenger sort of way.

We started to walk together.

"Oh my God, so, wait—were you and Trey Simons really flirting or was I delirious?" I asked quietly.

"Who?" she asked.

My jaw dropped. "Trey Simons! The guy you were just talking with for the past—"

She put her hand to her cheek and blinked exaggeratedly. "I'm sure I don't know who you mean."

I sighed. "Okay, you got me. But you could have meant it; I never know with you. Don't forget that the minute I first saw you at my condo, you were running away from that thug Darren Neville. I just never know with you."

"If you want to know a secret," she said, "*I* also never know. It's always a surprise to me. And I just can't wait to see what comes next."

Chapter Eighteen

Crosby

Working for Mardie was harder than I could have imagined. For two weeks I went to her place and tried to pull stories out of her, and for two weeks I came back in the evening and checked the dictation app I'd gotten to see if it had understood her any better than I had. It hadn't. Which was disappointing. My hope had been that I could rearrange the pieces of what she said into a coherent narrative, but it was impossible.

Even when she stated what sounded like a single fact, I'd repeat it back to her to make sure I'd understood correctly, and she'd snap that I had it wrong, and I'd be back at zero.

Incredibly, throughout all of this, I could tell that *she* was getting sick of *me*. And I didn't know what to do about it. The nicer and more accommodating I tried to be, the more annoying I was, even to myself.

Yet showing my own frustration was a huge blunder; I'd made it only once.

"Mardie, I'm writing *your own words* down and you're telling me it doesn't sound like you. It *is* you."

"No, it's not, you're not doing it right."

There was no way to argue with that. "I'm sorry." It took all I had to just say that and leave it there, but it seemed to satisfy her.

"Just take notes of *exactly what I say* and then it will sound like me."

Why hadn't I thought of that? Why hadn't I done that every day for weeks? God, she was so frustrating. But all I said was "Okay."

More and more, I realized that I had had the opportunity of a lifetime with my first book, and I should have been *so* much smarter about saving the money. It was a mistake I'd never make again.

"I was thinking about Trey last night," she said out of the blue.

That made two of us. My ears perked up but I was careful not to say anything that might spook her off the subject. "Oh?"

"You want to hear about him, right?"

"I want to hear about whatever you want to tell me," I said carefully. *Please tell me about Trey, please tell me about Trey.*

"*Everyone* wants to hear about Trey."

"True."

"Okay." She hesitated before speaking. "As you know, we met when we were kids. Really, really young."

"Right. On the show."

A single nod. "I don't remember *all* that much about those days, to tell the truth. We only did that for . . . what, three or four years? And then none of us saw each other for a *long* time after that."

The show had actually run two seasons, over a period of about a year and a half, though it had gone into reruns almost immediately and for long enough to hook Frances a few years later. I'd looked it up as some of my basic homework on Mardie.

"All right, well, so when did you and Trey meet up again?" I asked.

"It was the Teen Choice Awards," she said thoughtfully. "I was seventeen and up for my"—she scanned her memory—"second...no, third award. Which I won."

"Cool. So you guys reconnected then? Or you kind of were back on each other's radar?"

"Oh, for sure, yeah. I knew everyone in his band and they all knew me, but we hadn't actually *partied* together before that. After the awards, we went to a party in the penthouse of the Beverly Hills Hotel."

There was something kind of scary about all those über-famous kids partying it up, being given everything they wanted whether they could handle it or not. Dad's fame had been a much simpler one in a far more grounded time. Back then, there were four or five TV channels and they went off the air at midnight, so the world didn't have twenty-four-hour access to teenybopper fame. I don't even know if there were that many famous teens in his day. Actors, sure, but musicians? Only the odd prodigy, I think. Mardie was part of the early generations of mega-fame.

"So what happened at the party?"

"He kissed me." She smiled and her gaze grew distant, dreamy. "It was my first kiss ever."

I double-checked the recorder to be sure it was still going, then made my backup notes. "You were seventeen and he was . . ."

"Eighteen." She sighed. "He was really cute back then. Have you ever seen him?"

Yes, just the other night. "Yes, of course. He was cute. He *is* cute."

Somehow she half rolled her eyes. "He's getting old now." She hesitated. "Like the rest of us, I guess." Then she laughed a little too much at her own joke. If it was a joke. "I mean, he looks really different. Don't you think?"

She scanned me thoroughly. I felt overly observed.

"Yes," I said honestly, though I didn't think it would do much good for me to point out that he looked a hundred times hotter now.

She sighed. "He hosted *Saturday Night Live* twice."

"Did you watch?" I asked, imagining her alone, watching her old love on the screen just like the rest of us, knowing parts of him hidden beneath the surface that most people would never know.

Would I?

She lowered her chin, then raised her gaze to me. "Yes,"

she said, like it was a confession. "I saw. They wanted me to be the musical guest once but it didn't work out."

God, that would have been *amazing*. Good thinking on someone's part. Too bad it hadn't worked out. "You hosted too, though, right?"

"I think so." She nodded, and I tried to imagine how a person could be unsure of whether or not she'd hosted *Saturday Night Live*. "Have you ever been married?" she asked me suddenly.

"Nope. Engaged a few times, but never went through with it."

She stood up and moved to the head of the table where she could lean in close to me. "Tell me everything."

I was taken aback by the request. We were here to talk about her, not me. I didn't like talking about me, especially not about my failed love life. Yet how could I say that when I was asking her to do the same? Yes, I knew that this memoir wasn't about me, so it was a different situation, but I also knew Mardie would pull back if I did. I could just tell that about her. "What do you want to know?" I hedged.

"Tell me about your first engagement."

"No, no, that story is too long and *way* too boring. We're here to talk about you."

"How am I supposed to be honest about being me if you're not being honest about you?"

"The book is about you." I blushed; I could feel the heat and knew I looked like a clown with red cheeks. "That's why I'm here."

"You want me to trust you, right?"

It was so manipulative, but she had me in checkmate. I took a breath. "Marco. He was my first boyfriend. We started dating when we were like seventeen, and by nineteen we thought we knew everything and were ready to promise forever." Frances had actually talked me out of it. Out of making a huge mistake that would follow me forever. Or, as she had put it, out of hooking myself to a dunderheaded fuckwhistle who would never outgrow his high-school-jock mentality and would go to keg parties long, long after he was too old.

Thank God she'd talked me out of that one.

"Every now and then I see him on social media and I get a shuddering sense of relief that my sister talked some sense into me. Suffice it to say, we were young and stupid." I hoped that *would* suffice. I sure didn't need to think about him any more than that. "Now it's your turn. You dated Trey for a long time and eventually got engaged, right?"

"We were never engaged. People think we were, but we weren't."

For some reason I was glad to hear it. He seemed a world away from the woman before me. "No? Well, you might as well have been. You were a big-deal couple back in the day."

"Hell, I don't think anyone cares about that anymore." She frowned, drawing her face into lines that never fully disappeared.

"See, I think that's actually exactly what people want to hear about. Seriously, people eat this stuff up." I wanted every detail. I wanted to know if they'd ever really been serious or if it had been just a young dating thing with a hint of good publicity thrown in.

"There's not much to tell. I'm afraid if I talk about it, people will criticize me for going on about myself."

It had the unexpectedness of an ironic joke, but the tone was wrong. "This is a memoir."

"Does it have to be? Didn't I just sign a contract to write a book?"

"Well, there was a proposal you and your reps gave to the publisher. It outlined the things you were going to"—I searched for a nonintimidating word—"expound upon. It's most definitely expected to be an autobiography."

She looked thoughtful. "What do you think the world would do if we got back together?"

I blinked. "If who got back together?"

"Me and Trey."

I studied her carefully. Was this just theoretical, the rantings of a crazy person? Or was this an actual possibility? "Is that on the table? I mean, is there a possibility things are back on between you two?"

"Well, no. We haven't *talked* or anything."

Relief flowed down my spine, taking me by surprise. Who was I to be jealous of two celebrities who had a history like they did? "Is that something you want?"

She laughed. "I don't know, maybe I wouldn't. But it would be great if I wanted to put another album out."

I felt myself grimace and turned it into a smile. "I honestly don't know what to say to that."

"It's probably worth thinking about."

"I don't—" I paused. "Sorry. I'm not in the business, so faking a relationship seems—" I gave up. I had no idea what to say.

And she didn't care anyway. My opinion was of no use to her. "Any*who*," she said, and I thought less of her for it, "that's a story for another time. I've got stuff to do, so I'm going to have to finish for the day."

Glad to. I too had stuff to do, all of which entailed turning her half-thoughts into complete sentences until I couldn't see straight and then collapsing into a wad of frustration before pouring a stiff drink.

* * *

THAT WAS EXACTLY what I was doing when the doorbell rang.

Frances was out with some girlfriends she saw now and then but never introduced me to, and I was alone with my laptop and thoughts of applying for a job at Sephora since the writing thing was clearly not going to pan out. It was about seven.

I opened the door and saw a long narrow box with a ribbon around it and a card with my name on it. A quick glance up and down the sidewalk revealed no one, so I picked up the box and brought it in.

Does it say more about me or the times we live in that I was a little afraid to open the box? Visions of explosions, dead rodents, all kinds of "pranks," both benign and horrifying, came to mind. I had to stop watching the news.

Fortunately, I could smell the flowers inside the box. And there was a card. I opened it and read.

Crosby—

You're right, it wasn't hard to find you or get your number. Calling feels like a creep move without your permission, though, so here's my number. I hope to hear from you.

—*Trey*

My heart pounded. The truth was, it didn't matter that much that it was *Trey Simons*. The novelty of his celebrity had worn off pretty quickly the night I met him, fading in the much more interesting face of who the man actually was.

I opened the box and it was a simple bouquet of perfect pink roses. I closed my eyes and smiled. This was so *romantic*. Wasn't it? What did pink roses mean? Friendship? Red was passion. Did anyone actually think that way?

I tried to decide how and when to contact him. Calling seemed out of the question. Texting was less personal but also less chancy, so I was okay with that. But when? If I responded now, would I seem too eager?

Then again, he'd sent flowers. It would be rude for me not to acknowledge that they'd arrived safely.

That was it. I decided on a quick text.

The roses are lovely and so is the thought. Congratulations
on locating me, Sherlock, now you have my number too.

I hit Send before I could think about it anymore and then
waited.

It didn't take long before the phone rang. He was *calling*.
While I'd worried it would seem too pushy if I did it, I was
thrilled that he was.

"Mr. Simons!"

"Ms. Turner. How are you this evening?"

"Pretty good now! What a beautiful surprise!" How fast
could your heart beat before it became dangerous? "I thought
chivalry was dead."

"Not dead. Just a little green around the gills. So, listen, I
know this is last minute but I was hoping you'd go out for a
drive with me. Maybe grab a bite somewhere?"

"Tonight?" Did I have my loathing for Mardie written all
over my face? If so, could I cover it with makeup?

"I would have given you more notice but I didn't have the
number." He gave a laugh.

"Well, I *am* hungry. And I could definitely take a break
from work."

"What are you working on? Another fiction piece?"

Ugh. If he only knew. "Just a biography for someone impossible. You don't want to hear, believe me."

"Now I really do, but I'll cut you some slack. Can you be
ready in forty-five minutes?"

I would have agreed to any time frame so I was just glad

he'd given me a decent one. "Yup. You know where the place is?"

"Sure do." He laughed. "I dropped the flowers off."

* * *

AN HOUR LATER, I was in his car—a curvy little Lexus convertible (with the hardtop up) that smelled of leather—with a bag of egg rolls and tiny tacos from Jack in the Box on my lap and a bottle of chilled champagne at my feet. We were headed toward the Hollywood sign, as I'd mentioned I had seen it only from a distance no matter how hard I tried to get a close-up look.

"Are we going to be attacked by coyotes?" I asked.

"I hope not."

"Good enough."

He drove up a winding road into the hills and stopped at a dead end. "Ready?"

"I am." I handed him the bottle and held on to the bag and we got out of the car. "You know, the fact that you are a known person, so to speak, might be giving me a false sense of security."

He looked at me seriously. "I promise you have nothing to worry about. You might not like the food, and I could bore you, but I promise you can trust me completely."

I felt my face grow hot and I was glad he couldn't see. It wasn't the time to be flippant. "Thank you," I said quietly.

He put his arm around me and we started to walk. If I'd

known we'd be traversing fields and climbing fences, I might have worn more practical shoes, but it wasn't too long before we came to a clearing, and all the lights of LA spread out below us. It wasn't a total surprise, since I'd been able to see the light on the horizon, but that hadn't indicated just how beautiful it was to see them twinkling below. They stretched as far as the eye could see. It was breathtaking.

He turned me around, and there, behind where we'd been standing, perhaps twenty yards away, was the Hollywood sign.

It was strange, just a white ghost against the dark hill. There were a few lights on the top of the hill beyond, but the sign itself gave the strangest impression of being a forgotten remnant of the past rather than one of the most famous landmarks in the United States, if not the world.

"Welcome to Hollywoodland," Trey said. "Or what would have been Hollywoodland if they'd finished the development."

I did know the story of how the sign once had -land attached to it to advertise a housing development that was never finished. I'd always pictured it having the bones of unfinished homes dotting the landscape, but of course it didn't. This land was way too valuable to leave a ghost town on it.

He popped open the champagne and handed it to me. I took a sip. It was delicious, dry and yeasty. Made me long for a good slice of buttered baguette. But the fast food didn't sound too bad either.

We sat on a patch of grass and tucked into the food, washing it down with the excellent wine and even better conversation.

Turned out he'd grown up in the Midwest and had very solid, traditional ideals. By which I mean he thought people should be nice to each other, news anchors shouldn't yell at us, and everyday life shouldn't be designed to beat us down. Ideals I could wholeheartedly share. He liked good wine, craft beer, and comfort food. Someday he wanted kids and a house with land.

And all I could do was agree and hope I didn't sound like a sycophant trying to impress him.

I don't know what time it was when we finally went quiet for a while. I was looking at the sign, imagining all the stars and lives it had overseen from this hill, when the wind raised and howled lightly. I felt like it came from the sign itself but we were too far away from it to hear something so subtle. It was more likely the rocky hill and tall grass. Still, I shuddered. "It seems haunted," I said. "It's creepier up here than I expected."

"They say it is haunted."

"Really? By who?"

"Peg Entwistle. She was an actress who didn't make it as far as she wanted to and jumped to her death from up there."

"Which letter?"

"H."

I nodded. "I guess that makes sense. I don't know why, but I feel like it does. Poor thing. All because she didn't make it as a famous actress?"

He shrugged. "That's what they say. I have to think there was other stuff going on there, but Hollywood wasn't nice to her. Even after she died, one of the headlines said, 'I Am a Coward.'"

"Jeez." I couldn't help but think of Frances and how hard she was working to be in this business that could be so cruel. I'd always thought of her as being strong and self-assured but rejection was part of the game for a person auditioning all the time and it had to be difficult.

"A lot of people don't realize it's all an illusion," Trey said. "Acting, music, any performance. It's an illusion for the audience; you just can't buy into it. The toughest thing about it is counting on it to pay your bills."

"Wouldn't it be nice to positively yearn to be a CPA? People always need CPAs."

He chuckled. "You haven't done too badly as a writer from what I can tell. So who's the mystery person you're writing the book for?"

"Ghostwriters aren't allowed to tell."

"What if your name's on the book?"

"Then I'll tell. But I'm not sure she's going to go for that."

"Aha! So it's a woman!"

It was a detail I hadn't really meant to let out but it didn't narrow things down in any significant way. "Yes, and that's the only clue you get." I thought about Mardie saying she'd like to get back together with him for some good PR for a new album. And while I barely knew him, it was obvious to me that he would never go for it. He was light-years away from their relationship.

"All right, all right, I won't ask for more." He shifted

slightly and put his right hand on my left cheek. "Can I kiss you? I've been thinking about it for days."

"I wish you would," I said and held my breath as he moved closer.

When his lips touched mine, I swear it was as if an electric jolt went through my whole body. He was gentle but enthusiastic. He smelled delicious and tasted of champagne, not the junk food we'd eaten.

Kissing was a major litmus test for me. If the guy smelled funny or tasted like cigarettes or pressed too hard or brushed by like a butterfly, all of those were deal killers.

Trey was perfect.

And he was an absolute gentleman as well. Though we sat there making out for what felt like hours, he didn't fumble around trying to get further there where anyone could have walked up with a flashlight. Or, perhaps worse, without one.

With the view before me, I felt I was literally on top of the world.

We left when the sun was beginning to peek up in the east. As we cleaned up our stuff, I noticed there was still about half a bottle of champagne left. I wondered if he wanted to keep it but he shook his head and poured it out onto the grass, saying, "This is for Peg."

Tears pricked at my eyes. *For Frances*, I thought. *Here's to the audition for Fletcher Hall changing her life.*

Chapter Nineteen

Frances

It had been a long night. Not because I'd stayed up and partied with my friends for so long. We'd actually parted ways early, as two of them had babies at home and the other one had a day job that required the ability to think in the morning instead of just sleep. We were happy-hour friends who'd met five years ago when we all worked at the Chateau Lounge. Time marched on, each of our lives changed, but we still tried to get together once every month or two to catch up, though my sense was that all of us were feeling less and less inclined to keep it up.

So I'd come back to my place and, seeing it empty for the first time in a while, poured myself some wine and watched a few old interviews from *Inside the Actors Studio*. The more I watched, the more of a hack I felt like, yet I couldn't stop. I had perhaps one last shot and it was a big one. One could reasonably say I had waited a lifetime for it . . . assuming it was coming.

Jill swore it was, and if it was, I had to be ready.

It wasn't until almost sunrise that I forced myself to go to bed. I knew from bitter experience that if I didn't get enough sleep I wasn't able to think.

After some time, my phone buzzed and I turned my head painfully to see texts from FLETCHER HALL, whose name I had flanked with two red siren emojis.

I sat up so fast my head spun and I read the texts. The first one had come at nine thirty. The second had just come in.

The first read:

Good morning Frances—last minute audition opp today, you able to swing by the studio? 11:30 a.m.

He then listed the address.

The text he'd just sent said:

Haven't heard anything . . . on your way?

I glanced at the top of my phone screen. It was ten twenty-five. My hair was a mess. I looked barely alive. And getting there in under an hour was a tall order. None of that mattered.

Oh my God, this was it. *It.*

I sprang up and went to the bathroom, took a super-quick shower, dried my hair as fast as I could, and slapped on some makeup, making sure to emphasize my eyes. Ages ago, I'd heard that was important in an audition, to have expressive eyes.

I remembered to text Fletcher.

> Good morning! Great news, yes, I'll be able to make it. I apologize for missing the first text, I was doing some prep work. See you soon!

I rolled my eyes at just how bullshit that was but threw my phone back on the charger and then finished getting ready.

Clothes were a dilemma. After too many precious seconds wasted dithering, I put on a pair of black leggings, a black tank, and black flats, picked up a camel duster, and went out the door, grabbing my purse and a bottle of seltzer on the way.

Finally, just before 11:30, I got to the right address and hopefully the right parking lot.

God, it was hot. And *bright*. And I was *so* hungry.

I had tried to eat a Nature Valley granola bar ("Franola bar," Crosby would and has called it) from my glove box, but it was the driest thing I'd ever eaten and half of it ended up down the shelf bra of my tank and I was not looking forward to unearthing the crumbs later on.

I dropped my phone on the asphalt, and as my Ray-Bans slipped down the bridge of my nose, I said a small prayer to every god that the screen had not cracked.

It had not, and I whispered some disjointed words of gratitude as I took off running. If I had been Crosby, Darren Neville probably would have swooped by in a golf cart and given me a ride. Maybe a tipple of champagne as well.

I powered on and appeared at the right building at the right time in front of the right door of the right room. I was probably not the right person wearing the right thing about to give the right performance, but I was *there*.

Good for me, I thought, because sometimes you have to congratulate yourself on the little things.

I triple-checked that I was in front of the right door. It didn't seem right. The hall wasn't filled with sixty girls who looked like me or better. There wasn't a line. There weren't multiple things going on at once. It was just a big building with some people walking around, but not much else. Like going to a weird, specific doctor's appointment in the early evening when everyone was about to go home. I knocked on the door.

"Come in" said a voice on the other side.

I opened it and found a room that looked more like a black-box theater than anything else.

It was like time-traveling back to college. The smile that spread across my face was not the polite response to meeting people who control your fate. It was genuine pleasure at being in an environment that felt familiar.

"Frances, I'm so glad you could make it," said Fletcher, standing to greet me. He clapped his hands and gestured behind him. "Everyone, this is Frances Turner. Frances, this is Alex Chao, Sarah Penn-Wilder, and Natasha Juarez." He looked to them. "She's the one Jill told me about."

This was already unlike any audition I'd ever been to. This was so much more personal. Was this what it was like to have connections? Was this what networking (effectively) could do?

I'd met Jill only because I'd met everyone else I'd met. Like hopping from lily pad to lily pad or swinging from vine to vine. You just never know.

"Can I grab you a water?" he asked, shooting finger guns at me as he walked toward the back of the room.

"I'd love that, yes, please."

"It's finally getting cooler out," said Alex Chao. "Thank God, I couldn't take any more of the heat this year."

"I know, and my AC has been broken since June!" said Sarah.

I walked a little closer and saw there was a chair across from them, probably for the likes of me.

"How is that still broken?" asked Natasha. She had big glasses and a low bun at the base of her neck. She was androgyny incarnate, high office fashion's essence, and her very question made me feel like I needed to check and make sure my own air-conditioning was working. "I thought we got my guy in there."

"We did, it was just a fucking shit show. Apparently everything else is broken too. It's been fine, Christ; we've been spending half the time at the place in Malibu obviously."

"And the other half at my house, hiding from your children."

"Don't remind me."

"Here you go, hon." Fletcher handed me a small glass bottle of Evian. He cracked open the top of his own. "Your place in Malibu notwithstanding, we do have auditions to hold."

He sat down and gave me a smile. I smiled back with a *Don't worry about it* look.

"We were talking more about my terrible children and air-conditioning or lack thereof, but you're right. Okay, so how are you today? Have you prepared something for us?"

Fletcher spoke before me. "Actually, I didn't ask her to. I only texted her this morning. Sort of a more casual thing." He leaned back in his chair and crossed his arms.

Natasha narrowed her eyes and extended her legs. I could see that even without the three-inch heels she was wearing, she had to be over six feet tall. "What exactly did you want to do?"

Of course I had monologues and soliloquies galore in my head. Tired old things I'd performed over and over. I could have done one of those, probably could have done it really well.

But suddenly I didn't want to. I didn't want to do the same thing I'd been doing for years. Be the same *her* I had tried to be for years.

This was a terrible time to have an existential crisis, yet that's exactly what it felt like.

Fletcher kept talking. "As you know, I've been wanting to do this a little differently. I want these to be *people* in the show, not just actors standing in the background saying, 'Peas and carrots watermelon,' whatever." He gave an exasperated gesture with his arms. "Which is why I had that skinny white kid try to do the most offensive thing he could. Obviously he couldn't come up with anything, and he left without crossing any lines or getting a job, but . . ." He shrugged.

Alex and Sarah stifled snickers. Natasha grinned and shook her head at him.

My stomach was filled with acid. There was an intense cool-kid vibe here. Even the talk of air-conditioning was a power play to show me that they could discuss boring minutiae in front of me, someone who was hoping for a life-changing event to take place. Fletcher seemed pretty nice—they all *kind of* did.

But I could tell they weren't.

"You are the worst, Fletch," said Alex, wiping invisible tears from under her eyes. "That poor kid."

An exchanged look with Sarah sent them both back into hysterics.

The novelty of the experience was wearing a little thin. Or was it just one of those euphoric hangover waves that was so often followed by crushing reality?

"Okay, okay, settle down, settle down." Fletcher licked his bottom lip and lifted his chin to me. He was telling them to stop, but clearly he loved it. "So, what I'm going to have you do today is just sort of, you know"—he glanced at the others—"riff."

"Riff," I repeated.

"Yeah. You have a theater background, right? No television, no film?"

A beat. "Correct."

"And your age?" asked Natasha with the tone of someone teeing up someone else's punch line.

"Thirty-five."

They didn't laugh outright. Worse, there was a distinct air of *not* laughing. Of *not* looking at each other. Of *Going to talk about it later.*

I smoothed a cool palm over my hot forehead and drank some water. My fingers were shaking. I tensed every muscle in my hands to stop them trembling.

I wanted to be the sort of person who got mad and stormed out or who spit back some vitriol, but I was not. I just sat there, not even feeling comfortable enough to drink as much water as I wanted.

"So we'll give you a scene, and you just *go*," said Fletch with a shrug.

"Like improv," said Alex.

"Like theater," said Sarah.

Another slight curl of the lip told me this was another laughing point.

I had forgotten just how funny Hollywood found theater. I had forgotten just how pretentious it made me feel when I wanted to defend it. It made me feel like an unskilled rube who thought herself holier than thou. Which, in a nutshell, means you deserve all the laughter behind your back and the back of your high horse. Only made worse by the fact that said horse is actually three of your castmates covered in felt and Velcro and a horse's head with wide, unlidded plastic eyes. "Okay, sounds good!" *I hate myself.*

"Okay, so one of the actual scenes we have"—he laced his fingers behind his head and balanced on the back legs of his chair—"is a woman who is confessing to her husband that she doesn't want to try to have children anymore. They've been trying and trying and she's done." He sliced the air. "She's not even sure now that she *ever* wanted them."

I found myself nodding and picking through items in my brain—facial expressions, feelings, memories—then beginning to string something together. Did I really remember how to do this? Why hadn't I practiced?

Like angry meditation, I kicked that thought out of my mind with heels sharper than Natasha's.

"Her husband is—oop, she's ready." Fletcher smiled and turned to the women. "I guess she's ready."

I noticed all of that before I realized I had stood and set down my things.

Suddenly all eight eyes were on me. I scanned all of them.

You know, I thought to myself, I had truly *nothing* to lose. I would rather Fletcher go to Jill and tell her my audition was incredibly *weird* or uncomfortable or even *horrific* than have him say something polite.

So whatever.

I shook my head and bit the inside of my bottom lip and looked at Fletcher. I blinked and let my head lilt to the side before taking a deep breath and saying, "I'm sorry, I can't."

They all looked at one another.

I kept going. "I can't. I c—" I ran my hand through my hair.

Wow, I didn't even have to dig deep to find a situation to parallel. I meant every word I was saying.

"I've been trying for so long to do this," I said. "To do something I'm supposed to be able to do. I'm *supposed* to"—a sad smile came on my face; tears began to threaten in my throat— "I'm supposed to be able to do it. I'm less because I can't."

I licked my parched lips.

"I know people *know* what they're supposed to say. They're supposed to tell me I'm not less without this, without children, without fertility, or"—I looked skyward—"without good luck or good enough health or if it's survival of the fittest or whatever it is that you won't say. And the truth is I have been focusing everything on this for so damn long"—I let my voice go up in question—"that now it *is* all I am *and* I don't have it. My whole life became a question and now I'm finding that I don't have that answer."

I shook my head. I went on.

"Worse than that. I could find the answer and it could be worse. Worse than asking. The thing is, I've been asking for so long, I've been begging"—I laughed without an ounce of mirth—"for so long for some sort of miracle, sometimes even hoping for something to immaculately appear without my own help. Some miracle. Something that proves that this is more than what I want. More, certainly, than what you want. I want proof that it's what some God somewhere wants. But I'm starting to realize that I'm not digging. I'm not the shovel. I'm the hole. And while I grow bigger all the time, I am emptier and emptier, and the capacity for me to grow more empty is limitless."

My eyes burned. I fought off tears.

"So, no." My voice became a few notes higher. "I'm done." I thought of Crosby. Of how I'd let a lifetime of stupid resentment fall into this pit that had nothing to do with her. "And I'm sorry."

The last word was a whisper.

I stared at each of them. All amusement was completely gone from their faces. At some point Fletcher had moved from his back-row history-class posture to bent over with his elbows on his knees. Natasha's eyes were narrowed, but her thin lips were a line so firm I could see every wrinkle, one for every cigarette. Alex's chin was flush with her throat. Sarah looked like I had slapped her.

I turned and picked up my bag to go.

"Wow," said Fletcher, clearing his throat.

"Wow," said Natasha.

"So what would you think about coming in to read for— what do you think, for the part of Lauren?"

"Lauren, I was going to say Lauren."

"Definitely. Though she would be an interesting Pat."

"Oh, I like that."

I listened, thinking I must be misunderstanding. They thought that was an audition and not a soul-burning release of my chains. But . . . maybe it could be a release *and* an advance. Maybe by giving up my fierce hold on my need for everything to be *just so*, I had opened the doors for my future.

Chapter Twenty

Crosby

Two days after my date with Trey and the last time I'd gone to Mardie's, I got a call from Mardie's brother.

I had a day off with no plans at all. I was sitting outside on the roof of the building, soaking up the sun. I had a little spray bottle of water and a big jug of iced-tea lemonade; I had my speaker, Spotify, and the rest of my Jen Lancaster book to read.

I felt good warming myself under the sun in my yellow bikini—well, the bottom half of my yellow bikini, because no one was close enough to really see me, and if someone was going to take out binoculars, well, have at it.

I heard a woman scream.

It was loud and bloodcurdling enough to really grab the attention. It wasn't teenagers messing around. I didn't think it was anyone faking it, but it was Hollywood, so . . . who knew?

I remembered how Frances told me to stop calling all of Los Angeles Hollywood.

I was not going to. It was all Hollywood.

Anyway, I heard the woman scream, and I tore off my Lolita sunglasses, covered my bare top with my arm, and stepped over to the edge of the roof. Frances would have completely Franicked if she'd seen me that close to the edge.

I looked for the source of the scream but saw nothing obvious. All I saw was the swinging slat blinds in an open window across the way. Like someone had just been pushed through to his or her death.

It was like *Rear Window* except I was topless and I definitely wasn't dating and rejecting any stone-cold hotties like Grace Kelly.

Hesitantly, I looked down to the sidewalk under the open window, expecting the absolute worst, a crumpled female form surrounded by an expanding pool of red blood, but instead there was, if I was seeing correctly, a . . . sandwich?

"You asshole!" I heard faintly. "I wanted that!"

Another female voice, less distinct, answered in an equally angry tone, and someone gestured out the window, hitting the blinds again and setting them swinging.

If I was hoping for inspiration for another mystery novel—and I always was—this was a disappointment.

I sat down, a little reluctantly, and put my sunglasses back on, thinking that was still kind of a cute opening for a book. The innocuous beginning that turns deadly as the book goes on.

It felt good to start thinking creatively again. There was a reason Hollywood was the world of fantasy—the sun was like a charger for all things imaginative. And writing Mardie's book might keep me on the map, maybe even expand me into the true-crime world, so I'd be free to pick projects I was in the mood for.

I tipped my face toward the sun, willing the inspiration to soak my body and soul. My phone rang. I looked and didn't recognize the number, but it was an LA area code.

"Hello?" I realized then I should have one of those more professional answers, maybe just picking it up and saying my last name like a man with a Bluetooth on Wall Street in one of those business dramas of the early nineties: *Turner here*.

"Crosby Turner, right?"

Fear gripped me. Was something wrong? Were Mom and Dad okay? "Yes?"

"This is Conor. Mardie Mariano's brother."

"Oh. Right. Hi, Conor." Then it hit me that maybe something was wrong with Mardie. Maybe she'd had some dramatic backslide after her big confession the other night. I hoped she was all right. "Is Mardie okay?"

"Yes. So, listen."

Shit. I'd started a lot of conversations that way. Breakups. Quitting. Not going to make rent. Conversations that started this way never ended well.

"What's up?" I asked cheerfully anyway. Although not in the history of time has being a gleeful, pitiful recipient of bad news made the news less likely to hit you like a piano from the top story.

"I'm calling you about the book."

I sat up. He knew about the book?

He cleared his throat. "Mardie asked me to call you. She's going to have to take a few weeks off from meeting but she's hoping you have enough already to get the book done."

"Wait, so she's . . . checking out?"

He hesitated. "If there is any way I can fill in details, you can call me."

Oh my God, she was just flaking. She was flaking even though she needed the money and her brother knew it. "She's bored, is that what you're saying? She wants this done and wants to find another project to amuse herself?"

"She has a lot of interests."

"She has ADD."

"Call it what you want."

I gave a short laugh. "Wow, I thought I was kidding. Is she really not going to cooperate anymore?"

"Look, if you need specific information or reactions or whatever, I'm sure we can get her to talk about it, but this is why we never did a book deal before. Because she doesn't—" He hesitated. "She doesn't have the capacity to concentrate on one thing for very long. But we want her story out there. She *needs* this book out there. I'm just calling to say that if you can't get through to her, please try me and we'll try and muddle through."

"Wow. Okay." I have to say, I was glad it wasn't a total cancellation. If she'd sacked me, that would have been devastating. I was counting on the pay for this project. But I was also counting on her participation.

I thought about it. Really tried to be objective. I *had* spent hours with her. Days. She'd said a lot. It wasn't always in order and it didn't always make sense, but I had it recorded and it would be an . . . interesting . . . challenge to thread it all together into a cohesive timeline.

She'd told me the whole story of *Minus Four* and of meeting and dating Trey. Initially I'd hoped the latter would be more interesting, more salacious even, but as it turned out, I was glad it was a pretty tame love story. And it was possible that opened the audience up even more. I hoped so, anyway.

Conor and I agreed to stay in touch and hung up.

Suddenly my roof-sit felt way too hot and flashbulb bright. It was entirely up to me. He had all but given me permission to fictionalize whatever facts I couldn't get. It was going to take some real—and urgent—creative writing. Creative *thinking*.

The music that had resumed when we disconnected sounded loud and insistent and annoying and I wanted silence, but when I turned it off, the city sounded loud and bigger than me, like it knew more than I did. And it probably did.

Time and money were running out for me. If I didn't pull this off, by myself now, I wasn't going to get a dime. I had to somehow make sense of the hours of nonsense I'd recorded.

I picked up the notepad and pen I'd brought and started to write a new structure for the book.

This could be done. It *could.*

I could do it.

This was the biggest test of my life. And the longer I sat there, the more I thought I could do it. That maybe it would even be easier without her stopping every five seconds and telling me I had things wrong even when they were transcribed directly from her own words.

I was not only able to do it—I could do it well.

Eager to get started on the new view of my job, I put my top on, gathered my things, and stepped over the exposed plumbing and stapled electrical cables to the door. I put everything under my arm and reached for the handle; I was ready to run downstairs and knock out three or four chapters.

The door was locked.

No.

No, no, no.

Seriously?

I tried again. Multiple times. I looked around, as if some magical solution—or maybe an actual fairy—would appear behind me. But no, it was a locked door. This was how it was designed, so people couldn't just come down from the top and wander around the building without authorization. Granted, I didn't know how people would be able to get on top of the building, but it wasn't impossible.

I put everything back down on the filthy roof, fished out my phone, and hit the image of Frances's face.

She sounded irritated. "Hello?"

"I'm in a sitcom and I need to be rescued."

"Right, well, I'm at work, so I can't really help right now. Did you try Neil Patrick Harris?"

"I'm serious, I know you're at work, but I am trapped on the roof and it's a thousand degrees up here."

"*What?*"

"I'm not kidding."

"There's no way."

I looked around. "Beg to differ."

"Are you sure the door is locked? It's never been locked in my whole life living here. Ever."

I rolled my eyes, even though she couldn't see me. "I'm sure. I tried it a bunch of times; it's definitely locked."

"Well, I can't come right now, I'm doing this . . ."

I smiled. "Say it."

"I will not, I hate it."

"Gig. You're doing a *gig*."

"I'm freelancing for a caterer," she whispered. "It's a free-lance job. Extra money. Give me a break, I'm trying to be responsible."

"Okay, so quit and come home and save me." I almost told her I'd been fired but I didn't want to add undue pressure on her to fix my mistake.

"This is ridiculous."

I looked at the phone. "Sorry?"

"Not you, no, I just got told to get off my phone, like I'm a hostess at Applebee's or something. Look, I'll be back as

soon as I can. I'm going to try to stay and finish the g—job.
You'll be fine, it's not that hot out."

"It's California!"

"It's November!"

I sighed. "Fine."

We hung up.

I set up my little camp again. It's funny, I might have
stayed up here for six hours and never even thought about
leaving, but now that I couldn't, I was helplessly bored, hungry, hot, and suddenly I really had to pee. I was even painfully conscious of the limited amount of liquid I'd had, as if
I were going to get dehydrated and perish.

If there were a volleyball here, I probably would have
named it already.

The sun wasn't really all that hot. I leaned back and, after
a moment, put on the music and took my top back off.

I was there about an hour when my phone dinged. It was
evidence of how little I'd interacted with anyone besides
Frances that I just assumed it was her coming to rescue me.
But it was Trey.

I can't stop thinking about you.

My face broke out into an extremely uncharacteristic
smile and a little squeal even came from somewhere within.

I texted back.

Who is this?

Man, did that sound cooler than I was. Did it sound too cool? Like I really didn't know?

He didn't answer right away. I started to add something to clumsily clarify. Before I could send it, he answered.

> What are you doing right now? I know it's unlikely
> you're free, but I really want to see you.

I laughed.

> It's not that I'm not free, actually. It's more like I'm trapped.

He sent back a question mark.
I went on.

> I decided to eliminate a few tan lines by sitting out on my
> sister's roof. She left a few hours ago so I just came up here
> alone, and, well . . . I live here now. The door is locked.
> Low on water. Lower on cocktails. Tell them all I loved
> them, won't you, I'm not sure how long I can survive . . .

He said nothing for a few minutes and I felt really dumb. Then finally he sent:

> Same address?

I said yes.

I was wearing no makeup; my hair was in a messy (not

chic-sloppy) topknot, and I smelled like coconut sunscreen. There are worse things to smell like, obviously, but it wasn't Chanel No. 5.

Half an hour later, the door opened, and one of Earth's Handsomest Heartthrobs came through it.

I couldn't help it; I cracked up at the still-unlikely sight of him.

"What the hell is reality right now?" I asked him and the universe. "This is, I think, a fantasy for most people but my mortification."

"Mortification?" He laughed. "Why?"

"Well, because I pee over there now, for one thing." I gestured to the corner. "Oh, hello." I saw someone behind him.

"The super," said Trey. "Didn't think to call him, huh?"

"Now I'm thinking that was Frances's job. If not to call him, at least to remind me that he existed and *I* should call him. See, where I live, I don't have a super." If Julie did her job well, I wouldn't even have a house soon.

The super glanced at the corner, glared at me, then propped open the door resolutely with a brick that had been resting on the top step. He left.

"I don't think you can be a dick about something like me not knowing to prop it open like that. Like, *obviously*, the brick is here for a *reason*. No, doors are not supposed to be permanently shut."

He laughed. "I think it was probably more about poo corner."

Embarrassment swept hotly over my face. "It's *pee* corner."

"Sure. For now." He looked around. "This is a pretty sweet setup you got here."

"I'm a little over it, to be honest."

"Yeah? Well, good thing I'm here to save you."

We gathered my stuff yet again. "I'm glad you are," I said.

"I was thinking maybe a rooftop bar," he said.

I snort-laughed and he imitated me.

As I went through the door to freedom, I was half sure I was going to wake up any second.

* * *

IT WAS SO strange to see him in Frances's apartment. His presence seemed to puff and fill every crevice of the place. It seemed forever blessed now, like a devout Catholic's house after it was visited by the pope. One of the really good popes. Are there lots of good ones, or is it just this most recent one who thinks gay marriage is cool?

Anyway, he looked around with his hands in his pockets while I scrambled to get dressed.

Yes, I had a book to write. But actually, Conor's call had given me some relief. Some freedom. Perhaps I no longer had to worry so much about what she would delete or change her mind about. Now I could use what she'd told me honestly and put it into an order that made sense.

Meantime, there was no harm in going on a date with one

of the hottest men who'd ever lived. His past with Mardie made things a little complicated, but surely it wasn't that big a deal anymore.

Except I knew I had to tell him about the book, about my association with her, and I didn't want to yet. What if he thought I was trying to use him to get juicy details? Would it seem *too* coincidental that I was the ghostwriter of her book? Or would he see it as the plain old job it was to me?

Ugh, I couldn't think about that now. I'd think about it later. Tomorrow. Meanwhile, I had to look my best and enjoy the hell out of this. I picked a rust-colored Leith leotard, high-waisted dark denim jeans, and heeled leather boots that matched the black NYC leather jacket with a tapered back. I tied my hair in a loose bun at the nape of my neck and pulled out a few strands. I put on just a little Laura Mercier tinted moisturizer and mascara, one single poof of color on my cheeks, and a few dabs of Hug Me by MAC on my lips. Given the bloom of vitamin D from the sun and my sincere excitement, it was just enough. I looked healthy and happy and, I hoped, pretty from within.

That wasn't something I'd seen in myself in a while.

I didn't want to leave California. It was good for me. I didn't want to leave whatever was happening with Trey. But was there any justification in me staying now that my job was done? California wasn't exactly an inexpensive place to live. Neither was New York, though. And when I sold my house,

I would be able to spot myself for a while either way. Surely I'd be able to find work.

"Hey, what are you thinking?"

I looked at him and smiled. "That I'm really happy."

At that moment the front door opened, and a breathless Frances came in.

"What—" Her head practically vibrated. "You're not trapped on the roof. I just quit my job to come rescue you!"

"Sorry. I *was* trapped. Then Trey texted and thought of asking the super and . . . here I am."

She clutched her ribs and caught her breath. "Screw it. You're right. I hated that job. I'm never freelancing for a caterer again. I am done with"—she swept a hand over the air behind her—"everything I've ever known. Hi, Trey. I'm the adult manifestation of your biggest fan. You probably remember me from my dreams. And here you are. Second time I've seen you in a week."

"Hi, Frances." He looked at me. "I remember you from Jill's party too. We had some good times, huh?"

"Yes. Though they were interrupted too often by pop quizzes in math. I guess you get that a lot."

He chuckled but obviously didn't know what to say to that. He glanced at me and I winked.

"We were going to go get some drinks if you'd like to join us," he offered, not acknowledging her fangirling.

She thought for a second. "I pictured that invitation differently when I was thirteen."

"Bet you knew I'd be going, though," I said.

She gave a wry smile. "Of course." She shook her head. "You guys go on, I've got to change out of these clothes and . . . this life. Go, have fun."

"Are you sure?" I asked, really hoping she was.

She knew that was what I was hoping. She gave me a quick smile. "It's been a day," she said. "Really a hell of a day. No offense but I would love nothing more than to be alone with a big pile of magazines and a big bottle of wine. And some cheese. Go. *Go.*"

Chapter Twenty-One

Frances

After Crosby and Trey left, I started straightening up the living room and came across the stuff Crosby had taken sunbathing with her. A small Bluetooth speaker, towel, water bottle, and a notepad with some writing on it. Notes about the Mardie book.

It should have made me feel better, knowing that she had this job, but seeing the attempts at outlining what she'd already described to me as a mishmash of word salad just made me think she probably would have welcomed a more straightforward gig.

And I was the jerk who had kept an opportunity from her. Even knowing she was in a bind financially.

Maybe it was our fate to have this stupid dynamic where she would trump me at every move. Seriously. Look, I'm not being all Zen about this; like I've realized this is my destiny and so it goes. It sucks. I hate it. I'm not ashamed of having the thought not to tell Crosby about an opportunity to get a job on a project I might be rejected for.

I was ashamed of being small enough to follow through with that impulse. That was unquestionably wrong, at least as far as my personal code was concerned. So I had to do something about it. I had to try to find out from Jill if the offer was still good and if it was appropriate to give Crosby Fletcher's number, even though I hadn't heard anything back about the audition. (In my experience, in this business, no news is usually bad news.)

"Frances!" She always sounded delighted to hear from me. "How *are* you, sweetie?"

"Good, Jill. I was wondering if you had a moment to talk."

"Always, for you."

"It's about that text you sent me about Fletcher and the anthology. The screenwriting and whatnot."

"Oh, yes." She groaned. "Such a shame."

My gut plummeted. She knew something. Something bad. "I'm sorry?"

"I thought it was a go for sure. Anyway, even if it couldn't work out, I'm so glad you got that experience! You got back out there!"

They'd told her I was a psychopath. That I'd popped my clutch right there in front of them. "What, um"—I gave one shake of the head. "What do you mean? What are we talking about?" I laughed apologetically. "I'm out of the loop."

"I thought . . . Fletch said you were wonderful. He said it was a really unexpected"—she sounded like she regretted the word choice—"performance, that it was really, really good. He said you were a shoo-in."

My heart leaped. They hadn't told her I'd made a fool of myself! They'd told her I had the job!

"But," she went on, "then the project was shelved. For a couple years. I'm so sorry, I'm—I feel like a complete fool, I can't believe I'm the one to tell you that. I didn't mean to do that. Honey, I'm so sorry. Hell, I thought for sure they'd let you know already."

I could feel my skin getting hot. Not just my cheeks flushing but the kind of tear-hot that I get around the top lip, between my eyebrows, and at my temples.

"No." All this, all the angst, the wrestling with not telling Crosby—it was all for nothing.

"My offer still stands," she said. "As much as ever. I'd hoped you'd change your mind, but not like this. Not because of a disappointment."

"Jill, I'd never feel like working for you was some sort of consolation prize," I managed. I meant it. "This is just a matter of picking either apples or oranges. Forever."

"But, darling, of course it's not! Oh, I know the traffic is a bear, but it's not *that* far to get to LA if an audition or job comes up. We all know that's how Palm Springs became the actors' haven that it is."

I'd sat in traffic on the 10 too many times to write off the trip that easily. To me, going to the desert meant making a final career choice. Not a *bad* one, just not the one that had captured my heart since childhood. If I took the job out of town, it meant I would be committing to it fully, giving up the idea of following my star to Hollywood.

How do you know when something is meant to be versus just being something you wanted desperately as a kid? I guess the answer is that it doesn't matter—you just do what you have to do to make a living.

And I loved cooking. I had loved every moment of working for Jill; it was the best job I'd ever had. I had been terribly sad when I thought it was over for good. Now, picturing myself working in a bright Palm Springs kitchen, sitting poolside in the sun every day of the year, made me happy. Or at least it took a lot of the sting out of the disappointment. "I think I *am* going to accept your offer," I said. "It's too good to resist."

"Oh, how wonderful! Are you sure?"

Was I? Was I really going to finally give acting up completely?

I was. I had to.

"Yes," I said. "There are just a lot of loose ends to tie up here, but yes."

"I completely understand. And we will have *such* fun!"

I wrapped up the conversation with Jill, doing my best not to let her hear my voice crack before we hung up. My hopes on this one had been so high. Embarrassingly I'd *almost* bought a bottle of good champagne the other day when I was at BevMo because I was that sure I was going to get the Call any day. Any *moment*.

Now all of that was off the table. Completely gone, no

longer an option, no longer a hope, no longer so much as a faint possibility.

And the hard part wasn't even over.

I still had to tell Crosby the truth.

* * *

WHEN SHE CAME in later that night, she was on top of the world. A regular Eliza Doolittle, all but singing "I Could Have Danced All Night" in her glee. I don't really believe in love at first sight. I always thought it took time to build a relationship, time to withstand a few tests, maybe weather all the seasons first. But damned if Crosby didn't look happier than I'd ever seen her—maybe happier than I'd ever seen *anyone*.

It figured.

You're always smiling on the JumboTron right before getting hit in the face by a foul ball, right?

"Whoa, what's the matter with you?" she asked as soon as she saw my expression.

"The Fletcher Hall project is off."

Her face didn't register the news. "What does that mean?"

"They've shelved it. Canceled it. My audition was great—apparently I was almost given a deal—but then they decided to cancel the whole thing. It's over."

Now she understood. Her brow knotted, she came over to me. "Oh no! That's terrible! I'm so sorry, I know you were really hoping that would work out. Is it really totally over? Out of the question?"

"Totally over."

"God, what a shitty thing. I am so sorry."

I shrugged. "Palm Springs will be nice."

She looked shocked. "Wait, you're *moving* too?"

I felt myself deflate a little as I tried to show enthusiasm. "It's a great offer. I'd be a fool to refuse it."

"Well, yeah, but I was kind of thinking we were having fun here in LA. Like we were finally getting it together after all these years."

Now was my chance. Now I had to do it. "I'm not sure you're going to feel like that when you hear the rest of what I have to say."

"Don't say that. The past is the past; let's just let it go and move on." She was being so kind. It would never have occurred to her at that moment to be mad at me. "You've been my saving grace. Want some wine? I got some bubbly and cheese at Trader Joe's on my way home."

"I'll get the wine," I said, getting up. "Could you maybe sit down? Seriously, I have something I have to say."

She frowned and I felt the tension arc from her like electricity. "That doesn't sound good."

I tightened my jaw, got the wine out of the fridge, grabbed two glasses, and went back to the sofa. I poured her a glass and handed it to her, then wondered if maybe glass was a bad idea. I poured my own, took a long sip, and said, "I'm sorry. You need to know that right up front: I'm sorry."

She shrank away from me ever so slightly. "This is a really bad start. Can you just"—she snapped her fingers a couple of times—"out with it?"

"I wasn't the only one who stood to gain from the Fletcher Hall project," I told her. "He asked for your contact information because he was interested in having you as a guest screenwriter. You know how they do, throwing different names into the hat to keep audience interest?"

She frowned. "He asked who for my contact information?"

"Jill."

Crosby looked relieved. "I thought you were going to say you, which would have been—"

"Horrendous."

"Yes."

"Jill told me. More specifically, Jill *asked* me to relay the message to you."

She cocked her head. "When?" She drew the word out.

"A couple of weeks ago." I swallowed. "And, just to be very clear, I purposely didn't tell you about it. I thought you were doing great with Mardie and would get everything you needed from that book, so I didn't want to tell you about Fletcher because I was afraid you'd get that job too." I closed my eyes for a moment, then opened them again. "And that then I wouldn't."

She looked stunned. "You didn't tell me. On purpose. Because . . . you were afraid I'd get the job?"

I knew she wanted to hear she was misunderstanding me. She wanted me to correct her on the part of it that was hurtful. The part I couldn't correct because she was understanding it perfectly. "Yes. It was wrong. Selfish. I'm just so sorry."

"Why are you telling me this now?"

"Because I couldn't live with myself if I continued to keep it from you."

"Coincidental timing, isn't it? Now that the show is off and no one can work on it."

"Hey, I could have said nothing and you'd never have known."

"Do you want a prize for that?" Her face flushed. "Some commendation for doing the bare minimum a sister should do? Maybe a *thank you*?"

It was then that I realized I'd been blindly hoping she *would* see some nobility in confessing when it no longer mattered, but to say that would be to say that the choice had been my luxury. To grant to her or not. But that wasn't true; I *had* done the bare minimum.

"I don't know what else to say," I told her. "There is a lifetime of history driving this and I made a bad choice."

"A *lifetime of history* driving this? What does that even mean?"

"You know what it means. Ever since we were young, when I was doing something, you'd sweep in and outdo me. No matter what it was. School plays, writing, boys, *everything*."

She tensed all over. I saw it. "*Boys*? Are you fucking *kidding* me?"

I sighed. "I don't mean to deflect. None of that is the point right now."

Evidently, for her it was. "What *boys* did I *outdo* you with?"

"You're right, that isn't the point." I didn't want to do this right now. I didn't want to *feel* all of this right now. It was one case where I knew I wasn't wrong, but I still didn't want to go through it right now.

Her race to rage was breathtaking. "No, I want to know what you meant."

Boy, it was tempting, but I tried to act like an adult. "That has nothing to do with the issue at hand."

"Apparently it does. Apparently you have been holding a whole lotta stuff against me for a really long time and that led you to just go ahead and fuck me over when it really mattered." She stood up and paced before me. "Who was it you're thinking I tried to take from you? Little Randy Guiseman? Who wanted to play kickball with me and my friends instead of doing gymnastics with you? You went crying to Mom and Dad about that."

"Give me a break, that was fourth grade."

"Yeah, that's a long time to hold a grudge, isn't it? I mean, who else could you reasonably think was as affectionate toward me as he was toward you? I can't even think. *Dad*? After all, you'd had him for two years before I came along and blew it for you."

She was pissing me off now. Yeah, I'd had an ignoble couple of weeks here, but she was purposely mocking me.

"How about Tyler?" I asked, nearly against my will. "I never said anything about it, but did you think I didn't see you go into the barn with him that night at the field party? Did you think *everyone* didn't see you? I wouldn't sleep with him so he tried going for a cheaper version of me and, lo and behold, you fell right into his arms."

Her face went white. There was a very long silence before she spoke. "Fuck you."

I couldn't see why she thought she had a reason to be self-righteous. There was no denying the facts. And that, arguably, had been more damaging than keeping a secret for a few days when it ultimately didn't matter one bit. "I called Jill to try to get that opportunity *back* for you, and it was only then that I found out the whole thing had been canceled. So, really, I'd delayed telling you about an opportunity for just a few days and then it fizzled out to nothing, so"—I shrugged—"no harm, no foul."

"You just told me you have a *lifetime* of resentment toward me and then you have the absolute *gall* to mention Tyler? You don't even—oh my God, just fuck you."

I could not believe her nerve. Yes, it had been a long time, but come on, she'd humiliated me in front of everyone we knew. This had been a slight that never left me. It had never been resolved. It was the most basic of betrayals and she was acting like it was a youthful indiscretion that she owed me no apology for. "Fuck you too! Not that your sputtering objections aren't compelling, but yeah, that mattered, okay? It mattered because everyone at that party knew you guys were hooking up before I did, and every one of them thought I was a pitiful fool letting it happen literally right in front of me. Who *does* that? To *anyone*, much less a *sister*."

"You apparently have no idea what happened."

"Okay, enlighten me." Part of me didn't even want to know. Had there been a Hallmark-worthy romance between them before they went their separate ways for the cliché of college? "Did you two continue to date after I dumped his ass? Did you elope? Was there a big wedding I wasn't told about?"

She looked at me with absolute disdain. "For your information, your *boyfriend*, who you felt just *fine* about bringing around your family, was a pretty shitty guy."

Clearly. "So you dumped him too? Got sick of him?"

"One night," she said, "*that* night. He . . . I drank way too much, like a dumbass, and thought I was going to puke in front of everyone—which would *also* have embarrassed you, I know—so he offered to help me to the barn where I could have some privacy. But it wasn't *my* privacy he was worried about, it was his. He . . . whatever. *Really* great guy, Fran, I'm sorry you lost him to me."

"What are you saying? He kissed you?"

"Yes." She gave me a challenging look. "He kissed me."

It's what I'd always figured had happened. "Why didn't you ever tell me?"

She hesitated. "Because I was so ashamed of what I had 'done'"—she did sarcastic finger quotes—"to *you*. I thought you would feel *exactly* the way you are saying you feel now.

Imagine that." She gave a humorless laugh. "I didn't want to hurt you." Her eyes grew bright with tears.

This was so confusing. And so much time had passed, erasing the sharp contours of memory that might have made it clear. "What if I'd stayed with that asshole? Would you have *ever* told me?"

"I don't think you would have believed it wasn't my fault." The tears spilled over onto her cheeks and she was instantly a mess. "I couldn't tell anyone." She sniffled. "Not even Mom."

I thought back to that time. It wasn't like rewinding a movie, I hadn't committed my whole life to memory, but since that had been so soon after the party where they'd gone in the barn, I did remember how she had clammed up and been pretty antisocial with me. At the time, I thought it was because she knew she was wrong. "So you were too embarrassed to tell me? To just apologize?" This was so confusing. It wasn't *that* big a deal.

"I—uh." She shook her head. "You know, there is a lot more to this than I think you're getting but we're just not able to communicate. We never have been able to. I think I should just pack my stuff up and get the hell out of here."

"Fine."

"Sorry I've been such a burden on you all your life."

"Ditto."

She looked at me, took a breath to say something, then shook her head and stalked off to her room. I could hear her angrily tossing things onto the bed and muttering. She was checking out and I was glad. Did that make me a bad person?

Exactly how much of this did make me a bad person? And how much was on her?

Guilt nagged at me just for having the thought, but our problems were not just a one-way street.

She came out of the bedroom a short time later with her suitcases. Her face was devoid of emotion.

I felt like mine was too.

"Thanks for letting me stay here," she said. "I appreciate that."

"Right."

She rolled her eyes. "I don't know how you can turn this around so *you're* somehow the aggrieved party."

"You're sitting there telling me what a terrible sister *I've* been without taking any responsibility for your part in it. Yeah, I'm aggrieved."

"What did you want me to do?"

"Read the room now and then. Shut up when it was my turn to speak. Or cry. Or anything. Even at that party. If you got yourself drunk, maybe you could have told *me* you needed help. Or anyone other than the guy I'd come with."

"That's not fair."

At this point, I honestly didn't know if it was or not. I shrugged.

"Here's the thing," she went on. "Maybe we just don't *like* each other. Maybe we're trying to force something that only builds resentment." She looked me over and I knew she meant her, not *us*.

"Maybe."

"We just don't have anything meaningful in common. It seems to me it's just best to do our own thing and not look to each other for help or, you know . . . *sisterhood*."

At the moment that sounded just fine with me. "Right. So where will you go? Trey's?"

She laughed but her eyes were cold. "You really don't know me at all, do you? No, I'm not going to call the guy I've known for five minutes and ask if I can move in."

Put that way, I was glad she wasn't. That *would* have embarrassed us both.

"Make sure you let Mom and Dad know where you land. I don't want to get shit for not babysitting you well enough."

She threw one last hostile glance my way then stepped out and slammed the door behind her.

Chapter Twenty-Two

Crosby

It was true, there was no way I was going to impose on Trey when I needed a place to stay. That would have been psycho. Instead, I went on a last-minute-hotel app and found a place I could afford. Fortunately it wasn't that far away, and while it was *very* modest, it was also clean.

But once I was there, I didn't know what to do with myself besides wallow around in my thoughts, trying to puzzle out who was right and who was wrong when, most likely, the answer was both of us.

I guess that's life, huh? The goal was to learn to roll with it, to reach self-actualization or whatever the term is, but I was not good with unexpected detours and workarounds. I needed things to work logically and go the way I expected them to. Even if I expected the worst.

I just wasn't good with surprises.

That might surprise most people. They'd expect Frances

to be the one who needed order and emotional stability to function. I, they used to say, was the wild one. But that was never true—I was only able to be wild when my world was absolutely sane.

So it had made perfect sense for me to come out here and ghostwrite a memoir. What could be easier? It's a life story, from beginning to end, however you define *end*. It had already been lived, so all I needed to do, as the writer, was write it down. Correct the grammar. That's what I expected, anyway. I never thought there was any question that the job was straightforward.

That said, I also hadn't expected any additional offers, like screenwriting. It would have been really good if that had panned out, even though I didn't know anything about the craft. Maybe I would have failed. Maybe that would have embarrassed Frances. Maybe all of her fears were spot-on.

But was I pissed at her? Absolutely.

Privately I knew if I hadn't let myself fall into such a huge financial hole, I wouldn't be here depending on others for work. The old me had the confidence to write a book and do all the accompanying edits, so it would have been awesome if the present me was still doing that and didn't *need* any little crumb that was offered.

The truth was, I was just really embarrassed that Frances could see through me so completely that she knew, before even talking to me about it, that I was so capable of freezing in the clutch.

That still didn't let her off the hook, though.

We'd been sisters for a long time. We had great parents. If we were going to get our shit together, we would have done it years ago. Around the time we became adults.

Instead, we'd taken the other fork in the road.

My biggest challenge now was to face that and accept it.

* * *

I MANAGED TO stay in the Clean Hotel, as I'd come to think of it, for two nights without anything to do and without any progress in my life besides telling Julie to make a counter-offer on my house.

Turns out the renters had not, in fact, been interested in buying, so what I'd thought would be a fast, painless process turned out to be a little tougher in terms of both waiting and net profits.

Finally one night at seven o'clock my time, ten o'clock hers, Julie called and said they'd accepted my offer. She could e-mail me the documents and we could be under contract immediately.

Without any idea what I was going to do next, I agreed. Because no matter what I did next, I needed the money from that sale to make it possible.

Gathering my nerve, I texted Trey.

Just sold my place in New York. Care to celebrate with me?

This time he didn't answer right away so I figured I'd just made an enormous ass of myself by even asking. That was it, that was the final sign I needed. It was time to pack up my life and go back to New York to regroup. Beg my parents to let me stay there for a few weeks, if necessary, while I found a new place to live.

At 8:30, a text dinged in.

Just got in from Joshua Tree. No reception there. I would love to see you and celebrate if it's not too late.

I smiled and held the phone to my chest. God, what a relief. This was just what I'd needed.

I'm not at my sister's place anymore, I typed. Care to come meet me at my hotel and pretend we're strangers? It was a joke because we really were still strangers almost.

Call me Boris, I'll call you Natasha, he responded. I'll pick up the champagne.

I gave him the hotel and room information and took my computer over to the bed to look at what I had, all told, for Mardie's book. My lawyer said she had a number of liens on her properties and thought it would be hard to get money out of her even if I was successful in suing. But, he'd pointed out, if the publisher pressured her about a deadline, maybe she'd change her mind and want my work so far. Enough to pay for it.

It seemed like the only shot at getting blood from that stone.

When I got into the files, I was surprised at how much I'd managed to put together. It was considerable. Despite everything that had conspired against me, I'd done a pretty good job.

My self-congratulations were interrupted by a knock at the door.

Trey! Heart pounding, I jumped up and ran to the door, stopping only for a quick look through the peephole. Can't be too careful. It was him and he looked absolutely gorgeous. I couldn't believe this man was here to see me.

I opened the door and threw my arms around him. "Thank you so much for coming!"

"Hey, hey." He laughed. "I've spent two days freezing in the desert and thinking about you so I'm really glad you allowed me the dignity of not having to try and play it cool for another few days."

"Play it cool?" I gestured at the simple surroundings. "I'm about as uncool as a person in Los Angeles can get right now."

"You're the most beautiful thing in here," he said. "I can't even see anything else."

I felt my face grow warm and I laughed. It was so stupid, but I was loving this flirtation. I was not too cool for this at *all*.

"So, you sold your place," he said, producing a bottle of Bollinger.

"Yup."

He started pulling the foil off the top. "Does that mean you're staying out here?"

"I honestly don't know *where* I'm going to go. I'm completely open." I shrugged. "I'd kind of like to stick around for a while, at least."

"That gets my vote." The foil was off and he was twisting the wire hood. "Glasses?"

"Oh, crap." I looked around. There were two mugs by the coffee machine. I grabbed them and rinsed them thoroughly in the sink. "I saw a horrifying exposé on hotel cleanliness," I explained.

"I think I saw the same one."

I shook the cups out and brought them over.

"Ready?" he asked, thumb on the cork.

"Do it."

He pushed it off with a *pop*, and fine champagne sprayed all over me—my face, my hair, my arms. I stood in complete shock for a moment before cracking up. "I'm going to take this as a good sign," I said to him.

"That's the spirit."

"But if you could just give me a minute." I set the mugs down on the desk and went into the bathroom to wash the wine off before it got sticky and gross. I was rinsing myself off when it occurred to me that I'd left my computer open on the bed. I hoped to God the champagne hadn't gotten on it because it was the only laptop I had and I couldn't afford a new one. Once I'd spilled a little water—it was water, I swear it—on the keyboard of another computer, and that had been the end of it. I'd been able to hire someone to transfer the contents of my hard drive, but the machine itself had never worked again.

I hurriedly dried myself and opened the door.

Trey was next to the bed, a foot or so from the open laptop, facing me with an expression I couldn't unpuzzle.

"What's wrong?"

He took a deep breath. "I wasn't snooping—this was just sitting here."

It was only then that I realized the champagne wasn't my only worry. I'd left it open on the documents for the Mardie book.

"Oh. I know how this looks." But then realizing how really bad it might look, how really famous he was—especially to people who weren't me—I saw how this might seem exceptionally shady. "I mean, I *guess* I know it looks weird, but I'm writing a book for Mardie. Her memoir." I was so flustered that I could barely even spit the truth out. "She was the one I told you about, the one I've been so frustrated with." I said the last part fast and loud, like that might help.

"Not that I did anything unethical or anything," I continued. At this point I wished I would just shut up, but I couldn't. "It was nothing to do with you; she doesn't even know we've met. There isn't anything explosive about you or anything. If that's what you're worried about."

Trey sat down, which was better than leaving instantly, which is what happens at the eleven-minutes-to-the-end mark of every Hallmark movie.

"I'm waiting for the part where seeing me was just a coincidence," he said. "And not calculated."

"It was! When we went to the party, I had no idea you'd be

there, and trust me, by then I knew I couldn't get anything worthwhile out of Mardie. She hired me because she liked my previous book. See, she was at one of Jill's parties, where Frances was working or something, and then they started talking. I met you by coincidence. Because I was invited to Jill's party. And then we talked and, yes, okay, I knew who you were, but I wasn't associating you with Mardie or the book or anything. Not really."

A muscle twitched in his tightened jaw and he looked at the ground. "That's a lot."

I couldn't shut up. "Honestly, I know it seems sketchy, I always sound like I'm lying when I'm really telling the truth. This is probably why I'm kind of a failure. If I were cut out for this stuff, I would have come up with some interesting scheme like arranging to meet you or something. But . . . I didn't. I guess the only proof is that I didn't seek Mardie *or* you out, and I really didn't even associate you with her once I met you both." My brain hooked on this. I put my hands on my hips. "Hey, yeah, you can't possibly think I did anything wrong here. You're the one who came up to me and who contacted me first. So."

He raised his eyebrows.

"Anyway," I said, looking up to the ceiling. "Um, I'm sorry and I would try to lessen the blow by taking you out for a drink but . . . I'm soaking in it." I looked back at him, hoping the joke had landed.

He shook his head. "I'm kind of at a loss here."

Something suddenly occurred to me. "Why? Are you still in love with her?"

"No!" His answer was fast and strong. "I don't know that I ever was. But I'm still in that earlier part of the story with her and obviously you know it. What would you hope to get from me?"

"Nothing! I swear it! I'm just trying to piece her childhood together." I stopped. This wasn't right. This wasn't the way I wanted a relationship to go—me begging and pleading that being myself was okay only under certain circumstances.

I didn't owe Trey, or anyone, an explanation for my decision to take a job. And I didn't owe him an explanation for my doing that job. Whether he believed it or not, I hadn't been using him. I hadn't gotten information from him or even tried to. In fact, the reason he was so shocked by finding out that I was writing Mardie's book was that I hadn't asked him for one whit of information about it.

"I'm sorry," I said. "I was going to tell you at some point, if only because of the coincidence, but things went so fast that I didn't get the chance. You're barely even a celebrity to me."

He raised an eyebrow.

"Okay, obviously you are, but not to me. I honestly haven't even really made sense of the fact that you're the guy who"—I shrugged—"sang all those songs about Skype sex when I was eleven."

"That wasn't me."

"Whatever. You know"—I couldn't believe what I was

about to say—"I think it's probably best if you go. I don't see us seeing eye to eye on this."

"Wait." He looked genuinely confused. "What?"

But the feeling was growing stronger. An exhaustion of some sort. I was weary of conflict. Sick to death of apologizing. "Yeah, maybe I should have told you about this sooner, but Mardie wasn't really in the forefront of my mind. If that adds up to a problem for you, I'm sorry, but I can assure you that I'm not taking anything you said to me privately and using it. In retrospect it sounds stupid, but I haven't really been associating the two of you."

"I'm glad to hear that."

I shrugged. I liked him so much but how could we have a relationship at all if it started off on the wrong foot like this? "It's the truth, but I don't think it exactly clears the way for us. You don't trust me. I see why, but that's just not a hurdle I know how to get over."

"I didn't say that I don't trust you. But this was a surprise."

"I know. I get it." I looked at him and couldn't believe the words I had to say. "Honestly, Trey, this isn't going to work. We've known each other five minutes and we're already butting heads."

He was quiet for a moment, looking at me. "It seems pointless to argue this with you. I'm not going to beg you when you seem to have made up your mind."

Answering felt like an out-of-body experience. I couldn't believe I was saying this. But I didn't know how to stop. "I'm really sorry."

He gave a slow nod and turned to go. As I watched him, I ached to stop him, but why? To what end? What could we build on this foundation?

I stood there, watching nothing after he closed the door.

My phone buzzed on the desk. I glanced at the clock. It was late for any call. I went to the desk and looked on the phone.

It was Frances.

Not now. She'd tell me I was crazy and I already knew it. I pushed Decline and then saw on the home screen there were four calls from my mother and this one from Frances.

Something was wrong. I hit the button to return the call to Frances.

"Dad's had a massive heart attack," she said when she answered. "We have to go home right away."

Chapter Twenty-Three

Frances

*D*on't cry," Crosby whispered in a voice that wasn't quite her own. Fear had a solid grip on both our throats. Suddenly our argument was behind us, at least for the moment. "They'll kick you off the plane."

I glanced at her through tear-blurred eyes. "They don't kick you off the plane for *crying*."

She shook her head. "Google it."

"I'm not *Googling* it." I sniffed and tried to compose myself, then took out my phone and looked it up. Sure enough, there was a story of someone crying on the way to a funeral and being kicked off a flight for "upsetting the other passengers."

"See?"

"I didn't look that up."

"Yes, you did, I saw you."

"No, I didn't."

"Let's see your search history."

I held my phone away from her. "No!" Passengers glanced in our direction and I made a show of turning it into a laugh. "Don't be ridiculous," I added, a bit weakly.

"Do you have some sort of weird porn search there or something?"

"Obviously not."

Crosby nodded to herself. "Besides, he's going to be fine. Don't send all that fear out into the universe; that's just going to make everything worse."

"Are you saying *I'm* responsible for his health now by *worrying* about it?" I was all too ready to believe that. Part of me had been accusing myself of that already.

"No, I'm saying you're not doing him any favors by worrying about it."

Obviously we had much more immediate things to talk about—or a reason to not talk at all—but I think we both felt like we were just trying to stay afloat by being who we always were. There was no room to have an emotional heart-to-heart about anything other than Dad.

The plane began to taxi to the runway. I vigilantly moved my seat the quarter inch from reclined to straight up and down. I could argue this with Crosby but at the bottom of it all, it was true, worrying never helped anything. And if I showed up at Dad's bedside exuding worry and fear, it was only going to make him feel worse. I took a deep breath, held it for a moment, then let it out slowly.

Crosby dug in her purse and took out a small bottle of Finesse hair spray. She unscrewed the top and handed it to me. "Quick. Drink this. It will make you feel better."

"Hair spray?"

"It's *vodka*," Crosby rasped hurriedly. "Just down it before the flight attendant sees and thinks something weird's going on."

"Why is it in a Finesse bottle? Where did you even find that? I haven't seen that stuff for decades."

"Is that the point right now? Really?"

"You can use regular three-point-four-ounce travel bottles, you know."

"Yeah, well, they're a little more conspicuous, aren't they?"

"Right. Nothing conspicuous about drinking hair spray."

"Oh my God, fuck it." Crosby threw the liquid back, swallowed, then screwed the top on and put the bottle back in her purse.

"Hey, I didn't say no."

"You said a lot of stuff that wasn't 'Thank you, Crosby, I really appreciate you having my back like this even though I one hundred percent don't deserve it.'"

I wished I'd just said nothing and taken it. I envied Crosby the burning esophagus I knew she had right now. Neither of us usually drank anything stronger than wine, but three ounces of wine wasn't as strong as three ounces of vodka. In a couple of minutes, that burn would mellow into a tiny measure of relief.

My need for relief increased rapidly as the plane made its

final turn and started hurtling down the runway. I was not a fan of flying, though I'd gotten used to it, but somewhere along my phobia journey some asshole had pointed out that takeoff and landing were the most dangerous parts and I never forgot it.

"Fear and excitement feel almost exactly the same," my father had told me once in response to this fear. We were getting on a plane to London, where my dad was making a TV appearance on a talk show; I was going with him because I was fifteen and eager to trace the footsteps of the late Princess Diana, my idol, even though it meant an eight-hour flight over a dark, churning ocean.

As the plane taxied, I'd grasped my father's hand tightly, and he'd spoken in a calm, soothing voice. "Reframe what you're feeling as a thrill. You're going to England! Birthplace of the Beatles! Land of queens and kings. Your old man is going to be on Jonathan Dimbleby's show. Afterward you can have mushy peas—all the mushy peas you want! And a rib roast so huge it would embarrass Fred Flintstone!"

That had made me laugh. Before I knew it, we were in the sky, minutes, I supposed, from soaring over the vast Atlantic Ocean to Europe. Crosby had made noise about the route going north first, but back in those days there was no map on the back of the seat in front of you, and I could imagine anything I wanted, including (but not limited to) flying over the tragically romantic wreckage of the *Titanic* in the deep.

Now, however, we were just coasting over the uneven pavement of the runway at LAX, getting ready to fly over a whole bunch of states I'd rather skip entirely in order to arrive in a city I'd long thought of as the past.

The plane increased its speed and I closed my eyes and tried to breathe deeply. My heart pounded, and when I exhaled my breath wavered as if I'd been crying.

I felt Crosby reach for my hand and I grabbed on. We rested our joined fingers on my thigh and I kept my eyes closed and concentrated on breathing while the fuselage—I thought of it the way I was sure the news would report it later, the *fuselage*—rattled and cracked and all but split open on the uneven runway.

"I'm Daddy's favorite," Crosby whispered next to my ear.

My eyes snapped open. This again. "Oh, bullshit, you are *not*."

"I got the cool name."

"No, I'm the one he named for his idol. You got the leftover name because Grammy loved Bing Crosby and, no offense, but he was a wife-beater."

Crosby was unshaken. "That is not true, no one even alleged that, you've got your accusations wrong. And it doesn't matter because we're talking about Dad. He told me I was his favorite."

"He would never say that!"

Crosby made a show of shrugging, then leaned back in her seat, a small smile playing at her mouth. "Whatever. Believe what you want."

"If anything, you're *Mom's* favorite."

Crosby gave a laugh. "That's true too. She told me she thinks you're annoying."

My irritation grew. Why was she doing this now, of all times? "Oh, come off it, she doesn't even use that word." I looked at Crosby's amused visage and then glanced out the window next to her. "Oh, I see what you did. You were trying to distract me so I wouldn't notice we were taking off." It wasn't even clever, and she knew it.

"You're welcome."

Totally true—I would always rise to a competition with her. I gave her hand a grateful squeeze and then let go. "Thank you."

Crosby shrugged. "I just didn't want to listen to you dithering about it. I'm scared too."

"Of flying? Since when?"

"No, not of flying." She turned her gaze to me and the emotion in her eyes was like a punch in the gut. Here we were, bickering childishly about who was the favorite—as if our parents would ever declare or even *feel* such a thing— when the real issue was that this rock, this *Gibraltar*, in our lives was under threat. I was such a jerk for not seeing how she was suffering.

Somehow it was easier to take on a petty argument that had no ultimate meaning than it was to face the cold, icy reality that our parents were mortal. And in danger.

"I know," I said softly, looking for wise words but coming up short. "Of course I know."

"I'm really terrified."

I nodded and we sat in silence for a good long time before she spoke up out of the blue.

"You know why I love TJ Maxx so much?"

It was so conversational I wondered if she was talking to someone else, but there was only me. "Why?"

"Because it's designed to sell me a beautiful story about life, season after season. Summer? Try these sandals, they'll look great with this beach cover-up on your picnic date in Malibu where you'll make salad dressing with this fabulous rosé vinegar. Fall? How do you like these candles that smell like burning leaves? Won't you love having pumpkin beers on a crisp, cool evening and smelling these?"

I could picture it perfectly. "I bought some painted aluminum French fry tins there once, thinking they'd be perfect at a cookout. And I could call it a business expense but I never needed two thin metal cones with the word *fries* painted on them for Jill." I don't think I'd even imagined I would use them for Jill; I think somehow I'd fantasized that I'd have that cookout myself, but why? It would have been totally unprecedented.

"I think I saw those."

"With the little boardwalk scene?" Even saying it, I realized I'd buy them again right now.

"Yup."

We were silent for a moment, then I said, "That's what I like about the grocery store. It's always in the same mood, no matter what. Especially the florist corner and the soap aisle. Ever since we used to go to Giant with Mom and beg for Pop-Tarts, the grocery store has seemed like a place of simple, consistent pleasures for me."

"I can see that."

"I've had a box of Irish Spring soap in my bathroom for years, and every now and then I just sniff it for aromatherapy." I could conjure the scent in my imagination perfectly, even though I don't think I could pick notes out or describe it. "It smells like taking a shower in the locker room at the pool in the evening." Just thinking about it, I could feel the concrete floor of the neighborhood pool house under my feet and smell the mingled scents of soap, water coming out of old metal fixtures, and a little hint of the woods outside open doors.

"For me, it's Pantene shampoo."

We both laughed a little then drifted into silence for a while. I guessed that Crosby's thoughts from then weren't unlike mine—our dad picking us up from the community pool in his old 1982 BMW 320i ("Why replace it? It still runs great!"). Summer nights with Mom's vegetable salad— veggies cut into tiny dice and tossed with tangy, mustardy mayonnaise with a kiss of horseradish—and Dad's special hamburgers, with tiny diced sweet onions inside, cooked on the grill out back. What elevated them was the mix of meats and the way he "gently tossed the meat together, never packed it," though I now had a strong suspicion that it was the on- ion soup mix and tarragon he folded in and the Velveeta he topped them with that made them really special. Especially for kids—kids love cheese and nothing tastes cheesier than Velveeta or American cheese.

As if touching a bruise to see if it still hurt, I let my thoughts drift back to childhood, wondering what it was going to be like to return to the East Coast for the first time in years during the cooldown of fall into winter. Ever since I moved, our parents enjoyed coming to California to see me and visit their old friends and haunts in Laurel Canyon, which always made for an adventure in my own new hometown. It was fun to piece together old memories of people and places by seeing them with my parents in a modern setting.

The house that songwriter Rachel DeKeyser owned on Lookout Mountain, for example. As a child, I'd loved visiting it and watching the lights pop on in the distance at sunset. At the time, it had been a happy place to visit and play with the other musicians' kids in the backyard while the parents picked and plucked and harmonized by the pool. Songs that were synthesized walls of sound in the '80s and '90s sounded so pretty played acoustically outside at dusk.

It was a nice soundtrack as we'd run through the grass, spraying each other with the coppery-scented hose, tumbling down the hill and lying on our backs watching the clouds form shapes overhead.

"It's Mickey Mouse!"

"I see an elephant!"

"There's a flower with a long, long stem . . ."

What a life Crosby and I had had, and we hadn't even realized it. Kids didn't live like that anymore. They were all on their devices, holed up in their houses, not tumbling in the grass under the wide-open sky.

We'd had that, though.

We were so lucky.

That wasn't being snuffed out now; it couldn't be. Our father was on the mend—not only had Mom said so, but I could hear it in the relief in her voice. Crosby and I weren't going east for goodbyes, we were going for long-overdue hugs and encouragement and reassurances that he was important to all of us.

There were going to have to be lifestyle changes, Mom had pointed out. And of course he'd be resistant to that. Every-one was resistant to that. But I was coming to re-create some of his favorite dishes in healthier versions. Not that Mom couldn't do that too, she absolutely could. But her vegetar-ian cookbooks had been focused on cutting meat out of the diet, not being heart-healthy. That didn't matter, though—as a cook she was very savvy and would be even more clever at creating new favorites for him than I was. But she was dis-tracted, so if I could get things started, that was great.

And Crosby—well, no one would have said it, but Crosby *was* kind of his favorite. Certainly she was the most bold and obnoxious with him, so if anyone needed to bully him into exercising and sticking around for the rest of us, well, Crosby was the one to do it. And I had a feeling that might just be necessary.

I touched the screen on the seat in front of me to see where we were. Over Texas. There was still a long way to go.

But as long as we were in the air, here in Schrödinger's airplane, there was no news, and no news was good news. My phone wasn't going to ring. Nothing was going to go wrong. At least until we landed, everything was guaranteed to be all right.

Knowing that, I closed my eyes and drifted off into a light but troubled sleep.

Chapter Twenty-Four

Crosby

I forgot the sleep tincture I'd gotten in LA was weed oil and contained THC until we were at the stalled luggage carousel and they had a German shepherd sniffing its way through the bags.

Is this how it was going to go down? With everything that had gone wrong in my life, was the crescendo that I was going to be arrested for transporting Knock Out Dropz across state lines?

"Isn't that your bag?"

I jumped when Frances spoke. "What? No. Yes." The dog was sniffing around my black plaid suitcase.

I felt her turn to look at me. "What's wrong?"

"Nothing." I bit my lower lip. "Ugh, okay, I have weed in there," I whispered.

She blinked. "You have what?"

"Weed."

She shook her head in a way I'd seen before, that gesture that said she *had* to be misunderstanding me, even when we all knew she hadn't. "What are you talking about? You don't smoke."

"The sleep drops."

"Oooh." Then realization came into her eyes. "*Why?* You can't take those out of California. That's illegal."

"*I know.* But I wasn't thinking about that when I was packing. It was just like packing toothpaste or something."

We stood together, tension arcing between us, and watched as the dog hesitated at the handle.

"Oh my God, this is how it ends." I groaned. "*This* is my riches-to-rags finale. Mom and Dad do *not* need this right now."

"Calm down," she rasped. "He might be stopping there for another reason and you're acting like Pablo Escobar with a bag full of powder."

"For what other reason? My fine taste in clothing? Crest toothpaste? The Conquer Blonde shampoo that probably exploded when the air pressure changed and spilled dark purple toner all over my stuff?" I didn't have any patience for her trying to gloss over what was obviously imminent doom.

"You also have soup bones in there," Frances said. "That's more likely what he's sniffing."

"What? No, I don't. Why would I have soup bones in my suitcase?"

At least she had the grace to look a little ashamed before saying, "I packed them for Roger."

Roger is our parents' sweet golden retriever / pit bull mix. They rescued him when his previous owner left him tied on a short leash to an air hose at a gas station off I-95 in Georgia, where they'd stopped on their way to Florida a few years ago. "You put soup bones in my suitcase with illegal drugs?" I whispered harshly. "What is *wrong* with you? Why would you do that?"

"Well, for one thing, I didn't know you had illegal drugs in there, so don't act like *I'm* the idiot here."

"You are! What a gross thing to stick in someone's luggage! At *best*, that's going to make my clothes stink."

She rolled her eyes. That was something else I'd seen her do a lot. I'm not a violent person but it made me want to slap her. "Oh, come off it, you and I both know you brought dirty laundry and the first thing you're going to do is put it in Mom's washer."

"It's dirty *now*." But she was right; I hated going to the laundromat.

The dog moved on and the carousel resumed its movement and I breathed for what must have been the first time in ten minutes. People rushed forward to claim their things. I got the suitcase and examined it for visible signs of grease around the zippered edge.

"I packed it in multiple Ziplocs," Frances commented, as if reading my mind. "I'm a professional, you know."

"Do *not* try and act like this isn't fucked up." I shook my head. "It's not like dog bones are expensive. Totally not worth transporting."

"Not true—he's going to love them. They were simmered in a rich broth with tarragon and rosemary and just a kiss of butter."

"Of course he's going to love them, he's a dog. He'd happily lick that *kiss of butter* off the bottom of a shoe."

She retrieved her bag, and we walked together toward the parking garage, following the signs for the shuttles to car-rental companies. I'd rented a car for us, and like a fool, I'd taken the discount that came with letting them pick the car instead of checking the weather and knowing we'd need something snow-worthy. That usually ended up meaning a tiny two-door economy car. It was thirty-three degrees out with a chance of snow, so I was hoping I'd be able to talk the rental clerk into giving us something with four-wheel drive without too much of a price hike.

"You don't have to criticize me for having a kind impulse toward the dog," she said to me, then lowered her voice. "*Especially* not when you're the one who just transported an illegal substance across the country."

"It's *legal* here!"

"With a medical card! And it's *never* legal to transport it like that. And stop throwing this back in my face, you know you're the one who's wrong."

"This is so typical of you."

She didn't answer and we spent the next twenty minutes in silence, riding over bumpy roads in a miserable little van that might as well have been a pogo stick out of the airport to the car-rental lot, far into the gray landscape of upstate New York.

When the van finally arrived at the satellite lot, Frances looked and said, "How much of a discount did you get for picking the company closest to Canada?"

"At least I thought of renting a car," I countered. "You would have just had Mom come pick us up."

"That's not true, but I would have—" She threw her hands up. "I'm sorry. I'm glad you rented a car, I honestly didn't think of it. It's just been a long day. As you know."

"I know."

It was about to get longer. Twenty minutes later, we were presented with our rental, a two-door ragtop convertible. Apparently, all of the all-wheel-drive and even all of the front-wheel-drive economy vehicles were spoken for.

"Oh, this is crazy, they can't give us this car," Frances said. "It's going to *snow* tonight."

"It was a mix-up," I said, "give them a break. It's not a big deal. If we need more than one car, Mom and Dad have two."

"True, but they took good money for this and it's wildly inappropriate. Did you book a Jeep or what?"

"Um," I hedged. "I *did* click Manager's Choice, so I guess I took the chance."

She shook her head. "This is completely unacceptable. I'm going to talk to someone and have them search through the reservation history—"

"*Please*, they don't need to do a forensic analysis of the reservation, Francy Drew, give it up. Let's just go. You're trying to avoid facing our reality, but that's not going to make it go away. Just shut up and get in the car."

She took a deep breath and nodded. "Fine. But only because we don't have time to argue."

"Agreed."

She got in the passenger seat and I got in the driver's and punched my parents' address into the GPS on my phone to help us find our way out of this labyrinth three miles (apparently, though it really felt longer) outside the airport.

By the time we were well on our way, it was ten thirty and the traffic was about as light as it would get for the day. Which is to say it was considerably better than it ever was in LA. It was moving, for example. Traffic rarely did that around LA.

I hadn't been gone from this area very long, but it felt foreign already. I knew the roads and yet I felt like I didn't belong anymore. It was a place I'd known so well once, and now the familiarity itself was alienating. Like when you visit your elementary school as an adult and the bathroom stalls are much smaller and lower than you ever realized. And the trees outside are bigger.

All along the drive, I had pangs of remembrance. Of taking this turn to a little pub where my dad used to sing occasionally. Taking that turn to the mall, which was barely a mall at all by city standards. I had a lot of weekend dates along the shore of Cayuga Lake in the autumns of my teenage years. For picnics, coolers of sandwiches from Wagshaw's Deli, frozen candy bars, and smuggled beers.

And finally the turn that put us on the two-lane road that loped over gentle hills to the house where so many of my childhood memories took place.

We could hear Mom yelling inside before the door was even open all the way. "No! Alexa! Stop! Alexa, cancel timer for sixteen hours!" A muffled response and exasperation from Mom. "Alexa, set timer for *six minutes*."

Another voice, this one electronic. "Okay, here's what I found on the web for syphilis."

We rounded the corner just in time to hear our mother tell her electronic assistant to fuck off.

"Oh, I *hate* Alexis," I grumbled.

"I know what the problem is," Frances said, putting her bags down and hurrying into the kitchen.

Hearing her voice, old Roger scrambled up from where he'd been lying in front of the refrigerator and came over to us with a big smile and a wagging tail. His face seemed more sugared with gray than the last time I'd seen him, but surely not—that had only been a couple of months ago. It felt like time had passed so quickly here while I was away.

It was Roger's movement that got her attention. "You're here!" Our mother's face lit up and she held her arms out to us. Right away we were all crying and hugging and I felt like a child again, afraid to let go. At this moment, everything was still okay. If we stopped, if anyone said anything, that might change. I held on tight.

We might have stood there for two minutes or ten, but by the time we let go we were all tear-streaked messes and yet I felt better than I had since we'd gotten on the plane.

Frances sniffled and swiped the back of her hand across her eyes. "The problem with having one of those things in the kitchen is—"

"—the government is listening to everything you say," I finished, anticipating the usual argument.

Mom laughed. "You sound like your father."

"He's probably right," Frances said.

"People like to say that, but the real problem is she doesn't understand anything, and as time goes on she just gets stupider. Or maybe her speaker gets blocked up in the kitchen. Anyway, mine doesn't speak the same language as me."

Roger wagged his tail crazily, like he was in on the joke, and I remembered the bones in my suitcase. Frances might have packed them but I got to be the hero who gave them to him, I thought with a laugh. Who didn't love giving a dog a treat? "Come here, I've got something for you, bud." I went to my suitcase and he followed along with blind faith that I'd summoned him for a reason. Sure enough, there was a matryoshka-esque collection of Ziploc bags inside one another, tops all facing different ways, with two large bones in the center. She was right, I had to admit it, there was no way any juice was leaking out of that. I handed him one of the bones and he ran off with it immediately, as if I might change my mind and try to take it back.

Meanwhile, Frances was saying, "The *problem* is I think

cooking near one puts a film on it and it can't hear so well after a while. I have the same issue."

"So Alexa isn't gaslighting me?"

The device lit up. "According to Wikipedia, the National Aeronautics and Space Administration is—"

"Alexa, stop!" Mom said automatically. Then she looked at us. "She's definitely driving me crazy. Funny thing is, Dad has no trouble with her. He's always playing *Jeopardy!* or *Name That Tune* or whatever and the thing operates perfectly for him." She shook her head. "Imagine being so charming that even inanimate things fall in line for you."

"It's a curse." I put the other bone in the fridge. "What's cooking? It smells great."

"Oh! It's probably ready." She went to the oven, opened it, pulled out her old mint-green Pyrex casserole dish, and set it on the island before us. "Macaroni and cheese with San Marzano pesto."

"Oh my God," I breathed. I could smell every individual note, or thought I could, as always with Mom's cooking. I couldn't cook but I could eat. She had a way of taking good, simple ingredients and making them into a symphony. To be honest, Frances had gotten that from her. I could doctor some Campbell's soup fairly well, and I had a résumé of three decent chip dips, but other than that, I was an order-out girl. These two were geniuses.

Frances asked for the details of the recipe and got them while I sat like a begging dog waiting as Mom scooped some into a bowl and slid it over in front of me. The buttery cracker top still sizzled from the oven and I could taste the creamy cheese before I even got it in my mouth. She'd topped it with a fragrant garlicky tomato condiment. It couldn't have been more comforting and warm if it had been an actual angel wrapping me in a fluffy soft blanket.

I didn't realize how hungry I was until I started eating, and I zoned out while Frances and Mom talked until they got to the part we'd all been avoiding. About Dad.

"It was a major cardiac event," Mom said, then gave a short, humorless laugh. "That's what they call a massive heart attack these days. I think it's meant to sound less doomed, but at this point every medical term they throw at me lands like a dart."

"When are the visiting hours?" I asked. "I want to see him as soon as possible.

"He's in the ICU," Mom said. "They don't limit the hours. We can go as soon as you've gotten some nourishment in your bodies." She clicked her tongue and looked us over. "You both look way too skinny."

I wasn't sure about that, but I'd been feeling pretty solid lately and Frances was definitely looking healthy, so I knew my mother wasn't to be believed about that. Frances, though, looked pleased with the comment so I withheld my input. This wasn't the time for teasing.

After two helpings of lunch, we cleaned up and went through the laundry room to the garage, where Mom's reliable Toyota Highlander sat, as it had for at least a decade, next to Dad's impractical 1965 Ford Mustang convertible.

Had fate given us that rented convertible to honor him in some small, idiotic, and ultimately impractical way?

We chatted nonstop on the way to the hospital, but I couldn't tell you what we talked about. I think all three of us were aware that silence would be much too loud, so we sliced through it with talk of traffic in the area, why we'd never had cats (Mom is very allergic), old friends who used to live in a neighborhood we passed, a restaurant we loved on Old Benefort Road, not far from the hospital, and, once we got to the hospital, what a wild pain it was to park there these days.

When we started walking in, though, the atmosphere got too tight to speak. I searched frantically to find something to fill the silence but came up empty and I suspect they were feeling the same way. It took every bit of concentration to put one foot in front of the other to get to the antiseptic chamber where the larger-than-life man who had hosted our greatest happinesses and dried our most desperate tears lay on a thin, bent hospital mattress, looking as if he were caught in a spider's web of tubes and wires. The obligatory heart monitor—something I associated more with soap-opera scenes than real life—beeped next to him.

We shuffled in slowly and stood by his bed, three fallen angels looking over him, powerless to help.

A sob escaped Frances, and Dad's eyes flew open, startling all of us. It was akin to a corpse sitting up in a coffin. Suddenly what had been a somber and silent room was filled, first with adrenaline-fueled gasps, then with laughter.

"This is a bed, not a casket," Dad said, reaching his hand

out to his elder daughter. "No need for tears. Come on, girls, you're making me feel old."

"Don't say that," Mom warned. "I'm a year older than you are, Sparky."

"Shhh . . ." He put a finger to his lips, and I noticed the gesture looked weak. "No one would know if you didn't say it!"

"How are you feeling, Daddy-o?" Frances asked, using the old nickname. She touched the side of his face. "I haven't seen you for such a long time. Too long."

"I miss my girl," he said, putting his hand on hers.

I was so ashamed of the jealousy I felt. Frances was and would always be the golden child.

Now she was gazing at Dad like a Renaissance painting of the Holy Mother looking down at a symbolic man-baby. "I miss you too. You and Mom." She turned to look at our mother, then back at him. "So much." Tears spilled over onto her cheeks. Honestly, I don't think I ever realized how emotional she was. But it touched my heart so much to see how tenderly she looked at him.

"In the old days, families all lived in one small house together, forever," Dad said with a small smile. A beat passed before he added, "Imagine what a hell that would be."

Everyone laughed, but Crosby and I laughed the loudest.

"In the old days, there was typically one bathroom," Mom said. "Hell indeed." She smiled at both of us. "We love you both so much but we always wanted you to spread your wings and follow your dreams." She heard herself and shook her head. "And every other cliché you can think of. But it's true."

"A hundred percent," Dad added. "The shame is that we haven't been out to visit you more. California is a nicer destination than the shivering East Coast. Especially around February or so."

"It's supposed to snow here tonight," I said, feeling the thrill I always did when snow was in the forecast. The first day of it was always great. Then it inevitably got packed down into dirty gray and black ice that lasted for what seemed like forever. "It might be a long winter. Every single spring I remember thinking April and May should be warmer here. They never are. *Never.* I have no idea where I got that idea."

"Oh, you know," Dad said. His voice was raspy and weak. Had he been intubated before we got here? "The past. It always seems so golden." He closed his eyes for just a moment longer than a blink, and Mom was suddenly on alert.

"Are you tired, hon?"

"Pretty bushed." He sighed, and when he did it seemed like he got smaller. He turned his head to look at the monitor and I noticed for the first time how much of his blond hair was now gray. Was that sudden or was it a change I hadn't noticed when I was nearby?

I glanced at Frances and I could swear she was thinking the same thing.

"Girls," Mom said. "I'm going to stay here. How about you come get me in the morning?"

"The hell you will," Dad said before either of us could answer. "You don't feel good when you don't get enough sleep, and you don't sleep good with me here. You spent last night in that damn chair and I felt guilty every time I woke up and saw you there. Your neck must be killing you."

She instinctively raised her hand to her shoulder and rubbed it. "It is a bit sore, but I'm going to sleep far worse at home."

"In that big bed without me snoring?"

"I can't sleep well without it these days."

He leveled his gaze at her. "You know that's not true. If you stay here *I'm* not going to be able to sleep well. You make the call."

"Well played, Dad." I laughed.

"Fine," Mom said after a moment. "You call me if you need anything. At *any* time. I'm going to be mad if I don't get at least one middle-of-the-night call, do you understand?"

"Are you asking for a booty call?" he asked, then winked at us.

"Gross," I said.

"Do you even know what means?" Frances asked him.

He simply raised an eyebrow.

Mom shut it down. "I love you so much," she said to him, bending down and putting her cheek to his before kissing him briefly on the lips. "You scared the hell out of me."

"Not all of it, I hope."

She gave a laugh. "No, not all of it."

The shift nurse picked that moment to come in for vitals,

so we said our goodbyes with promises to come back soon, and sooner than soon if he needed us.

I was the last one out the door and I stopped and looked back as the nurse checked his IV and made some notes. For the first time in my life, he seemed small. And for the first time in my memory, he was, most definitely, not in charge of what happened to him or any of us. And I couldn't help the feeling that we were all going to have to get used to that because now it was clear that he wouldn't—he couldn't—be here for us forever. I'm not saying death was necessarily upon him, only that this brush with it showed us all what we all already knew. There is only one endgame and everyone has to play it eventually.

And now we all knew we couldn't win.

In bed later that night, I read an old Baby-Sitters Club book of mine that I'd found on the shelf. I wished everything were as simple for grown-ups as those books had made the adolescent me think they'd be.

Chapter Twenty-Five

Crosby

I could not stop crying.

And I don't know why, because I was really positive my father would be all right. He'd survived *the big one* and now he was indomitable. I hoped. But just seeing him, having him see us, showed me how strong the life force in him was.

So it was a pretty big surprise when, a little before sunrise, my mother called on the house line, which was next to both Frances's and my beds, and roused us both, and said Dad had had another heart attack and that maybe we should head on over.

Right away.

Apparently she was already there. I'd suspected she might sneak back there after the rest of us—including Dad—were asleep. This is actually what I would have expected from either of them, the noble protest and then the inability to respect such a stupid request.

I could hear Frances in the room next to mine hurriedly getting dressed, and I knew she felt as frightened as I did. Things had to be really bad or Mom wouldn't have called at this hour. Much as she'd tried to sound calm and soothing, she hadn't fooled me. And from the sound of the frenzy next door, she hadn't fooled Frances either.

We emerged into the hall at the same time and just looked at each other wordlessly. We'd bickered on the way in, played nice in front of Mom and Dad, and would have bickered our way back west, but now we were all balanced on the head of a pin and didn't know what to do.

"Can you drive?" I asked her when we got to the hall table where the keys were kept in a huge glass bowl.

"Sure." She picked them up, a big key ring—obviously Dad's—with keys to everything on it. "His car is heavier than the rental," she said. "Probably better in the snow."

It wasn't ideal but we'd spent plenty of time in our lives maneuvering through the winters here, so she managed all right. Ice you couldn't mess with, four-wheel-drive or no, it would be insane even to try. But with snow, you just had to know which back roads had the best grip and to get to the county roads because they got salted and plowed the minute the flurries started coming down.

It seemed like it took forever to get to the hospital, but I think that was partly a function of what I was afraid was going on there. As on the plane, I had the illusion that time stood still in transit. The visual landscape just enhanced that idea. It was so strange how the snow made everything into black and white. There was no color to be seen on the road or trees before us and beside us. Only dark silhouettes of trees hunching toward the ground and the far expanse of gray sky overhead. Behind the clouds, there was a full moon, so the clouds were extra-bright with that spotlight behind them.

It looked fake.

I pushed the CD button on the radio, curious what Dad had last been listening to in here, and "Perfectly Good Guitar" by John Hiatt started playing halfway through. Much as I wanted to read significance into it, I couldn't come up with anything.

So I willed the second song to have the meaning I was looking for.

It has to be said that I really do believe this was a random CD of his and this was all probably a coincidence, but it was "Don't You Worry 'Bout a Thing" by Stevie Wonder. Which, arbitrary or not, was exactly what I needed to hear.

While I half-heartedly sang along, Frances said nothing, just kept her grip on the wheel and drove. It was, of course, something I'd seen for years—ever since she got her license at sixteen she'd always been very serious about road safety, but there was no denying that things were different now.

The parking lot felt like miles from the hospital, and the space we found was at the back. We got out of the car and walked away from it in silence apart from the light click of her hitting the lock button on the key fob.

The whole way in, I just wanted to turn and run away. Classic magical thinking for me. As long as I didn't hear bad news, there was no bad news.

Once we walked through the automatic doors and into the lobby, I started to feel the lump in my throat. Usually I'm not a person who hates hospitals. I volunteered in this very one when I was a teenager and I'd visited two friends here after they gave birth. This was not a place I had negative memories of.

Yet this time I found myself noticing everything and wondering if these were the motifs of future thoughts. Would these overly sterile white walls haunt me forever? Would the near-cartoonish oil painting of the patrons of this wing haunt my dreams?

The ghoulish thoughts repeated themselves until we got to the floor where Dad was and saw Mom, pale and small (oh, so impossibly small), in the chair next to his bed.

The machines next to him, which yesterday had been alive with spikes and beeps as they'd monitored his vital signs, were off. Completely off. Not even the obligatory blood pressure and heart rate LEDs were scrolling by.

And so I knew.

"Dad," Frances said, hurrying over to him, taking his hand. But she drew back instantly. In shock.

I stood there like a coward.

"He's gone," Mom said, then immediately started sobbing. "About fifteen minutes ago. I'm so sorry, girls. He tried to hang on but—" She dissolved into unbridled tears.

Frances moved closer to her and put her arms around her. "We're here and we love you. We'll stay as long as you want us to."

I tried to find something to say but I couldn't. I was frozen. Looking from a distance at my father on an electronic bed, with all the needles and tubes still hooked up, somehow made him look even more . . . gone. They'd left them there like that. I didn't understand it.

And so I went to him, past my mother and my sister, and started to pull the tubes out.

"Crosby! What the—what are you doing?" Frances's voice was sharp behind me.

"He's gone," I said. "He deserves the dignity of not having to be all wired up. Why did they leave him like this?" I glanced at my mom, but she looked down, no answer.

Because there was no answer.

They had a protocol in the ICU and they'd get to it all when they could. Admittedly, this was a time when the hospitals were tapped out. Anyway, I didn't care. I couldn't do him any harm at this point, so why not?

The sun was high in the sky when they finally came and took him away, forcing Mom to leave the scene. She would have stayed there as long as he was there, and while I understood it I knew she needed food and rest.

Outside, snow was falling, silent and thick and white like the sweetest sugar. As if nothing horrible, terrible, devastating had happened at all.

"I'll drive Mom," I said to Frances while she walked between us like a wordless child.

Frances nodded, snowflakes dotting her hair.

When we got to the Highlander and got in, Mom said, "Take a detour by the liquor store, please."

She hadn't worried about judgment and she didn't get it. "Gladly," Frances said.

* * *

WALKING INTO THE house and kicking the powdery weak clumps of snow off my shoes, I noted it was the first time I could remember that I had *not* felt warm and safe there. All I could feel was a hollow cavernous echo, and the wispy ghosts of a lifetime of memories all crowded around like gory wounds, daring me to look.

I knew how this worked. Grief was no stranger to me. The initial shock, horrid and electric, eventually faded to a new normal, and someday my head and heart wouldn't be completely consumed by his absence, but right now that was still unimaginable. Right now the relentless lack of him was more solid than any piece of furniture in the house.

As soon as we arrived, Mom excused herself to go up and take a shower and change her clothes. Get the hospital off her, she said, though I thought she needed to be alone. Frances and I set about putting together huevos rancheros (Fran) and margaritas (me), at Mom's request.

Cooking was never my thing but I was a pretty damn good mixologist. My margaritas were legendary. And strong. My hope was that we could get some nutrition into Mom via the huevos and that she'd be asleep by midafternoon. It had been a very tense few days for her—for all of us, but especially her—and the most healing thing she could do at the moment was sleep.

I wondered how long she would need to sleep to have a more comfortable distance from the huge sadness of today. Would ten years do it? Or would she only awaken to find her long love gone and have the shock of it hit her all over again?

How long did it take to tread, awake, through the hours, days, and weeks following a death until finally the memories brought smiles instead of tears?

I didn't know the answer, but more to the point, I couldn't have controlled it even if I did know the answer. There was nothing profound I could do to help my mother, or my sister, or even myself through this.

There was only the nebulous concept of time.

Frances and I worked in silence. I wasn't feeling the anger at her now, so it wasn't that our silence was stony. There was simply nothing to say. And everything to say. We were walking through the gates of hell, side by side, and it was a long slog through sadness before either one of us could reach the other side.

When Mom came down, she was wearing jeans and an old Jimmy Turner Band T-shirt.

"Whoa, that brings back memories," I said. We all used to have those T-shirts. They were unsold merchandise from a very early tour. Musicians with a single hit didn't tend to sell out stadiums.

She smiled faintly. "He'd get so embarrassed when I'd put this on. But I think he secretly liked it."

"Hey, I'd protest if you wore a shirt with my book on it, but I'd secretly be thrilled," I said. "Fran, too, if you, you know, wore a shirt with broccoli on it or something."

Frances shot me a look but I could see the smile she was trying to hold back. "Brunch is almost ready," she said. "Start pouring, Crosby."

"Please," Mom agreed.

I did, pouring the citrusy concoction into tall water glasses rimmed with my blend of sugar and salt.

We raised our glasses. Frances tried to say "To Daddy" but broke and we all lost it.

"How is this possible?" Frances asked after we'd all taken healthy gulps. "How does something like this happen, so fast, so unexpected? He was *way* too young for this. And too healthy." She shook her head. "I can't accept it. Can't wrap my brain around it."

"He didn't even want to go to the hospital," Mom said. "At first. He thought it was heartburn. But I just had a feeling it was more. And I think he did too because he didn't argue too strenuously when I insisted. You know how he normally feels about any kind of doctor's appointment. *Felt*," she amended, and looked down.

"Did he know you went back last night?" I asked. "Did you get to talk?"

She shook her head. "He arrested shortly after I got there. They thought they'd stabilized him, but they told me then that it wasn't looking good. They intubated him. I asked the doctor to tell me the truth, to tell me what he would do for his loved ones in this situation. He said that we were headed in a bad direction."

"You should have called us then," Frances said.

She took a deep, shuddering breath. "I'm sorry. But I knew it wasn't what he would have wanted. He wouldn't have wanted you to watch that and be haunted by it for the rest of your lives." The tears overtook her for a moment but she collected herself and added, "That is not the way he would want you to remember him."

We both knew what she meant. Despite the millions of other memories we had, the trauma of that would always find a way to attach itself to them as punctuation. Death was so cruel that way, carrying endless grief, presenting itself with every memory, like a stupid hat that doesn't go with the outfit.

No one ate much, though the eggs were delicious. I think we were all just trying to get enough in our bodies so that the alcohol would have something to land on besides an empty stomach. As the bottle got emptier and we got louder in our nostalgia, I could tell that Mom was getting tired. Finally we managed to talk her into going to bed, assuring her that we would let key people know what had happened so that she wouldn't have to relive it time and again.

When she'd gone upstairs, Frances and I moved to the family room and sit down on the sofa.

For the first time in hours, I picked up my phone and there it was. A little Newsbreak item, right on the home screen.

Jimmy Turner, One-Hit Wonder, '70s Ditty
"Happily Never After,"
Dead at 65

I didn't click to read the article. "It's on the news," I said to Frances. "Did it show up in yours?"

"What?"

"Dad's death." I turned my phone around and showed her. BREAKING NEWS, it said. It was hard to decide if that was good or bad.

"Oh God. No, I turned those alerts off years ago. How did they find out?"

"I'm sure Mom called Steve right after she called us." Steve Sullivan had been Dad's manager since the early '80s. He was the go-to for the press if they wanted any accurate information. She would have known that if this got out as a human-interest piece, there was the danger of the facts getting muddled.

"What do you think we should do? Should we put his things away or leave them out where he left them?"

"I don't know."

"Let's just clean the kitchen, put something easy to nibble in the slow cooker, and ask her when she wakes up. I don't want to sanitize the place of his recent existence."

"Good plan."

We went to the kitchen and set about doing the dishes and boxing the leftover food. We fell back into silence as we worked. No radio, no conversation. My sense was that we were both uncertain about how to feel about *anything*, much less the very real problems between us. There was no way to fit them into our shock and grief. So we just did what we could.

I was digging under the sink for steel wool to clean the stainless steel when suddenly it hit me. He was really gone. Dead. Forever. Yesterday he had been here and there was hope. Two days before that, he was going to live forever, everything was fine.

And now he was in some cold drawer in the basement of the hospital with a tag on his toe and no one there to watch over him.

The tears started and I couldn't stop them. I sank to the floor and leaned against the cabinet.

The sobs came from someplace deep inside of me. It was soul-scraping.

The heels of my shoes dragged over the tiles over the floor until I kicked them off. My elbows were on my knees, my forehead on my forearms, and I cried into the cavern created by my body. I smelled like chips and lime and tequila and salty tears. I became hot and my skin pulsed with my escalating heart rate.

I wiped my tears away like a child, impatiently swiping at my cheeks and sniffling indelicately, snot still running out of my nose.

Frances, who had come over and crouched next to me balancing on her heels, stood up. She found a dish towel, folded it, covered it in cool water from the sink, wrung it out, then came back to me, gathered my hair up, and placed the cloth at the base of my neck.

It felt incredibly soothing.

It was probably ten minutes before I could breathe and remember English well enough to speak.

Finally she said, "I know."

"Now part of me is gone," I told her. "And part of you and part of Mom. And all of Dad. Life just changed without *any* of our permissions and I don't know if I can roll with it."

"You don't have a choice."

"I know!" I was trying not to wake Mom. "I know, but it *just* happened. It feels like we should be able to do . . . I don't know, *something* really fast and reverse it. Or find out it's a big mistake or misunderstanding."

"I know."

We both cried.

Then finally Frances said, "You know what we have to do. We have to chop wood and carry water."

Chop wood and carry water. Dad always said that. Whenever anything got us down, that was the answer. To get back to basics, to do the most basic things we could. Since he did the wood-chopping and we didn't need to carry water, that meant mop the floor, scrub the bathroom sink, vacuum, cook, go for a walk, breathe. To do whatever we could use our energy for that didn't require diving into our minds.

Never had that advice been as important as it felt at that moment.

Chapter Twenty-Six

Frances

When we had finished all the cleaning we could possibly do, we moved to the living room and turned on the TV. The Hallmark channel was in the holiday season it trained all year for, and the cheerful romantic foibles of the characters on-screen were the perfect antidote to the reality of our current life.

Every once in a while, Mom came down and got a cup of tea or picked up a book, but I think she was checking on us even though she needed to save her energy for her own self-care. She'd look at the TV, give a small laugh, and inevitably say, "Oh, we watched that one."

The snow continued to fall outside, though it had tapered down to light flakes dancing on the cold breeze. It got darker and darker and finally I turned on the lamp on the table next to me and the whole room seemed to explode in light.

"How long have we been sitting here?" Crosby asked, blinking against the brightness.

"Hours. Days. I'm not sure."

She nodded. After a while she said, "Do you want to build a snowman?"

"What?" I looked at her.

She shrugged. "It doesn't have to be a snowman."

"Are you seriously *Frozen*-ing me right now?"

She sighed and stood up. "Okay, bye." She turned and walked toward the kitchen, and I thought I might have misunderstood the whole thing.

"Wait."

She stopped.

"I'm sorry, I didn't mean to—"

She gave a small shrug. "I was totally *Frozen*-ing you. But we could probably use a walk."

"No snowman?"

"I don't have the patience, do you?"

"Probably not." But being able to go out and walk around in the slow silence of snow and just breathe felt like the thing I wanted to do more than anything.

We hit up the front hall closet for the winter coats that had been there for eons and still fit. Ours, Mom's, Dad's, it didn't matter; there were always coats for everyone at the ready for times just like this.

Roger watched us with mild curiosity, the bone I'd brought him hanging pitifully out of his mouth. I took his leash from the side hook in the closet and asked if he wanted to go for a walk. Even though he looked ancient compared to the last time I'd seen him, he did the dance of excitement I knew so well from his early days, and I hooked the leash to his collar and we all three set out, down the lane toward the middle school, where the best sledding hill in the county was.

For a long while we just walked in the thick silence, our boots whispering muffled crunches in the night.

Then Crosby asked, "What happens to Mom now?"

I was struck by the fact that she was asking me. It seemed we were always competing over who was smarter or more mature but now she seemed like the little girl who'd once looked up to me and thought I was the wise one.

It was terrifying, really. I wasn't the wise one.

But I did know one thing. "That's not up to us. She won't want us butting in and acting like she's too frail or weak to make her own decisions. We're support staff now; we don't turn into the parents."

Crosby nodded. "It's hard to think of one of them without the other. Hard to think of half being whole."

"I know what you mean. But she is whole. And she's grieving a loss we only know one part of. Like looking at one facet of a diamond. They had so much that we weren't there for. If we try to insist she do anything we think is *best for her* we won't be respecting the fact that there's a whole other side of that moon."

Crosby looked surprised. "Nicely said."

"Thanks."

"I might have said there were a lot of other facets to the diamond, but moon works."

I nodded. "I see your point."

We walked without speaking for long stretches, up the hill to the edge of the field the junior high used for soccer, baseball, and field hockey back when that was the thing. There was a black asphalt walkway into the woods that bordered the field and led to the top of the sledding hill.

We started on the path. "Do you remember going for walks on this path when we were little?" Crosby asked. "And Dad said this was the way to the Big Bad Wolf's house?"

There had been initials and stuff carved into the asphalt when it was still wet and he'd said they were directions out of the woods. "Yes."

"Was that fucked up?"

"What? No!"

"Really, though." She didn't look so sure. "I mean, it's kind of scary. This path into the dark woods. I don't think he realized how sophisticated the concept was."

I smiled to myself, remembering. "I think he was just trying to think of fairy tales in the woods. Dad wasn't very good at making up stories. Great at songs, but not super-good at making up a sustained story. I don't know where you got it."

She looked at me and smiled. "You think I have it?"

"The evidence would suggest you do. You can't become a bestseller just for looking pretty."

She stopped. "You think I'm *pretty*?"

I stopped too. "No. So it's a good thing you can write."

She smiled and we started walking again. "People say we look alike, so . . ." She felt like she'd stolen a compliment, I could tell.

We kept going until we got to the top of the hill. It was late and all the sledding kids were gone, though you could see the tracks and the pushed snow that were evidence of a lot of activity there earlier. It was coming down fast enough again that the boot- and blade-made peaks were disappearing before our eyes. There was a softness to the air that felt so cozy, despite the bite of cold.

We sat down at the crest and looked over the school we'd gone to, then across its low roof, past streetlights and an empty road, to the houses beyond. It was still our neighborhood, and we'd had many friends in those houses once upon a time, though they'd all moved on now. Some parents remained, but far more had moved once their kids had gone. These were big houses for just one or two people.

When I was little, it had been my greatest hope to grow up and be just like my mother. To move into one of these farmhouses and have my own kids. To live the TV-commercial life with the freshest air blowing through the cleanest sheets in a home with the tastiest fried chicken and the cleanest tubs. Those women always looked so *happy*. And my mom was happy too—we'd come home to all kinds of cookies, muffins, soups, whatever her recipe testing led her to. We'd try everything and she would delight in our enjoyment of her cooking. I think that's what got me interested in cooking myself; I'd seen both sides of the food exchange and it was love no matter how you looked at it. Plus, some of my happiest moments had been in the kitchen cooking with her, learning from her.

Maybe equally happy were the moments I'd stolen as a child alone in her kitchen. When she was away, I'd take to the kitchen inventing my own dishes, with varying levels of success. There was the mistake of the root-beer cupcakes, sweet cake cut with lava slopes of pure root beer extract. That had been god-awful. Also, I don't know where my mother had gotten root-beer extract or what it might have been intended for, but I don't think it's available at Giant or Safeway anymore.

But there had also been the triumphant success of "French hamburger" from some obscure French cookbook I'd found on the shelves. It called for onion powder, which Mom would never have had, so I chopped up onions very fine, then added an egg because I liked them in my mom's meatballs. The burgers were light and tender, and when I took the wine Dad had left on the pantry shelf from his steak dinner with Mom the night before and followed the directions to make a butter red-wine sauce for them, it was bliss.

Until they got home and realized what I'd done with the last third of their three-hundred-dollar special-occasion wine they'd left to finish that night with some cheese after dinner while watching *Survivor*.

I sat on that hill in the snow with Crosby, still hearing a tiny echo of that suburban life that had called, so loudly, to me in my youth.

"I thought you'd marry Sam Dratch," she said to me, breaking the thick silence.

I remembered him, the boy from science class who made my heart skip a beat every time I saw him in the hall. A nice guy. Never tried to be too cool or badass, but at the time, to me, he might as well have been Justin Timberlake. I wondered what had happened to him. "You did?"

She smiled. "I think you adored him so painfully aggressively that a person couldn't be around you without feeling it too."

I laughed. "He never even noticed me."

"Too bad." She moved her feet, crunching the snow in front of her.

"I thought you might end up with Hans Sumner."

"*Hans Sumner*! He was the weirdest guy in school. He was into LARPing before it was a thing. I can't say *before it was cool* because *it was never cool*. Ugh. Why him?"

"Oh, I don't know." I shrugged. "He was imaginative."

"He was *costumed*. That's different." She shuddered. "He did try. He asked me out a few times, always to strange events with fringe people from school who kind of scared me. People who had chain mail and play swords. Weirdly enough, I preferred a knight who was not in *actual* shining armor."

"He's probably rich now."

"Super-rich." She sighed. "There is something sweet about thinking we'd all live happily ever after in this neighborhood near Mom and Dad. Forever, I guess. I sure didn't plan on ever losing anyone."

"That's always part of the plan. We just pretend it isn't. But I sure didn't think we'd lose him so soon."

"No. We should have had decades more. He was so huge in my esteem. But when we went today, he looked small and helpless, tied to that bed, tied down like Gulliver by the tubes and IVs."

She was right. Tears burned my eyes before I had a moment to even think. "I know." I covered my face with my hands, remembering. And knowing that I'd never forget him there, in that bed. "I missed so much time with him by moving and not coming back."

She nodded and a moment passed. "It's probably your fault he had the heart attack."

If anyone had been eavesdropping, they would have thought that was a monstrous thing to say, but I got it. I laughed. "Yeah."

"He wanted us to fly," she said after a moment. "He *wanted* us to follow our hearts wherever they led. You are the perfect illustration of *exactly* what he wanted for us. He wasn't trying to make you feel bad, he was telling you he loved you and he was glad for what you'd done."

"Oh." I smiled to myself. A faint memory came to me: Sitting next to Dad as he held little Crosby and sang to her, to us, about little birds spreading their wings and taking to the sky. "Do you remember him singing 'Summertime' to us?"

"'Summertime'?" She frowned and thought about it. "No."

It was crystallizing with greater and greater clarity in my mind. "He should have recorded it. I remember him dancing around the family room, whirling you up into the air, and singing it to you." I leaned back, the soft crunch of snow cushioning me. "That and 'Up in the air, Junior Bird girl.' I don't remember all the words to that but I remember how it *felt*. I could just see soaring into the blue sky, free and happy, not a care in the world."

"Mmm." She faced the distant clouds. "I'm positive that's what he'd want you to take away from that. I mean, don't we all want to soar off into the wild blue yonder? Isn't that the most beautiful illustration of the future there is?"

"I've always associated it more with death than with life," I said honestly. "But maybe it is about life."

"It is."

A few more minutes passed. The snow looked like it would never end.

"Do you remember when we used to go to that house in Laurel Canyon?" I asked.

"Yes!" She sat up. "It's so weird but I remember that *so* well. We haven't been since I was, what, like five? Six?"

"Seven," I said, and I had to smile. "We were at Percy Bay's house, which is where we always stayed when we went there, and it was my ninth birthday. Percy gave me Ringo."

"Ringo? That beanbag dog?"

I nodded. "Someone said it was also Ringo Starr's birthday so I named him Ringo, though I don't think I knew who that was at the time." And then he'd lived in my room for the next decade until I went to college. He was packed in a memory box now, somewhere.

"I don't remember that."

"You should, you were pretty irate that you weren't also getting birthday presents."

She nodded. "That tracks."

I closed my eyes and remembered the day. Usually when we were there, at least a couple of people had guitars and there would be singing on the air, along with lively conversation, laughter, and charcoal smoke under Mom's miso veggie kebabs. That day some of the luminaries of the music world were there, though I only realize that now, as an adult. I remembered them doing acoustic versions of songs I knew from the radio and thinking how much prettier they were stripped down to their elements.

"What is that?" Crosby asked.

"What?"

"That song. The song you were humming."

I hadn't realized I was. "Just an old song they used to sing there on the hill sometimes. I don't even know what it's called."

"I remember spinning around in circles and then trying to stop and stand up straight without tumbling down the hill. Was that there?"

I remembered it too. "Yes. There was a tiny steep incline and we'd dare ourselves to try and stand still at the top without falling."

"Yeah." She nodded slowly. "And we'd lie there on blankets, watching the clouds change shape. And the blackbirds flying overhead."

"That's right." It was a memory I sometimes used as my peaceful place during the meditation portion of my yoga class.

"And were there . . ." She sat up straighter. "Was there something called a Fuck You tree?" She frowned hard. "That can't be right, can it?"

Until that very moment, I hadn't remembered that. "Yes! Those trees that look like three fingers, the middle one sticking up. I mean, they really do look like they're flipping the bird." The memory came on so strong I couldn't believe it had been gone so long. "Holy cow, did they really make that joke in front of us?"

"What *are* those trees? I've seen them near your place."

"I think they're some kind of cypress. They're everywhere." I laughed. "I can't believe I didn't remember they called them that. But they really do look like they're giving you the finger."

"No wonder I felt so unwelcome at first."

"Well. You were *kind of* unwelcome at first. Kind of. Despite your famous Welcome Wagon." This wasn't easy for me to admit. "I was worried that if you came in, my whole life would fall apart. You'd win everything and I'd lose everything. And that was me," I hastened to add, "it wasn't your fault. It was me being insecure and scared."

"That's nuts. You were always first, older, smarter, better. I was the pale imitation."

"You're dating Trey Simons."

She gave a single laugh. "Kind of. I really wanted to tell Dad about that."

"He always told us not to date musicians."

"I know. I was looking forward to telling him that."

I closed my eyes for a moment, then turned to face her. "I'm really sorry I didn't give you Jill's message about writing for Fletcher Hall. As embarrassing as it is to admit, I was too—"

"Worried that I'd be in over my head and would look like a fool," she supplied. "And that would have been embarrassing for you. I get why you'd worry about that."

"No, I was going to say I was too afraid you'd outshine me. In fact, I could pretty easily envision a scenario where I didn't get so much as the role of Distant Cashier Number Four and you got to write whole episodes that didn't involve me. You'd go on to be the favorite party guest at Hollywood dos, and I'd end up wearing a hairnet and heaping mashed potatoes onto plates at a ten-dollar buffet somewhere on the outskirts of town."

"Are you joking?" she asked.

"No."

"Well, that's funny, because I saw you becoming the next big thing in some TV anthology while I lost everything to become a *failure* at writing the story of a famous person with a fascinating life and so I had to, instead, become a cashier at Sav Mor and quietly seethe at the signs that say *please don't lean on counter* with *please* in inappropriate quotation marks."

I had to laugh. I'd been to Sav Mor when I needed to stock up on canned goods whose brand didn't matter. I knew exactly what she meant. But it didn't change the fact that she had successfully outdone me more times than I could count. "As much as I enjoy that visual—and believe me, I do—there are way too many stories of you swooping into my school, my friend group, my life, my *whatever* and shining like a beacon while I became shadow outside of your glow."

"That's not true!"

"I know you believe it isn't. That's what's even harder. There was never any way to ask you to stop because you were just *being you*."

"I can't help that."

"I *know*. But it's like—" I paused, trying to think how to be succinct. "Okay, it's like when we were talking about the thing with Tyler What's-his-name. You got drunk and went off with him to the barn, he made a pass at you—which I believe, I'm not saying that's the issue—and the takeaway for you was that, because you were afraid if you told me I'd blame you, this became your torture."

She looked at me, silent.

"So then *I* end up thinking I did something wrong because it's always you just being you and me being told I'm not patient enough and—"

"Winchester."

"What?"

"That was his last name. Tyler Winchester."

"Right. Okay, well, that's not really the point, is it?"

"I think you've misunderstood something." Her voice was quiet. She wasn't looking at me.

"Oh, I'm sure I've misunderstood a lot. What is it this time?"

"Tyler didn't just *make a pass* at me." She met my eyes. "He *forced* himself on me. He raped me." She cleared her throat and said it again, stronger. "He raped me."

"I don't understand. You said he kissed you."

She nodded. "I did. But I was trying to protect you. Or me. Or something. But didn't you know?"

"No! Didn't I know? My God, I thought he kissed you and you kissed him right back, a teenage betrayal. Rape? Oh my God."

"I remember him trying to get closer and me trying to push him away, but I guess I, I don't know, I passed out? Because I *did* drink too much, that was stupid, that was on me. But when I came to, I was alone and in pain and . . . it was obvious what had happened."

"Oh, Crosby. He just . . . *violated* you and left you there?"

"Yeah, well—yes." She took a shuddering breath. "Yes. I guess you'd know more about that part of the timeline than I do." She shuddered visibly. "I hate going through this again. I never wanted to think about it ever again. Especially on a day like this."

"But I didn't know! I swear, I had no idea!"

"I do know that. I believe you."

The anguish was indescribable. "I thought he'd made a pass at you and that you . . ." I thought she'd let him; I thought he'd kissed her and she'd kissed him back and I'd carried that stupid little idea with so much resentment for so long. "I'm so sorry I blamed you for any part of this."

"That's the thing, right? Some part of it, at least, *was* my responsibility. Not what he did to me but the fact that I put myself in a position where I couldn't, or didn't, protect myself adequately. If I'd been sober, there is no way that sonofabitch would have been able to get away with that."

"*I* was sober," I said. "I shouldn't have watched you go to the barn with him and been all pissed off; I should have gone to find out what the fuck was going on."

"But given what you thought was going on, that you thought we were both betraying you, it would have been completely out of character for you to go get in the middle of it."

"I should have trusted you more."

"Yes, you should have. But the way we were with each other at that moment in time, I don't know if I would have reacted any differently than you did had the situation been reversed."

The cold around me felt like a blanket. I couldn't have felt more chilled if I were naked. "What a lot of time we've wasted," I said, really looking at her. "We had so many good times together. We are the only two people on earth who know what our lives were like, how we've lived, what wonderful parents we have. Had." The tears came again. "You're the only person on earth who could understand this exact loss and I pushed you away because I was afraid you'd steal my thunder."

"Your thunder can't be stolen, Frances," she said seriously. "Do you think I ever would have even joked about our relationship if I thought there was even a *remote* possibility that you weren't an absolutely *incredible* life force? You don't call a guy who's actually short *Shortie*."

"Wait, we both know a guy named Shortie."

"What are you *talking* about?"

"He was—" I remembered and started laughing. "Oh my God, I'm going to hell. He was on the basketball team, remember? He never got off the bench, I don't think, but he was the *nicest* guy."

"Oh no, that's right. I *do* remember. God, what a terrible example. Erase that. Seriously."

I shook my head, still laughing.

"Perfect case in point. Would I have said *that* if I thought it was actually true?"

"I'm honestly not sure."

"Let's go with no."

"All right." I sighed, and it puffed out of my mouth as a white cloud and rose into the air. It felt like the whole world was on mute. "I never meant to hurt you," I said.

"I believe you. And I never meant to hurt you. I worshipped you. I wanted to be your best friend."

I looked at her. "I think you are."

"That's sad." She broke into a smile. "You're mine too. It would be so great if we didn't hate each other so much of the time."

"Yeah." And I meant it. "Do you think we should head

back? In case Mom wakes up and needs us? Or worries that we're not there?"

"Sure." We got up and dusted ourselves off and started the trek home. It felt like it had gotten twenty degrees colder since we'd headed out. I wondered if that was our inactivity or just the way the world would be now, without Dad in it.

Chapter Twenty-Seven

Crosby

It would be impossible to forget the night my father died. I know for the rest of my life, I will remember it with the crystal clarity of the snow Frances and I sat in, finally telling our truths at a time when, maybe, we should have been celebrating his life.

Then again, wasn't telling our truths and breaking the barriers doing just that?

We were walking through the quiet darkness, past houses that used to be the homes of friends we'd play with. Mailboxes we'd put Christmas cards in on late-night runs with Mom. Street signs and landmarks that I couldn't help thinking my father had passed so many times but his eyes would never see again.

And someday the same would be true of me.

Of all of us.

One by one.

These morbid, sad thoughts were as easy for me to fall into as a pool of warm water, and I could swim in the misery indefinitely if I didn't force myself to stop. I had to think of the good times. The funny times. And all of the things that had been the stuff of our *lives*.

"We had an amazing upbringing if you think about it," I said. "We met so many cool people. Got to hear our father singing at pubs and fairs and festivals and then also at weird random times, in the grocery store, on the radio at work. We're still going to hear it at random times. That's going to be crazy. Comforting. I think."

"It played in a bar once when I was in college and making out with a total stranger," Frances said. "I felt like I was going to get in trouble. Like Dad was right behind me."

"Really? What did you do?"

"Turned and hightailed it out of there. I never saw the guy again."

"He must have thought you were insane."

"Right? And this other time it came on the radio when I was on a first date and before I could shout, *This is my dad!* the guy said, 'I hate this fucking song.'"

"Ha! Wow. That's a bad omen. For him."

She shrugged. "We never went out again. His choice, by the way. I could live with him hating *that fucking song* but he couldn't face the girl who said, *But it's my dad!* It ended up being a test of character."

"No offense, Fran, but you have dated some duds."

She feigned insult. "Wow. Easy for Trey Simons's girlfriend to say. Just *wow*."

"We're not seeing each other." My heart deflated at the thought of it. "Flash in the pan."

"Whoa, I'm sorry," she said. "I thought . . . well, it doesn't matter. I guess I was just expecting that things would go how they do for regular people, not stars."

"I guess he was too big a star for me."

"I didn't mean just him. You too."

"Oh." This was a surprise. "Well. No. Not for either of us. All of that is a world or two away."

But it wasn't. All of our friends were going to hear this as a news blip, a sad *where are they now*? So many of my friends now didn't know him; he was just a trivia question to them.

I thought about it. "Can I tell you something? I used to kind of feel like Dad had failed. It was cool the first time I told someone that was his song when it came on, like on a date or whatever, like you said. But he didn't have anything else out there that he performed so people tended to think he'd tried and failed."

"He didn't! He wrote so many hits for other people!"

"I *know*, but that's not what people understand. And now I'm a one-hit wonder, though not on the scale of Dad. And I've got nothing to back it up. I'm only *trying* to write the hits for someone else now. And I'm not doing a banner job of that either. But he managed to keep on doing what he loved without doing the mentally grueling part that he hated. He wrote his own playbook."

She nodded. "Because of that, we're the products of parents who wanted to be there for us all the time and who slipped their work in *around* raising their kids. We're the luckiest people in the world."

"We are." The cold was starting to seep through my coat and the snow turned into little ticks of ice hitting the ground. The wind raised against my cheek and I could *feel* it turning bright pink. "Has it always been this cold here?"

"Why do you think I moved to California?"

We neared the end of the sidewalk.

"You know," Frances went on, "to this day I feel a tingle down my neck that the Big Bad Wolf is behind me on this path."

I nodded. "Maybe Dad was a better storyteller than I give him credit for."

She made a noise of agreement and we kept walking. Several steps later, she said, "Maybe he told us that story so that someday we'd have this exact conversation."

"Maybe." A moment of silence. "But it was still a fucked-up story."

* * *

WHEN WE APPROACHED the house, the light was off in Mom's room. So many times I'd come over and seen that top left window lit up and I'd known they were up. I'd walk in and

Dad would be watching football or whatever seasonal sport was on and there would be delicious smells drifting out of the kitchen with Mom in there listening to her beloved history podcasts.

These were such simple things I'd taken for granted. Worrying about *my* life. Like they were just my permanent support system.

We got to the back door and entered the mudroom, pulled our boots and icy coats off, then stepped into the warmth inside. I half expected to see the usual scene of my parents but it was completely quiet.

Something deflated within me.

Would it have been better if I'd realized their vulnerability? I wondered. Would I have appreciated the normality more? Did I *need* to? While I could flog myself for my ignorance now, the truth was that I'd had the luxury of *not* worrying about them. For years. Not like Frances, who worried about everything all the time. And I'm not saying that as an insult; I know she hates it. But in some small way Dad's death had probably validated that part of her personality.

I went to her and just hugged her hard.

It took her a minute to return the hug. "Are you having a stroke?" she asked into my shoulder. Our old joke, used a thousand times.

"I don't know."

She tensed. "Should we . . . call a doctor?"

"No." I pulled back and held her upper arms and looked into her wide blue eyes. "We should just fucking get along."

She looked at me, then down, then let out a long breath and said, "I don't know what's wrong with my flawed character, but it is so fucking hard for me to say *I'm sorry* to you. Even that, right there, that was really hard."

Tears were burning in my eyes now. I bit my lower lip. "I thought I was the one who needed to apologize to you for the rest of my life."

"*You?* Why?"

"Because." I was full-on crying now. "I didn't realize how it felt for you to have me coming along behind you and threatening to embarrass you or even just horning in on your relationships with friends, with teachers. I see now how you didn't get to have a totally independent identity because I was coming up right behind you all the time, taking the spotlight or shooting a slingshot at yours."

"No." She gripped my shoulders. "It's not your fault. It's mine. I'm the worst sister in the world."

"No, you're not!"

"You've told me I was a hundred times!"

I felt my face grow warm. "Well, yes, okay, but that's just a thing I say."

A muscle tensed in her jaw. This was Frances feeling something fiercely. I'd seen it a million times in my life, usually before she told me what I'd done wrong.

Not this time.

"This ends now," she said. "It has to. For Dad. And, even more, for Mom. We have *got* to get ourselves together."

"You're right." I put my arms around her. "The past is over for me. I love you."

I felt her shrug. "Why?"

"I guess someone has to."

She sobbed.

Chapter Twenty-Eight

Frances

So we didn't end up building a snowman.

But I think we started to build a bridge.

Half an hour after we came in from the snow, we were sitting on the sofa, each with a glass of warm watery margarita in hand. My eyes were red and swollen and they hurt, as did my skin from all the salt water running over it, and Crosby was less red but looked worn out.

"So I want to thank you for what you said," she said carefully. "I am as bad at accepting apologies as you evidently are at giving them, so we can just leave it at that."

I gave a limp shrug. "That's probably my fault too."

She nodded. "Agreed. Second, I owe *you* an apology for not being more sympathetic to your losing your job with Jill in LA and your hope with Fletcher. Though I think you can't give up on acting. Look, I've recently learned what it's like to have the financial rug pulled out from under you and I don't honestly know how you do *anything* productive when you're worried about the power being turned off or the water being turned off or some thug coming to the door to change the locks—"

"Oh, I don't think that stuff really happens in real life."

"It happens," she said. "Believe me." She closed her eyes and took a deep breath. "But that's not the point. The point is that you can't give up on your dreams. You just can't."

"There comes a time when a person has to realize when things aren't going to work."

"Maybe. Maybe not. But it's not that time for you."

"The ship of opportunity has sailed. I'm old enough to be cast as the *mother* in movies now."

She blanched. "You're bad at math."

I threw up my hands. "Hollywood isn't fair." It wasn't. It was random and played favorites and paid back favors and bullied and sexually abused—yes, still—and it was a flat-out miracle to make it there without weird extenuating circumstances. "But I'm glad you've mentioned this because I have something way more important than work to bring up."

"Which one of us Mom will live with first?"

"Oh my God, no. You're out, she's in here. Are you kidding? Find yourself some new digs."

"We can argue about that later."

"Or you can accept it now. Because you know what? As much as it pains teenage me to say this, you have a huge relationship to pursue. And it doesn't involve having a full-time parent around."

She frowned. "You're not saying—"

"I am. Trey. And you know it, Crosby. For fuck's sake, to use your own verbiage, you two are ridiculously perfect together. And now that you're almost finished with the first draft, he can *see* there's nothing negative about him in there."

"True, but he didn't trust me to—"

"Do you *blame* him?" I could absolutely see his side. And I could see how little that would matter once he saw the manuscript and the two of them moved away from Mardie entirely.

She was silent for a long moment, thinking about it. "I can see why he was suspicious."

"Good. Make a humble pie and offer it to him while you say that. Meanwhile, we have our careers to figure out."

"Funny you should say that," Crosby started. "Because I had an idea that might save us both—"

"And you know what makes it the hardest? Not knowing what to do."

"I'm sorry?"

Her words registered. "Wait, what were you going to say?"

A bloom came into her cheeks. "I got an idea. It's just a seedling, really, but I have to do it. *We* have to do it."

I couldn't even imagine what our combined talents or experiences could add up to. "What is it?"

She beamed. "A one-woman show."

A familiar defense stacked up inside of me. I was here to be backup again. Which, fine, I deserved. "What woman?" I asked, knowing the answer.

"You!"

"And what are you—*me?*"

She nodded. "I mean, you'll be an amalgam of our experiences, a story of growing up with famous parents and fighting each other for third place in line. Of course, I'm no performer at all, so"—she shrugged—"you."

Hope nudged in me. "And you're going to write it?"

"I've already started. In the notes on my phone, but still. I haven't had this much energy for a project in . . . ever. I don't think I ever have."

"But . . ."

"But *what?*"

"I decided to stop the acting thing and take the job with Jill in Palm Springs. It's time for me to be realistic."

"*Realistic?* Did our father's life teach you *nothing?* You've got to follow your passion! What better tribute to him? Show the world that Jimmy Turner lived life to the fullest and raised people to do the same."

I gave a laugh. "That's so corny."

"Exactly the way he'd want it."

It was true. "I can't believe this," I said. "But I think it's a good idea. In fact, I think it might be a really good idea."

"It absolutely is. Think about what we've been though. The people we've met through Dad, through Mom. Remember when we met Julia Child and I thought she was doing a joke voice?"

I cringed, remembering. Back then I had no idea just what a luminary she was or how much I would give now to ask her just one question: Is there *really* a worthwhile use for eggplant?

"What about the time you asked Chris Martin if he'd seen Chris Martin at that party?"

"He looked so different in person!"

"Hey, if you hadn't done it, I might have."

"We've done a lot," I mused. "Seen a lot. Maybe this could work. I really think if anyone can write it and make it hilarious, it's you."

She raised her glass. "Here's hoping."

I raised mine and dinged it against hers.

"Speaking of following your passion," I said. "Have you come to your senses about Trey yet?"

Her expression darkened. "It's just about all I can think about. That's why I dove so hard into this project."

"You can do both, you know. Create art and be in love. Ask any poet who ever lived."

"We started out on such a bad foot."

"No," I said firmly. "You started out with a weird coincidence, that being you happened to be writing a book for his long-ago ex. If it was anyone else, someone who wasn't famous, you would see that it was just happenstance. But you're holding him to a higher standard because of his fame."

"I'm not holding *him* to a higher standard. *I* was the one who ruined everything."

"By not knowing how to tell him about Mardie? You would have gotten there. And it wouldn't have been a big deal. Instead, you broke things off to beat him to the punch.

It makes no sense to put yourself through pain in order to avoid maybe going through some pain. It's like"—I searched for an analogy—"cutting off your toe because you're afraid you might stub it."

"That's bad."

"I know, it was all I could come up with. My point is, how can you sit there and preach to me about following my passion if you're not willing to follow yours? Can you not see from our own past that it is an absolute bullshit waste of time to *assume* you know what someone else is thinking? *Especially* when it's based on what it *appears* you are doing? Come on. How long will it take for you to leave a little room for misunderstanding?"

"Wow." She looked stricken.

I wasn't concerned. "Yeah. Think about it."

"You're right."

"I know it. In this case, I am definitely, definitely right."

"I'm such an idiot."

"You're right too."

"I should call him."

It was impossible not to roll my eyes. "*Definitely* you should call him."

"And tell him what? That I'm going to be another LA free-lancer working at whatever I can, always looking for a better place to live?"

"No, tell him the truth. See what he says. I think you'll be surprised. So, actually, yes. Say all of that. Exactly."

"Okay . . ." She considered. "You know, I was planning on

going back to California anyway. If it's okay with you, that is. I don't want to horn in on your territory but it makes the most sense for us to work together and, you know . . ."

My first reaction was to be glad. But I didn't want to scare her by being too out of character. "I guess that could work."

"Don't worry, I'll pay my fair share of rent."

"Wait, you think you're moving in with *me*—"

"Oh, it'll be fun," she said. "You'll see. We'll watch movies and play games and do each other's hair and do all the things girls do at sleepovers, only we'll get to do it every single night!"

"How long are you thinking this is going to go on for?"

"Just until we get the project done and start making our millions. A year. Two. No more than that. Probably."

"Oh God."

"It'll be *fun*," she said, putting an arm around me. "Just wait and see. Mom's talking about coming out too. See how this all fits into the show? It's about all the millions of pieces that go into making a single life. How you never know what all the moving pieces are behind the story."

"Yeah." I nodded. "I like it."

"I've even got the perfect title."

"Tell me."

She smiled and it all came together. *"One-Hit Wonder."*

Acknowledgments

Thank you, Annelise Robey, for your always-brilliant brainstorming and editorial notes. Your patience astounds me, and I'm so lucky to have you as an agent but even more lucky to have you as a friend.

I also owe huge thanks to the whole team at William Morrow, including my dazzling editor, Lucia Macro. Also to Asanté Simons, Eliza Rosenberry, Amelia Wood, and the art and design team who make my books look so good! Thank you!

Many thanks to Paige and Jack Harbison for reading and brainstorming and gabbing on together late into the night. Not many people are lucky enough to have such great, smart, funny, helpful people in their lives, much less as their kids. I'm so proud of you both and so glad we get to spend so much time together, laughing and drinking cheap bubbly.

Much love to Adam Smiarowski, for way too many things to list. Your love, your kindness, your support, your thoughts, your humor . . . How lucky I am to have you.

Thanks to Mike Beall and the precious memory of George

Bennett for being our first guests when we got to our new home. And, actually, our only guests as we stayed there in quarantine. October 9 will always be special in my heart and mind for what should have been.

Isaac Babik, you entertain and inspire me so much; what a way you have with a story!

Finally, I want to give heartfelt thanks to Mark Hicks for giving us such a lovely landing spot in California when we up and moved across the country to start a new life. I have been grateful for your help in making a new home, and honored to feel the soft memory of Julie around us on Surrey and Torremolinos as I wrote this book.

About the author

Read on

Insights,
Interviews
& More . . .

Meet Beth Harbison

Chandler Schwede

New York Times bestselling author BETH HARBISON started cooking when she was eight years old, thanks to *Betty Crocker's Cookbook for Boys and Girls*. After graduating college, she worked full-time as a private chef in the DC area, and within three years she sold her first cookbook, *The Bread Machine Baker,* to Random House. She published four cookbooks in total before moving on to writing bestselling women's fiction, including the runaway bestseller *Shoe Addicts Anonymous* and *When in Doubt, Add Butter.* ∾

Playlist for Frances and Crosby

1. "She's So High"—Tal Bachman

2. "Careful"—Guster

3. "It's a Miracle"—Trashcan Sinatras

4. "The Things I Hate Look Great on You"—Thalo

5. "Torn"—Natalie Imbruglia

6. "There She Goes"—The La's

7. "We Used to Be Friends"— The Dandy Warholes

8. "Breakfast at Tiffany's"— Deep Blue Something

9. "More than Words"—Extreme

10. "It Never Rains in Southern California"—Albert Hammond

11. "Speeding Cars"—Imogen Heap

12. "A Girl Like You"—Edwyn Collins

13. "Follow Me"—Uncle Kracker

14. "No Rain"—Blind Melon

15. "Perfectly Good Guitar"— John Hiatt

16. "Roll to Me"—Del Amitri

17. "Kiss Me"—Sixpence None the Richer

18. "Forever Young"—Youth Group ▶

Playlist for Frances and Crosby *(continued)*

19. "Don't You Worry 'Bout a Thing"—Stevie Wonder

20. "Wonderwall"—Ryan Adams

21. "To All of You"—Syd Matters

22. "Fix You"—Coldplay

23. "Ooh Child"—Beth Orton

24. "Closing Time"—Semisonic ॐ

Recipes

Avocado Egg Rolls

This is so easy you won't believe it! If you're a cilantro fan, chop some up and include it in the avocado mixture before creating the egg rolls. Likewise, you can use fresh parsley or basil, just make sure you chop it finely so it doesn't become one long string when you take a bite.

2 large Hass avocados, cut into small chunks
2 tablespoons diced red onion
2 tablespoons diced ripe mango
1 large tomato, diced small
2 sundried tomatoes in oil, drained and chopped small
1 teaspoon garlic powder
Salt and pepper, to taste
2 cups vegetable oil, for frying
2 eggs
8 egg roll wrappers
Ranch dressing, for dipping

1. In a medium bowl, mix the avocados, onion, mango, tomato, sundried tomatoes, garlic powder, salt, and pepper. Combine gently to keep the avocado intact.

2. Crack the eggs into a small bowl and stir vigorously.

3. Lay the egg roll wrappers out and spoon ⅛ of the avocado mixture into the center of each one. One at a time, brush the outside edges with the egg (this acts as a "glue"), then, starting from the bottom, pull one corner of the wrapper up and over the mixture. Next fold the two sides in over the avocado mix and the corner you just pulled up. Then simply roll it up to the top corner and press to seal. ▶

Recipes *(continued)*

4. In a medium saucepan over medium-high heat, heat the vegetable oil to 375°F.

5. Fry the egg rolls for 30 to 45 seconds per side, until golden brown. Drain on paper towels, then serve with ranch dressing or your favorite dip.

Sandy's Wild Mushroom Risotto

One of the secrets to this recipe is that it doesn't have to be wild mushrooms. You can use frozen gourmet mushrooms, or any fresh mushrooms you like. There is no magic that will turn something you don't like into something you do like when you cook it, so just start with ingredients you like!

3 tablespoons olive oil, divided
1½ pounds mushrooms, thinly sliced and/or diced
Salt and pepper, to taste
2 shallots or 1 small white onion, peeled and diced
1½ cups arborio rice
6 cups chicken broth
¼ cup (½ stick) butter
⅓ to ½ cup grated Parmesan cheese
Fresh chopped parsley, for garnish (optional)

1. Heat 1 tablespoon of the olive oil in a large skillet over medium heat. Add the mushrooms, season with salt and pepper, and sauté until gently browned, about 5 minutes. Remove the mushrooms to a bowl.

2. Add the remaining 2 tablespoons olive oil to the skillet and heat to shimmering. Add the shallots or onion and sauté for 2 minutes, then add the rice and stir to toast for 4 minutes.

3. Increase heat to medium-high, then slowly add the chicken broth, allowing it to absorb into the rice along the way, about 1 cup every 5 minutes, stirring constantly, until most of the broth is absorbed.

4. Once thickened, turn heat off and add the butter and Parmesan cheese. Stir to melt and incorporate the cheese, and remove from the heat. Stir in the cooked mushrooms.

5. Garnish with a little sprinkling of fresh chopped parsley (which makes it prettier but isn't necessary if you don't have it). Serve warm. ▸

Recipes *(continued)*

Mac and Cheese with San Marzano Pesto

You can use almost any cheese for this, so choose your favorites.
You can also top it with bread or cracker crumbs and butter, but
I prefer it without a crust when using the tomato pesto. It's up to
you, whatever you like!

1 (28-ounce) can whole San Marzano tomatoes
2 teaspoons brown sugar
2 tablespoons butter
6 tablespoons flour
2 teaspoons dry mustard powder
5 cups milk
6 ounces shredded white Cheddar cheese
6 ounces shredded Fontina cheese
4 ounces shredded sharp provolone cheese
½ teaspoon cayenne pepper, optional
Salt and pepper, to taste
1 pound elbow macaroni, cooked according to box directions
2 tablespoons olive oil
4 cloves garlic, peeled and pressed
3 tablespoons pine nuts or walnut pieces

1. Preheat the oven to 400°F.

2. Place the tomatoes on a parchment-lined sheet pan. Top each
   with a little of the brown sugar and roast for 20 to 30 minutes,
   until the tomatoes are dried and have dark brown spots.
   Remove from the oven and let cool.

3. In a saucepan, heat the butter until melted, then add the
   flour and mustard powder and cook until golden, about
   4 minutes (you're cooking the flour so it doesn't taste raw,
   so this is important). Slowly add the milk while stirring
   until it becomes thick and creamy.

4. Add the cheeses, a handful at a time, and stir in. Add the
   cayenne, if desired. Taste for seasoning and adjust as needed.

As soon as everything is melted and smooth, remove from the heat and set aside.

5. Mix the cooked pasta into the cheese sauce. Combine well.

6. Meanwhile, place the cooled tomatoes, olive oil, garlic, and nuts in a food processor and puree to make your pesto.

7. Put a dollop of pesto on top of each serving of the mac and cheese. Serve hot. ▶

Recipes *(continued)*

Pork and Scallion Purses

Like the Avocado Egg Rolls (page 5), these are very easy and they're so good!

Purses

4 ounces ground pork, cooked and cooled
2 scallions, whites and halfway up the greens, thinly sliced
2 cloves garlic, pressed
1 teaspoon grated fresh ginger
1 teaspoon umami or oyster sauce
1 teaspoon toasted sesame oil
1 teaspoon soy sauce
1 egg
8 wonton wrappers
⅓ cup vegetable oil, for frying

Dipping Sauce

¼ cup soy sauce
2 teaspoons honey
½ teaspoon sriracha
1 clove garlic, pressed

1. **Make the purses:** In a small bowl, mix together the cooked ground pork, scallions, garlic, ginger, umami or oyster sauce, sesame oil, and soy sauce.

2. In a separate small bowl, beat the egg.

3. Set the wonton wrappers out and put ⅛ of the pork mixture into each wonton. Then dip your fingertips generously into the egg and twist the wrapper shut over the pork mixture, creating a little "purse" or bag shape.

4. Heat the oil to 375°F in a large frying pan with a cover. Drop the purses in and fry for 2 to 3 minutes, turning them to cook on all sides. Then remove the purses from the oil and drain

on paper towels, wipe the pan clean, and return the purses to the pan over medium-high heat. Add 1 cup of water, cover the pan, and allow the purses to steam for 7 to 10 minutes.

5. **Make the dipping sauce:** Whisk the soy sauce, honey, sriracha, and garlic in a small bowl. Can be made ahead or last minute. Serve alongside the purses. ▶

Grilled Cheese Sandwiches

Honestly, you can use whatever cheeses you want for this, you just need to end up with a smooth paste, similar to the consistency of hummus. You can keep this, covered, in the refrigerator for up to a week.

If you want to add caramelized onions, slice yellow onions thin and cook in butter with a pinch of salt and sugar in a frying pan over medium heat until they become a deep brown. Add to the sandwiches before topping them with the bread. Thin slices of peeled apple and/or tomato are also wonderful add-on options.

4 ounces Gruyère cheese, roughly chopped
4 ounces Morbier or Fontina, roughly chopped
2 ounces Brie or similar, rind removed
2 to 3 tablespoons white wine
½ teaspoon freshly ground nutmeg
1 teaspoon Calabrian chilis, optional
8 slices sourdough bread
Softened butter
Mayonnaise

1. Puree all the cheeses, wine, nutmeg, and Calabrian chilies (if using) in a food processor. Spread it on four bread slices, then top each with another piece of bread (come on, you know how to make a sandwich).

2. Lightly spread both sides of the sandwiches with butter and a little bit of mayonnaise. Fry to golden brown on both sides.

3. Serve with or without Cream of Tomato Soup (page 13).

Cream of Tomato Soup

This is adapted from a Cooks Illustrated *recipe that I made so many times I had to streamline it. One of the keys to it is to use good canned tomatoes. For me, that means San Marzano. They're a little bit more expensive but well worth it.*

4 tablespoons butter
4 shallots, peeled and chopped
½ teaspoon ground allspice
2 tablespoons all-purpose flour
2 cups chicken stock
2 (28-ounce) cans whole tomatoes
Salt and pepper, to taste
2 tablespoons brandy or dry sherry
½ cup heavy cream
Cayenne pepper, optional

1. Heat the butter in a large saucepan over medium heat. Add the shallots and cook until they're translucent, then add the allspice. Stir for 30 seconds until the scent rises and blooms.

2. Next, add the flour to the pan and cook it in the butter until it starts to brown a little (you do this so you don't end up with a raw flour taste in your soup).

3. Slowly add the chicken stock and whisk for 1-2 minutes to thicken and get rid of lumps.

4. Add the tomatoes and their juices straight from the cans and use an immersion blender to puree them smooth. (Alternatively, you can use a countertop blender, then return the puree to the pan.)

5. When it's heated through, taste for seasoning, adding salt and pepper as desired. ▶

Recipes *(continued)*

6. When ready to serve, add the brandy or sherry and cook for 2 minutes. Then stir in the cream and cayenne pepper (if using), ladle into soup bowls, and serve with or without Grilled Cheese Sandwiches (page 12).

Cream of Crab Soup

I'm from Maryland, where everyone has Old Bay in the pantry and an old family crab soup recipe up their sleeve. This recipe uses hollandaise sauce mix to add to the creamy flavor, but if you like tarragon, you can use béarnaise sauce mix instead. It's not a cheat, it's an ingredient.

1 pound backfin lump crab meat
3 tablespoons all-purpose flour
1 package hollandaise sauce mix
4 cups half-and-half, divided
¼ cup (½ stick) butter
1 cup heavy cream
½ teaspoon dry mustard powder
Pinch allspice
1 tablespoon of Old Bay seasoning
Splash of decent sherry (use something drinkable but not
    expensive)
Fresh chopped parsley, for garnish (optional)
Pinch of smoked paprika, optional

1. Pick through the crab meat for pieces of shell, even if the packaging says it's already been picked. No matter how much you paid, you'll find some. Set aside.

2. Add the flour, sauce mix, and 2 cups of the half-and-half to a bowl and whisk until smooth. Set aside.

3. Melt the butter in a saucepan over medium heat, being careful not to let it brown. When it's melted, add the flour-hollandaise mixture, stirring constantly, until slightly thickened. Add the crabmeat, remaining half-and-half, the heavy cream, dry mustard, allspice, and Old Bay and taste for seasoning.

4. Finish with the sherry, cook for one minute, then remove from heat. Garnish with parsley and a pinch of smoked paprika before serving. ▶

Huevos Rancheros

A very easy and comforting breakfast, and it comes together really fast, even when you're making your own salsa. If you want it even faster, you can, of course, use store-bought salsa, but it always requires a little more than you think it will so get two jars instead of one.

1 (28-ounce) can crushed tomatoes
1 jalapeño pepper, ends cut off and seeded
1 small red onion, peeled and coarsely chopped
Lime juice, to taste
Salt and pepper, to taste
Tortilla chips (flavored are okay—up to you!)
8 eggs
Grated Cheddar or Pepper Jack cheese, for garnish
Sour cream, for garnish

1. **Make the salsa:** Put the crushed tomatoes, jalapeño, and red onion into a food processor and process for five or six pulses, until thoroughly mixed. Add the lime juice and salt and pepper to taste.

2. Put half the salsa in a large pan and heat over medium heat.

3. Layer about six tortilla chips into each of four good-sized bowls. You want them large enough to pile on more salsa, cheese, sour cream, etc.

4. Crack the eggs, one at a time, into a bowl (to ensure you don't get any shell in the pan) and pour each egg individually into the pan of salsa. Do this in two batches of 4 eggs each. Cook to desired doneness. Scoop 2 eggs with salsa out at a time and onto the layer of chips in each bowl. Repeat with the remaining eggs and salsa.

5. Top each bowl with cheese and sour cream before serving.

French Hamburgers

Found in an old French cookbook I can no longer remember the name of, this is a delicious entrée. While I think a side of mashed potatoes goes with just about anything, including this, it also makes a lovely lunch or dinner with a mixed baby greens salad with a light vinaigrette on the side.

¼ cup finely minced onion
2 tablespoons vegetable oil, divided
1½ pounds lean ground beef
Salt and pepper, to taste
¼ teaspoon thyme
1 egg, lightly beaten
½ cup dried bread crumbs
Flour
2 tablespoons butter, divided
½ cup red wine

1. Cook the onion in 1 tablespoon of oil in a small pan over medium heat until translucent but not browned. Remove from the heat and transfer to a large mixing bowl.

2. Add the ground beef, salt, pepper, thyme, egg, and bread crumbs to the onion and gently toss to combine. Do *not* overwork the mix or it will get tough.

3. Make six patties. Dredge each through flour and tap off the excess.

4. Return the pan to medium heat, add 1 tablespoon of the butter and the remaining vegetable oil, and cook the patties to desired doneness, then remove them to a large plate or platter.

5. Increase the heat to medium-high and pour in the wine. Cook, scraping bits off the bottom, for 5 minutes, or until slightly thickened. Add the remaining tablespoon of butter, stir, pour the sauce over the patties, and serve. ▶

Recipes *(continued)*

Cali Shot

The famous "Cali Shot" detox drink has many variations. This is my favorite. When in California . . .

12-ounce glass of water
2 tablespoons apple cider vinegar (buy the kind with the "mother")
2 tablespoons lemon juice
1 teaspoon cinnamon
1 tablespoon raw honey

Blend all the ingredients together in a blender. If you're doing it by hand, put the honey and cinnamon in the glass first and stir to combine. Slowly add the lemon juice, continuing to stir, then add the vinegar and finish with the water. Stir once more before serving. ☙